# DROPOUT
## THE GOOD GUYS BOOK 3

BY

JAMIE SCHLOSSER

Janice -
Happy reading!

Cover design: Hang Le

Formatting: Rebecca Poole at Dreams2media

Editing: Kim Huther at Wordsmith Proofreading Services

Due to language and sexual content, this book is intended for readers 18 and older.

# DEDICATION

*In memory of Louise Bluhm*
*1918-2006*

*And to Grandma Judy—because if it wasn't for you,*
*I never would've finished that rag quilt, and I wouldn't*
*have an endless supply of fuzzy housecoats.*

## JIMMY

Over the past year, I've been called a lot of things. Slacker. Troublemaker. Party animal.

I thought I was on top of the world. Turns out, I was pretty close to rock bottom.

Now I have a new title: college dropout.

Talk about a reality check.

But I've got a chance to redeem myself. One summer to turn things around. Two months to prove I'm not a complete f*ck-up.

It's time to change.

I want to get back to being one of the good guys.

## MACKENNA

I have everything I need to live out my dream of being a reclusive songwriter—my guitar, my notebook, and blissful silence.

At least, I did until Jimmy moved in next door.

With tattoos, piercings, and mischievous green eyes, he's got bad news written all over him. And last time I got with a bad boy, it ended horribly.

Jimmy makes me feel things I shouldn't feel. Want things I shouldn't want. He's a hazard to my carefully laid plans.

But he's only here for two months.

I can resist him...right?

# PROLOGUE

THREE YEARS AGO

MACKENNA

> **Lindsey: You're such a bitch**
> **Tiffany: Everyone hates you now**
> **Sierra: Why are you doing this to Jaxon? I hope you don't plan on sticking around after graduation. No one wants you here**

I blinked away the stinging in my eyes as I read over the tag-team texts from my best friends.

Former best friends.

Or maybe they were never my friends in the first place. Either way, it was safe to say those relationships were officially over.

I didn't have anything to say to them, so I started to set the phone back down on the nightstand. Another chirp stopped me. This time when I looked at the screen, Jaxon's name showed up. I'd purposely ignored the eighteen texts he sent me tonight, but this one caught my attention.

> **Jaxon: I'm outside**

My eyes flew to the window, which I knew for a fact was closed and locked. My heart raced as I tried to remember if I'd locked the front and back doors.

I did. I was sure of it.

I typed out a short reply.

**Me: Go home Jaxon**

Then I buried myself further under the covers, wishing the layers of warmth could keep me safe somehow.

A few seconds later the phone rang in my hand, and I immediately pushed 'ignore' as I crawled out of bed.

I held the screen to my stomach as I made my way to the window, hoping he wouldn't see the light in the darkened room. Peeping through the curtains, I saw Jaxon's old red Jeep sitting in the gravel driveway, and I spotted his shadowed figure in the front seat.

My voicemail chime went off, causing me to jump a little. Reluctantly, I put the phone up to my ear while inching toward my bedroom door.

"Who are you spreading your legs for, you filthy cunt?" Jaxon's rage-filled voice made my breathing pick up as I tiptoed through the hallway. "Come outside or else. Don't make me come in there. It won't be pretty."

*Click.*

Panic bloomed in my chest, squeezing and crushing until I struggled for air.

Since the breakup three weeks ago, the stalking and harassment had been escalating. Jaxon followed me everywhere—to the mall, in the hallways at our high school, to my favorite coffee shop. Every time I turned around, he was there. And when he wasn't nearby, he was calling me relentlessly.

No matter how many times I told him it was over, he

wouldn't stop. I should've known he'd be watching the house, waiting for the moment I was alone and vulnerable.

I crept into my parents' room and dropped to my knees beside the bed. My hands shook as I attempted to open the small safe in the cabinet of the nightstand.

The phone rang again, and I slipped up on the combination lock.

I started over. All I needed to do was turn that dial and match up three numbers, but the trembling in my hands made it difficult.

A breath of relief left me when the heavy door clicked open, and I reached in to wrap my fingers around the cold metal of my dad's semi-automatic handgun. I had no intention of using it, but it made me feel better to have it.

Just in case.

Keeping a gun in the house wasn't something my parents took lightly. After my dad bought it, he took my sister and me to the shooting range to learn the basics. I was a terrible shot, but I knew how to load it and make sure the safety was on, which is exactly what I did next.

I hated weapons. I hated anything that was created for the sole purpose of inflicting pain. But I knew a gun wasn't required to cause damage.

Hands could be just as dangerous.

Setting the gun on the bed, I sat down on the floor. Hugging my knees to my chest, I listened to the latest voicemail.

"I'm sorry, sweetheart," Jaxon cooed softly, his tone a complete opposite to the previous message. "You know I just love you so much. I can't be without you. Do yourself a favor and listen to what I say. We can do this the easy way or the hard way. Come outside and see me."

*Click.*

Another chime rang out, which meant he must have left another voicemail right after the last one. I pushed play again.

"BITCH!" My body jolted at the outburst. "Open the fucking door. That's it. If we're over, then you're dead!" he shouted. I began to hyperventilate as fear took over. "I warned you. I tried to play nice. Now I'm coming for you."

Tears streamed down my face as I stared at the phone in shock. Would he follow through on the threat he'd made so many times before? Despite his abusive tendencies, I never wanted to believe he was unhinged enough to kill me.

Loud pounding on the door spurred me into action. I grabbed the gun and ran back to my room. Then I did the most cliché thing possible—I hid in my closet.

Although the walk-in was spacious, hiding places were limited. As I settled into the far-left corner, I also remembered there was no window.

No escape route.

No way out.

Not that it would've mattered. We lived in the middle of nowhere. This two-acre piece of land used to be my own version of heaven, but right now I felt like I was trapped on an island with a murderous psycho.

I heard a loud thud followed by another, and I could tell Jaxon was trying to barge through the front door.

Fumbling with my phone, I quickly dialed 9-1-1.

"911, what's your emergency?"

Refusing to be incoherent with panic, I took a deep breath and tried to sound level-headed. "My name is Mackenna Connelly. I'm at 1715 Old Orchard Road in Daywood, Illinois. My ex-boyfriend is trying to break into my house. His name is Jaxon Meyers. I think—I know he wants to hurt me."

"Has he ever been violent toward you?"

"Yes." A choked sob escaped along with the truth.

For the past two years, I had kept the ugly details of my relationship a secret from everyone. Admitting it out loud for the first time made all the emotions come to the surface—fear, sadness, shame.

I should've told someone. My parents or a teacher. Instead, I let them believe the sudden change in my personality was due to typical teenage stuff, because I was ashamed of the truth.

Being smart, kind, and independent didn't make me immune to guys like Jaxon.

Hiding the bruises on my arms with long sleeves had been easy, and if anyone ever saw I laughed it off as an accident.

I absentmindedly rubbed at the scar by my hairline. That one hadn't been as easy to explain.

"Miss, are you alone?"

"Yes," I answered, struggling to keep my voice steady. "My parents went to a movie and my sister is at a sleepover."

Date night. Mom and Dad had kept the tradition of going out once a month for as long as I could remember. I'd always found it adorable, but as I watched them walk out the door earlier, I wanted nothing more than to beg them to stay home. I held it in, though. If I had asked them not to go they would've wanted to know why, and I didn't want to lie to them anymore.

Thank God my sister wasn't home. Krista was only twelve, and the thought of her witnessing Jaxon at his worst made my stomach churn.

"How old are you?" The operator's voice was calm, but it did nothing to soothe me.

"Eighteen."

"An officer is on the way. Are you somewhere safe?"

The sound of glass breaking had my pulse skyrocketing and I shifted, realizing I was sitting on top of a bunch of shoes. One of my high heels dug into my thigh.

"N—no. I'm hiding in the closet. I think he's in the house now." My body trembled and I tried to control my sobbing, which had turned into hiccups. I gripped the cold metal in my hand. "I have a gun. Am I allowed to use it if—if I have to?"

"You have the right to defend yourself, but an officer is on the way."

"They won't get here in time," I told her, knowing it was the truth.

"Can you stay on the line…?"

Her voice faded away as I set the phone down beside me without hanging up. I needed both hands for what I was about to do.

Inhaling a shaky breath, I flipped off the safety switch and listened for anything other than the sound of my pounding heart.

Then Jaxon's voice made me jump.

"Mackenna. The games are over. Where are you?" He was just steps away from the closet. "I bet you're in here."

The door opened, and even in the darkness I could see the metal bat in his hand. Moonlight from the bedroom window glinted off the shiny surface, and bile rose in my throat when I realized what he intended to do with it.

He squared his broad shoulders before stepping into the closet, and although I couldn't see his eyes, I knew the brown orbs were hard and cold as he looked down at me.

"You really thought you could hide from me? I'd find you anywhere. I know the way you think." Tapping his temple, he chuckled darkly. "I know every step you're going to make, even before you know it yourself."

"You don't have to do this," I said, hiding the weapon under my leg. "You can just go home and it will be like this never even happened."

"I told you I wouldn't live without you and I meant it. I'm gonna bash your fucking face in," he slurred, swaying unsteadily on his feet. "Such a shame. It's a pretty face."

Any hope of talking him down vanished. When Jaxon was drunk or high, there was no getting through to him.

He raised the bat over his right shoulder, the way someone would when waiting for the perfect pitch. He took a practice swing, and the bat made a *whoosh* as it cut through the air. There was enough room for the full range of motion, but the end of the rod clipped a rack of clothing.

Shirts, dresses, and plastic hangers clattered to the floor.

Time seemed to stop as memories flashed through my mind.

For some reason, I thought of a tea party I had with my stuffed animals one summer afternoon when I was five. Stargazing with my mom when I was thirteen. The time I went car shopping with my dad and I begged him for that pink sports car, but he said no. I remembered how pissed I'd been. How I'd pouted all the way home like a spoiled child.

And now I'd give anything to go back to that day to tell him I was sorry, to tell him the blue Buick with low mileage was the right choice. In the long run, I would've hated having a pink car.

All the memories were so simple. The small events of daily life somehow became the most important in the forefront of my mind.

And I wanted a million more of those insignificant moments.

Suddenly, the inner strength that Jaxon had tried so hard to snuff out reared up inside of me. Fear turned into anger. Sadness turned into rage.

I was *fucking pissed.*

This couldn't be the end. I couldn't die huddled in the corner of a closet with a stiletto poking me in the ass.

"I love you so fucking much," Jaxon said quietly, lifting the bat.

Before he could take another step I raised my shaking hand, pointed the gun, and pulled the trigger.

# CHAPTER 1

PRESENT DAY

JIMMY

I heaved out a sigh as I dropped the large box onto my bed. That was the last of it. The last of the belongings I'd taken to college with me.

It felt like yesterday I was packing up my stuff, excited for what would come next in life. I'd had big plans. I was confident, cocky, and completely unprepared for the responsibility and freedom that came with leaving home for the first time.

And now here I was.

A college dropout. A failure. A disappointment to everyone I knew, including myself.

As I scrubbed a hand over my face, all I could do was feel shame over the past and dread about the future.

What was I supposed to do next? I had no idea what I wanted to do with the rest of my life, but I probably needed a degree to do it.

There would be consequences for my actions.

And I deserved it.

I'd had my chance and I'd blown it.

Everything looked the same in my childhood room.

The Aerosmith poster still hung on the wall over my bed. If I flipped my black comforter over, I'd see a charred spot in the fabric—an innocent mishap from a camping trip when I got a little overzealous about roasting marshmallows.

A shelf of trophies and ribbons decorated the opposite wall over my desk.

I wanted to tear it down.

Those awards represented my greatest accomplishments, but they meant nothing now. Baseball participation trophies, swim medals, and a second-place ribbon in the 8th grade spelling bee didn't make me a success.

A soft knock interrupted my self-loathing, and I glanced at the doorway to see Ezra. Immediately, my crappy mood improved.

My younger brother was one of my favorite people in the world. Only a year apart in age, we grew up more like twins. We were complete opposites, though.

While I got my dad's dark hair and olive skin tone, Ezra was lighter like Mom with blond hair, blue eyes, and a fair complexion. In fact, we looked so different some people didn't believe us when we told them we were brothers.

"Heard you were back," he said with a grin.

I smiled and went over to wrap him in a hug. Putting him at arm's length, I observed how he'd changed since the last time I saw him.

"You got taller," I announced before giving him a noogie.

Laughing, he pushed me away and went to sit down in

the chair at my desk. As he made his way across the room, I noticed his uneven gait was worse than usual.

"Your leg bothering you again?"

Wincing, he rubbed at his left knee. "I fell at school. Twisted it a little."

"You fell, or someone made you fall?" I asked, crossing my arms over my chest. His silence was the confirmation I needed. "Who's been fucking with you? Is it that AJ prick?"

"It doesn't matter." Ezra shook his head. "I'll be graduating in a couple weeks anyway. I can't wait for high school to be over."

I frowned, thinking of how he might've been treated since I left.

Ezra was shy, and because of a leg injury he suffered as a kid his physical abilities were limited. He often walked with a limp, and he couldn't play sports or even participate in P.E.

Lack of exercise had caused his body to be on the softer side, and he suffered from low self-esteem. It made him the perfect target for asshole bullies.

When we were in school together, no one dared to mess with him. Everyone knew I wouldn't stand for it. But he'd been on his own for the past year.

Ezra was one of the best people in the world. He may have been younger, but I looked up to him. Physical traits weren't the only differences between us. I was the risk-taker, the wild one. Ezra tended to follow the rules. He was a peacemaker, a voice of reason. Kind-hearted and good.

Out of the two of us, I knew who was the better man. Hands down, it was him. I just wished he knew it, too.

Sweeping the mess of hair off his forehead, he sat up a little straighter. "Mom and Dad are downstairs. Said they needed to talk to you." He looked sympathetic. "They seemed pissed."

I sighed. "I know. They should be. I messed up pretty bad."

"They wouldn't spill the details to me, but I'm guessing it has something to do with school." He swiveled in the computer chair and it squeaked with his movements.

I nodded. "Failed three out of my four classes."

Ezra winced. "That sucks. What about the fourth class?"

Shaking my head, I huffed out a laugh. "Not much better. I got a C in music appreciation, but I have no idea how because I snoozed through most of it. Pretty interesting stuff when I wasn't hungover."

"So what are you going to do?"

"I don't know."

"Are you gonna go back to college?"

Frustrated, I ran a hand through my hair. "I honestly don't know."

"Shit," he breathed out. "I guess I didn't realize it was that bad."

"It's that bad," I confirmed with a nod. "Don't have anyone to blame but myself."

"Well, good luck." He stood up before limping across the room. At the doorway, he turned back. "For what it's worth...I don't think it's too late to fix it."

"Thanks." I smiled, touched by his never-ending faith in me.

\*

When I got downstairs, Mom and Dad were waiting for me at the dining table.

That's how I knew I was in deep shit.

Only serious conversations took place in those chairs, unless it was a special occasion. We usually ate dinner in front of the TV, with those trays and everything. Some people thought you had to eat a meal around a table to connect and interact, but that wasn't true. The best dinner memories I have are of laughing with my family over Seinfeld reruns and Jeopardy episodes.

The gleaming mahogany surface mocked me as I sat down for what was sure to be an unpleasant talk. As I looked at the expressions of disappointment on my parents' faces, the guilt got worse.

Way worse.

Taking a deep breath, I rested my elbows on the table. It was time to face the music.

Mom broke the silence first. "We're so disappointed in you."

I knew that was coming, but hearing it out loud fucking hurt. That five-word sentence pretty much summed up the last eight months of my life.

Dad cleared his throat. "Well, we didn't send you off to college to learn how to do a 55-second keg stand, though that's pretty impressive."

Mom smacked him on the arm. "Matthew."

"I saw the Facebook video," he told her, then turned his eyes to me. "Quite an accomplishment, James, but not what we paid thousands of dollars for. We've spent almost half our lives building your college fund. Seeing you waste it pisses us off."

"I know," I said, hanging my head. Nearly two decades of saving, budgeting, and cutting corners, and it took less than a year for me to flush a good portion of it down the drain.

"What happened?" Mom said, and the hurt in her voice made my chest ache. "You were such a good student in high school."

She was right about that. I used to get straight A's without even trying very hard. But simply being smart didn't mean jack shit in college. Intelligence was useless if I didn't put in any effort.

"I fell into some bad habits," I admitted. "I partied too much. Skipped class a lot. Didn't study enough. By the time I realized how bad my GPA was, it was too late to turn it around."

Dad sighed. "Look, we know you were upset after things ended with Erica. Letting go of your first love is hard, but you can't let it ruin your life."

I thought about how I started drinking after my high school girlfriend broke up with me, needing something to numb my damaged ego. We'd been dating since our sophomore year. Blinded by puppy-love, we made a pact go to the same college, graduate together, and live happily ever after.

Seemed like a good plan at the time.

Then life happened.

In the real world, we realized we didn't have that much in common. We disagreed about everything, from what movie to watch on a Friday night to where we should live after college. It didn't matter what the subject was. If a topic got brought up, we fought about it.

Two months into the school year she called it quits, and getting dumped for the first time sucked.

I drowned my sorrows in a bottle of Jack, and suddenly I was the life of the party. I was the guy everyone wanted to hang out with. And for a while, I thought that was what mattered most.

My dad cleared his throat again, and I realized he was still waiting for me to explain myself.

"It's not Erica's fault we weren't right for each other," I said. "The partying might've started because of the breakup, but it continued because of me. I just got caught up in it. After a couple months, I was over her. And looking back, I'm not even sure we were in love in the first place."

Dad nodded like he understood and Mom sat silently. Her blue eyes searched my face, as if she was trying to find the boy she raised.

"James—"

"I prefer Jimmy now," I interjected softly, and Mom made a sound of distress.

"It's like you're this whole other person." She motioned toward me. "New name, bad grades, the tattoos."

"Mom, I'm still the same guy I've always been," I told

her. "Grandma has called me Jimmy forever, so that's not new. And if there's one thing I don't regret from this past year, it's the ink. I love my tats."

I didn't bother telling them about the body piercings hidden under my clothes. Adding insult to injury wasn't going to help my case.

"What about the maxed-out credit card?" She slid the bill my way, and my stomach lurched when I saw the total amount was in the quadruple digits. "What do you have to show for it?"

"Funny story about that—there was this guy hanging out on campus, offering free pizza coupons if we applied for a card. It seemed like a good deal..."

My parents didn't look amused.

"That's an expensive pizza." Dad tapped the paper.

"Some of that was for the tattoos, which are a life-long investment," I pointed out, then decided to go for honesty. "But most of it was for booze."

Dad coughed, and I suspected he was holding back a laugh. Mom shot him a look.

"And the fighting?" she continued. "You've never been violent before."

"It wasn't real fighting," I said, hoping that would make her feel better. "It was street-fighting."

"Well, I don't see the difference!" Her eyes shimmered with tears, and I felt like the biggest piece of shit ever for making her cry.

"The public disturbance ticket you got didn't see the difference either." Dad turned toward Mom, rubbing soothing circles on her back. "It's okay, Linda."

"The dude and I weren't pissed at each other. It was for money. For sport..." My lame explanation faded away as I witnessed the full weight of my bad decisions, and how they affected the people I loved most. When I came home over Christmas break with a banged-up face and a $250 fine, they were pretty upset. But, at the time, I was still in denial about the downward spiral I was in.

"When I taught you how to fight, I didn't mean for you to use it that way," Dad said sternly. "Bare-knuckle street-fighting is not boxing. You never know what kind of person you'll end up against when rules aren't en-forced. When you're not in a controlled environment, it's dangerous."

My dad had done college-level boxing back in the day. When I was younger, we used to spar with each other. Some of the best times I had with my dad included having those gloves on, learning how to bob and weave and block.

Looking down at my hands, I said two words that couldn't even begin to fix the mess I'd made. "I'm sorry."

"Do you have any idea how worried we've been? Your mom has lost a lot of sleep over all this."

"I'm sorry," I repeated. "I don't know how to make it up to you, but I'll do anything. Seriously, you just name it."

"Good. I hope you mean that because we have plans for you."

"I'll get a job and pay you back." My mind ran through the possible places of employment in our small town. "I can move back home. Take a year off school to get back on my feet."

"We had something else in mind." Dad paused. "Grandma Beverly isn't doing so well these days."

Alarmed, I felt the blood drain from my face. "Is she sick?"

"She's as healthy as ever," he reassured me. "But her house is deteriorating. Regular chores have become too much for her. She needs help but she's too proud to hire someone. Says she doesn't want anyone touching her underwear." He rolled his eyes and I chuckled.

"I'll do it," I said automatically, knowing what they were getting at. "I mean, not the touching her underwear part. But I'll go and help any way I can."

"Really?" Mom asked skeptically. "Just like that? I expected a little more resistance."

Leaning forward, Dad placed his elbows on the table top. "You realize it's for the entire summer, right? She's got a long list of things to be done, including yard work, cleaning, and painting her house."

"Did you guys think I'd say no?" I frowned.

Did they really think so little of me? I knew I'd done a lot of immature things, but I was still loyal to the people I loved. If Grandma needed my help, she'd get it.

Shrugging, Mom dabbed at the corner of her eye with a tissue. "After the way you've acted over the past several months, we don't know what to think anymore."

"I'd be happy to stay with Grandma. In fact, I can't think of a better way to spend the summer."

Dad let out a snort. "That's probably just because she'll be mixing your mojitos. I'm not sure she'll be the best influence on you."

I grinned.

Beverly Louise Johnson was the coolest motherfucking lady in the entire world. She was brutally honest, didn't take anyone's crap, and swore like a sailor. On more than one occasion, my parents had said they thought I inherited my wild streak from her.

They were probably right.

"There's one last thing," Dad added. "If you follow through with this and behave yourself... We'll pay your tuition in the fall. We believe in second chances, but you have to earn it."

A burst of hope filled me, because this was it—my chance to redeem myself.

Looking my dad in the eye, I made a promise I intended to keep. "I won't let you down."

*

"So, what's the verdict?" Sitting down on the edge of my bed, Ezra narrowed his eyes at the duffle bag I was packing. "You going somewhere?"

"Yep." I stuffed some more clothes in, not bothering to fold them up. "The 'rents are shipping me off to Grandma's for the summer. I leave first thing in the morning."

Ezra's eyes got wide. "Seriously? Do they realize what kind of mayhem you and Grandma could cause?"

I barked out a laugh. "I know. I think Mom's a little nervous about it, but Dad thinks it'll be good for me. I'll be at Grandma's beck and call for the next couple months."

"Well, I would say I'll miss you around here, but they're sending me to fat camp."

"What the fuck?" I stopped packing. "Are you serious?"

He laughed. "No. It's actually a physical therapy retreat. Supposed to help my leg. But it might as well be fat camp."

I went back to shoving handfuls of T-shirts into the bag. "You don't need to go to fat camp."

Giving me a look, he brought his hands to his stomach. "Yeah, I do. I have man-boobs."

"Ezra…" I warned. I hated it when he put himself down. "Don't talk about yourself like that."

"Well, it's true." He shrugged. "You don't know what it's like. Look at you." He pointed at my arms and chest. "You're like one of those statues in the art museum. A statue with tattoos. God, the girls must love you."

I couldn't argue with that. I didn't have any trouble attracting women, but dating wasn't in the cards for me. Probably not for a long time.

Casual hook-ups had been par for the course with the party crowd I hung out with. After Erica, the last thing I wanted was a serious relationship.

It'd all been fun and games until I woke up one morning with not one, but two half-naked girls in my bed—and absolutely no recollection of the night before. I had no idea if we were even safe about it.

I'd spent the next day freaking the fuck out until one of them mentioned in a text message that nothing happened. Apparently, I had passed out before they could even get their clothes off.

I'd never been more relieved in my entire life.

And ashamed.

And pissed at myself for being so careless.

The fact that I'd gotten so hammered I couldn't even remember if I'd had sex? That was some scary shit.

But it was the push I needed to turn my life around.

Immediately, I went to the clinic and got tested for everything under the sun, took a few scalding hot showers, and made a vow of celibacy. I stopped partying so much, distanced myself from my friends, and started going to class.

Unfortunately, it hadn't been enough to salvage my grades. And no amount of abstaining from sex was going to pay off that damn credit card.

"I'm done with women for a while," I told my brother. "Just wait until college. A bunch of girls will be flocking to you."

"I don't want a bunch of girls," he muttered. "There's only one I want."

"Is this the same girl you've been going on about for the last few years?" I asked. He blushed, which was something he did often, but not usually with me. That's how I knew I'd hit the nail right on the head. "Aren't you tutoring her?"

"No. *She's* tutoring *me*," he said, letting out a humorless laugh. "Not only am I a cripple, but I'm also not smart enough to pass high school math."

"Fuck, man." I sighed and sat down in my desk chair. "Would you stop with that? Any girl would be lucky to have you."

He shook his head. "It doesn't matter anyway. She's been dating the star linebacker since freshman year. Off limits."

"Well, you might still get your chance. High school relationships don't always last. I would know." I shoved the last pair of jeans into the bag and zipped it up. "Just don't do what I did if you don't get your way."

"Which was what, exactly?"

I smiled ruefully before summarizing my actions. "Throw an adult-sized temper tantrum."

# CHAPTER 2

MACKENNA

"Well, who do we have here?" Shayla Perkins drawled from behind the cash register. "If it isn't Mackenna Connelly."

"That's me," I said with a tight smile, nervously glancing around at the empty store. The Daywood Country Mart was surprisingly slow for a Sunday. Jazzy elevator music played through the speakers overhead, and the only other person I saw was Stan, the store manager, snoozing in his office.

"You still look the same," she said with a sugary-sweet smile. "Your hair's a lot longer, though."

"Thanks." I brushed some of the unruly dark strands away from my face, wishing I had at least put it in a pony-tail before going out in public.

"When did you get back into town?"

"A month ago," I replied. I should've driven the extra fifteen minutes to Walmart instead of coming here. The last thing I wanted was an impromptu high school reunion. And with bed-head, no less.

"You back for good, then?"

Nodding, I pushed all my groceries to the end of the conveyer belt, hoping she'd get the hint that I didn't want to stick around for conversation.

She didn't get the hint.

With a snail-like pace, she slowly scanned my items while asking me questions I didn't want to answer.

"So you, like, didn't hit it big in Nashville?" *Beep.* "Oooh, did you get to meet Tim McGraw?" *Beep.* "Where are you living now?" *Beep.* "Back home with your parents?" *Beep.* "I heard they moved to the other side of town."

Ignoring the question about Tim McGraw—who I didn't get to meet—I gave her the CliffsNotes version. "No, not with my parents. And it turns out performing isn't really my thing, so I'm a songwriter now." I let out a relieved sigh as the last item reached her hand. "And I bought a house in Tolson."

"Tolson?" She scrunched up her face and flung a lock of bleached-blonde hair over her shoulder. "Why on earth would you want to live in Tolson? There's nothing in that town."

"Exactly," I said before swiping my debit card.

Most people didn't want to live in a town with fewer than 400 residents. Most single, twenty-one-year old women wouldn't voluntarily move to a place where eighty percent of the population was elderly.

But I wasn't most people.

I wanted solitude.

After three years of city life, I realized something—I wasn't a city girl. The crowds. The constant noise. Public transportation. Some people loved the hustle and bustle of Nashville, but not me.

I tried to like it. I really did. But in the end, I had to be honest with myself. I wasn't happy there.

Tolson was the perfect place to settle down. It was peaceful and quiet, which was great for my occupation. Plus, my parents were ecstatic to have me back in the area.

"So, Jaxon's still in the slammer?" Shayla asked, bringing up the one subject I wanted to avoid.

My chest tightened, that old feeling of panic resurfacing. The sound of his name caused unwelcome memories to float up. A tight, bruising grip on my arm. A cutting remark about my imperfect body. The crushing weight of him pinning me down.

Swallowing hard, I kept my response short as she handed me my receipt. "Yep."

Still not catching on to the fact that I didn't want to chat, she continued. "I can't believe he's still in there. I mean, what happened with you two was ages ago."

My nostrils flared and I couldn't keep the anger out of my voice. "Well, that's what happens when someone is charged with attempted murder."

Shayla's eyes widened, finally realizing she'd crossed a line. "Oh, I didn't mean to make it sound like he didn't deserve it. Of course, I'm on your side."

"Of course," I said sarcastically as I picked up my bags, and made a promise to myself to avoid this store like the plague from now on.

"Let's get together soon," she called at my back. "It'll be just like old times!"

*Fat chance.*

I waved, but didn't bother to respond as I walked through the automatic sliding doors, out into the summer heat.

After putting my groceries in the trunk of my trusty four-door Buick, I started the ten-minute drive back to my new home. I rolled all the windows down, enjoying the way the wind blew through my hair.

As my old hometown disappeared in the rearview mirror, I wondered who else I might run in to. Since I didn't spend much time on social media I'd lost touch with almost everyone I used to know, so I had no idea who'd left and who'd stayed behind.

It was probably smart to steer clear of Daywood all together. Although Tolson residents attended the Daywood school district, I hadn't had any trouble hiding out in the tiny town.

Back in high school, Shayla and I used to be friends. We weren't close, but our class was so small it was hard not to know everyone. And she might've been welcoming now, but that wasn't the last memory I had of her.

After Jaxon and I broke up, everyone took sides. That is, to say, *his* side.

People I thought were my friends suddenly became enemies. I ended up eating lunch alone in my car because no one would sit with me in the cafeteria. My house got egged several times, and someone vandalized my locker by writing 'bitch' and 'whore' all over it with a Sharpie.

And that was all *before* I shot the abusive asshole.

Jaxon was lucky I had shitty aim. The bullet went clean through his right shoulder, so it wasn't fatal. However, he wasn't very good with the sight of his own blood because he'd passed out, giving the police and paramedics time to show up.

The harassment from my peers got worse after 'the incident'.

Turns out, shooting someone could really ruin a person's reputation. Good thing I was so close to graduation, or else I might've ended up needing to be home-schooled.

When Jaxon was convicted, and put away for ten years, I thought people would move on. Unfortunately that wasn't the case, and I knew I needed to get away from the only town I'd ever known.

So, I ran.

Before Jaxon, music was my passion. I got a guitar for Christmas when I was twelve, and I spent countless hours learning new chords and writing songs. I used to imagine myself in the spotlight in front of thousands of cheering fans. I even won a few talent shows in my early teen years.

But Jaxon knew how to extinguish that ambition, knew how to make me question my abilities and my self-worth. People like him, they knew how to strip away your confidence one thread at a time, until there was nothing left.

But screw that.

My hopes and dreams weren't going to chase themselves, and I wanted to prove to myself that I could do it.

The summer after graduation, I packed up and moved down to Nashville to pursue a career in country music. However, it didn't quite work out the way I'd hoped.

Sometime between the loss of my innocence and the reclamation of my freedom, I developed debilitating stage fright. Open mic nights became my own personal hell. My anxiety was so bad that I froze as soon as I got up on stage.

Needless to say, the audience didn't like that much. They came to hear good music, and most of the time I couldn't deliver.

Within a year I was ready to pack it in, tuck tail, and run from the city.

After all, running away was something I was naturally good at.

But it didn't go unnoticed that I rocked it in the recording studio. The same night I made the decision to leave was the night I met my manager. I'd gone to the studio for one last jam session, and Kelly listened in on one of my songs. She said my style was great, but not for country music.

After a long talk, she convinced me to try my hand at songwriting, and she hooked me up with a popular punk band.

And that was my big break.

The female duet, known as The Princess and the Pariah, liked my style so much that they hired me as the full-time collaborator for their next album. The payout was good enough for me to buy a small house and start my new life as a hermit.

And, so far, hermit life was good.

My trip down memory lane was interrupted when I saw a large combine tractor blocking the road in the distance.

In a rural area like this it wasn't uncommon to get stuck behind slow-moving machinery, especially during farming season. But this tractor wasn't moving at all. Smack dab in the middle of the country road, it appeared to be broken down, and a couple of older men in flannel shirts stood off to the side talking.

I came to a stop behind an ancient station wagon. Judging by the three cars in front of me, I could guess the tractor had been in the way for a while.

Feeling impatient, I tapped my fingers on the steering wheel.

It wasn't like I had anywhere to be, but the frozen food in my trunk was melting by the second. I would be sorely disappointed if my ice cream sandwiches didn't survive.

Just as I was about to put my car in reverse, my eyes zeroed in on the object hanging from the bumper on the vehicle in front of me.

Wrinkling my nose, I scoffed.

A ball sac. An oversized, wrinkly metal ball sac. The heavy testicle pendulum swung back and forth in the breeze.

Disgusting.

If you're going to get held up in traffic, the last thing you want is to get stuck with that view. What kind of douchebag could feel good about driving around with that on display?

Deciding I didn't have time for this nonsense, I did a three-point turn and took a different road back to Tolson.

As I pulled up to my house, I let out a happy sigh at the sight of the small beige bungalow. It wasn't big, or new, but it was mine. All mine.

The wooden shingles on the roof were a bit rotted in some areas, and the windows needed to be replaced. The interior décor was outdated, but it still had the original woodwork. It had character, and the small front porch was a great spot for me hang out and play my guitar.

Inside the front door, there was a staircase that led to two bedrooms. A living room with a wood-burning fireplace was off to the right.

I took a left, veering into the kitchen, and set all the bags on my tiny round table.

As far as eating spaces went, mine was pretty sad-looking, with barely enough room for two people. But honestly, that extra chair was overkill.

I put the frozen items away first, but not before tearing into the ice cream sandwiches. Just as I took the first bite my phone rang, and my mom's face flashed on the screen.

"Hey, Mom."

"Hey, honey. What are you up to?"

Putting it on speakerphone, I set it on the counter.

"Just got back from the store," I said, shoving a few canned soups into the pantry.

"You ran out of ice cream sandwiches again, huh?"

She knew me so well. "How'd you guess?"

"Seems to be just about the only thing you leave the house for these days."

"Are you saying you wouldn't make a special trip to town for ice cream sandwiches?" I accused.

"I absolutely would. You know that."

"Good. That means we can still be friends," I joked. "I just can't trust someone who doesn't like vanilla ice cream mashed between cookies. It's not right."

She laughed. "I hope you're eating other things, too."

"I got a wide variety of food groups," I informed her.

"You can't survive on just soup and Hawaiian rolls either."

Eyeing the items in question, I emptied the last bag. "I got chicken, too. There's this Crockpot recipe I want to try."

"Alright, alright." She sighed, and a long pause followed. I knew what was coming next. "When are you coming to visit? We'd love to see you."

"I just came over for dinner the other day."

"That was three weeks ago," she pointed out. "I just thought with having you closer, you'd be over here more often." Then she brought out the big guns. "Krista misses you. Her school year is almost over, and I know she's hoping to see you more."

"I'm sorry," I said, feeling guilty. "I'll try to make it over this weekend."

"I thought about stopping by your house yesterday, but I'm trying to respect your privacy..." She trailed off, and I could tell there was more she wanted to say.

"Don't hold back on me, Mom. What's the matter?"

"We thought you never wanted to come home because we were still living in that house." The words came out in a rush, like she'd been holding it in for a while. "One of the reasons we bought the new place is so you'd feel comfortable here."

Home visits were few and far between over the last three years. As much as I tried to overcome it, I couldn't even think about that closet without experiencing anxiety.

The new country property they bought earlier in the year was gorgeous, and I appreciated their relocation on my behalf.

"I swear I'm not avoiding you on purpose," I told her before popping the last of the ice cream sandwich into my mouth. "I've just been sort of unsociable lately. Living in the city, I was surrounded by people all the time. It's just been nice to get some time to myself. Plus, I'm really on a roll with my writing."

"I can understand that. You're my little girl, so worrying about you is in my job description. Just don't be a stranger, okay?"

"I won't. And Mom?"

"Yeah?"

"Love you."

"Love you, too."

After putting the rest of the groceries away, I sank down into my favorite chair. I had everything I needed— my guitar, my notebook, and blissful silence.

The weight of the six-string Martin felt familiar in my hands, and a calm came over me as I plucked at the strings. Notes turned into melodies, and satisfaction flowed through me. This was the elusive peace I had been chasing for so long.

I was home.

# CHAPTER 3

JIMMY

As I pulled up in front of Grandma's house, a feeling of nostalgia washed over me. This place held some of my greatest childhood memories.

My parents weren't kidding about it needing a face-lift, though.

The white brick exterior was a little worse for wear, and the metal porch overhang was rusted and sagging on one side. The landscaping was beyond neglected. Overgrown bushes and weeds lined the perimeter of the small one-story home.

There would be no shortage of tasks to keep me busy. And out of trouble.

I walked across the dandelion-covered lawn, and Grandma's screen door opened with a loud creak. Her head of short dark curls popped out.

"James Peabody Johnson!" she greeted with a huge smile.

Slipping off my sunglasses, I laughed on the way up the porch steps. "Let's go easy on the full-name stuff, huh? Maybe save that for reprimands only."

"Well, then I'll get to say it at least once a day," she quipped. "Come on in. It's hot as hell outside."

When I walked through the door, the distinct smell of her arthritis cream hung in the air, reminding me that she was getting older. The same yellow and brown floral couch sat in front of the old box TV. Pictures of family and friends sat on the built-in shelves above the rocking chair in the corner. And I knew when I went into the kitchen, I'd see wallpaper with bright orange flowers, old veneer cabinets, and avocado-colored appliances.

The whole house seemed to be stuck in the 1970s.

No matter how many times my dad tried to convince her to upgrade, Grandma wouldn't budge. She swore if she bought new stuff, it'd just end up breaking six months later. Said they didn't make things like they used to.

It was fine with me. I loved everything about this place. Besides, she was probably right anyway, and I wasn't foolish enough to get into an argument with Grandma—I would lose every time.

"You been knitting again?" I asked, running my hand over the new bright pink afghan on the arm of her couch.

"Heavens, no." She chuckled. "I had to put away my knitting needles for good. These old hands just won't let me do it anymore. The little girl next door made it for me. She just moved in a month ago."

"That's nice of her." I smiled.

Grandma looked the same as always, a firecracker in a tiny package. Her thick-rimmed glasses were a little too big for her face, and she was wrapped in a fuzzy pink housecoat that was way too warm for summertime.

I dropped my duffle bag to the floor. Running my foot

over the old shaggy brown carpet, I noticed it needed to be vacuumed.

"So, what's up first on my list of duties?" I spread my arms. "I'm at your service."

"There are no duties," she said. "All you have to do is hang out with me."

Confused, my eyebrows furrowed. "Mom and Dad said you needed help. Isn't that why I'm here?"

She lovingly patted my cheek. "Jimmy, dear. I just said that so you wouldn't have to put up with their belly-aching all summer." She smiled, and a smirk spread over my face.

"You're shitting me."

"Nope. I might have a couple projects to keep you busy, but I really just want your company."

Grandma was one sneaky devil.

"Well, here I am." I went in for a hug, wrapping my arms around her petite frame.

After pulling back, she placed her hand in mine and passed something into my palm. I didn't have to look down to know it was a twenty-dollar bill. The 'shake 'n slip' had been her signature move for as long as I could remember. Mom and Dad frowned on her spoiling us, so she'd gotten sly about it. What appeared to be a simple handshake was really a way for her to give out $20, undetected.

"You know I love you, right?" I put the money in my pocket. "I'll do whatever you need. Mow your lawn, paint the house, anything."

Standing back, she smiled. "Can you do something for me right now?"

"You name it."

"Take a shower. You smell like you've been sitting in a sauna all day." Her nose wrinkled and I laughed. "Don't you have air conditioning in that old car?" She gestured out the front window at the beat-up station wagon I bought off Craigslist a few years ago.

I shook my head. "It broke."

The five-hour drive from Heyworth, Ohio to Tolson, Illinois wasn't that bad, but with temps near 90 and no A/C, I spent most of it sweating my ass off.

"Take it down to Hank's Auto Shop soon. Those boys can fix anything. Now—" She placed her hands on her hips. "—if you're gonna be staying here, I have to lay down a couple rules."

Raising my eyebrows, I wondered what kind of crazy shit she was about to say. Grandma didn't have many rules.

"I know what you're thinking. I've always been lenient with you boys," she said, reading my mind. "But you've grown up. The kind of trouble you can get into now is different. When you get older, mistakes are harder to fix. I gather you learned that lesson recently?"

"Yeah." I nodded. "I learned the hard way."

"Good. You won't forget it then." She smiled. "Back to my rules. Number one—you know where the liquor is in this house and you're welcome to it, as long as you use it moderately. And don't ever get behind the wheel of a car when you're drunk."

I held up my hands. "I don't drink and drive. Besides,

where am I gonna go? I'm stuck here in middle-of-no-where Illinois."

"Rule number two," she continued. "No hanky panky in the hot tub. I've never broken that rule and neither will you."

I made a face. "Grandma. No offense, but gross."

She shrugged. "Those are the rules."

"You don't have to worry about either of them. Like I said before, I don't think there's much trouble I could get into here, and I highly doubt this town is crawling with eligible ladies."

"You never know." She headed toward the kitchen and turned back with a smile. "It's good to have you, Jimmy. I'll get some snacks ready while you clean up."

Grandma and her fucking snack cakes. She didn't discriminate between Little Debbie, Hostess, Twinkies, or Ding-dongs. If it was covered in sugar or filled with frosting, she bought it. I was probably going to gain ten pounds over the summer.

I dumped my luggage in the guest room and gave the small bed a skeptical look. The twin-size mattress used to be perfect when I was younger. Now, at 6'3", I was pretty sure my feet would be hanging off the end.

It didn't really matter. I'd slept in less comfortable places. Back at school, I'd passed out on someone's front lawn more than a handful of times and woken up to find inappropriate pictures drawn on my face with permanent marker. At least I wasn't in danger of that happening here.

Then again...

Maybe I was. I wouldn't put it past Grandma to play a prank like that. Amused by thoughts of Grandma wielding a Sharpie, I went to the bathroom to peel off my sweaty clothes.

After the shower, I dried off with a pink towel before tying it around my waist. With matching walls, curtains, and carpet, the entire room looked like it'd been coated with Pepto-Bismol.

Whistling a random tune, I went to my bedroom to get dressed and unpack. Just as I was about to stick my hand into the duffle bag, something inside started moving.

"Oh shit!" I jumped back three feet as I heard a loud squawk. "What the fuck?"

Grandma came running into the room like the house was on fire.

"What's going on?" she asked, sounding panicked. "Where is he?"

"Where is who? And what is *that*?" I pointed to the little orange head popping out of the place where the zipper was open.

"That's Sweet Pea. My parrot." She made clucking noises as she bent down to pick up the intruder, and I swore he muttered "*motherfucker*" while glaring in my direction.

"Did he just cuss at me?"

She grinned, stroking his brightly-colored body. "Isn't he smart? He has a very colorful vocabulary."

Scoffing, I couldn't keep the sarcastic remark to myself. "I wonder where he got that from."

She shot me a look and Sweet Pea gave me the side-eye. He climbed up Grandma's arm and found a spot on her shoulder. He let out another squawk, then uttered a very clear "*fuck you.*"

I pointed at him. "He did! He did cuss at me."

I was a little confused. I'd never known Grandma to be an animal-lover. She said cats were assholes and dogs were too much work, so I had no idea what possessed her to get a rainbow-feathered devil.

"When did you get a bird?"

"Sweet Pea is a Sun Conure." She beamed with pride before her face got serious. "Bernice from my knitting club passed away a couple months ago. No one in her family would take him, so I volunteered."

"No one would take him? That's so hard to believe," I deadpanned.

With a smile, Grandma went back to petting his feathers. He nibbled at her fingertip before taking flight, disappearing into the dining room. He came right back with some kind of dangly toy in his beak, landing on her shoulder once again.

"You just let him fly around here like he owns the place?" I waved my hand through the air.

"Of course," she replied, as if it was ridiculous to suggest otherwise. "He lives here, too."

Shaking my head, I huffed out a laugh. This was definitely going to be an interesting couple of months.

Keeping a firm hold on the towel—because the last thing I needed was for my grandma to see me in my birthday suit—I bent down to grab some jeans out of my bag.

But when I looked inside there was bird shit. Every-fucking-where.

Making a sound of disgust, I glared at the bird. "Tweety Poo took a dump all over my clothes."

"Well, you know where the washing machine is," Grandma said, as if having all my things get crapped on was completely normal.

Letting out a growl, I snagged a pair of underwear from one of the outer pockets that was unaffected by Sweet Pea's literal shit storm.

"I don't have anything to wear," I said, holding out the scrap of material that wasn't going to cut it. There was no way I wanted to walk around here in only my briefs.

"Oh, don't get your panties in a twist. I'm leaving anyway. I've got a date, so I won't be around to see you in your skivvies."

"A date?" I asked, my eyebrows going up. Then I remembered meeting her boyfriend last Christmas. "Oh, yeah. Your neighbor. Ernie, right?"

Smiling, she nodded.

I couldn't help feeling grateful for the old man who'd made her so happy. Grandpa passed away more than fifteen years ago, and my memories of him were fuzzy but pleasant. I remembered coloring books, Matchbox cars, and the smell of cigars. He had a way of making me feel like I was 'one of the guys', even though I was just a little kid.

The watch I always wore on my left wrist had been a gift from him the Christmas before he suffered the massive heart attack that took his life. It stopped working years ago, but I never broke the habit of wearing it. When he gave it to me he'd told me his dad had gotten it for him, and I was glad to have something passed on to me, even if it was an old watch.

Over the years, I'd wondered how Grandma coped with her husband being gone and all her relatives living in different states. That was what sucked about living so far away—I always hated to think of her all alone.

But, thanks to Ernie, I didn't have to worry about that anymore.

"Well, tell him I said hey."

"Will do. By the way…" She pointed at my chest. "What the hell are those?"

Glancing down, I looked at the recent changes on my body. "Ah, are you referring to the tattoos or the nipple piercings?"

"All of it." Her eyes landed on my upper arm, then her voice got quiet. "Are those peonies?"

Nodding, I turned a little so she could see the full picture. "Because they're your favorite."

"Well I'll be damned, Jimmy," she said, looking misty-eyed. Then she motioned toward my chest again. "What about the piercings? Did that hurt?" Looking down at her housecoat, she added, "Maybe I should get some."

A rude sound escaped at the awful suggestion. "Grandma…no. God, no."

"Seriously. I think Ernie might like it."

Mortified, I ran a hand over my face. "Please stop talking."

I loved my grandma, and there wasn't much we couldn't talk about. But the subject of nipple piercings was going too far.

She laughed and pointed at my horrified expression.

"Boy, I really had you going. You're white as a sheet!" Bending over to slap her knee, she let out a cackle. Sweet Pea made a sound of protest when he almost fell from her shoulder, and I cracked a grin.

"Funny. Really funny."

Grandma straightened back up and adjusted the glasses on her nose. "This is going to be the best summer ever!"

# CHAPTER 4

MACKENNA

After nailing down the lyrics for the song I'd been working on for the past week, I shot off an email to my manager to let her know I should have a demo ready in a few days.

Then I decided to head next door.

My neighbor was the only person I saw on a regular basis. I met Beverly when her parrot escaped through an open window. Sweet Pea had flown straight to my front porch, where I was lounging on my swing. He perched on the armrest, cocked his head to the side, then pooped on my leg.

It was love at first sight. Sort of.

Without bothering to clean up the mess, I continued strumming my guitar and started to sing. The bird began to dance.

As I softly let out the melody, I realized my stage fright didn't extend to parrots. For the first time in a long time, I performed without a hint of nervousness.

And my audience enjoyed it.

When I was done, he bobbed his head while letting out a series of loud screeches, which alerted his owner to his location.

Beverly had rushed over, apologized, and handed me a handkerchief to clean myself up when she saw the mess on my jeans.

I'd jokingly asked her if I could have playdates with Sweet Pea, and she seemed thrilled about the idea.

Such a sweet lady. She had a tendency to drop an F-bomb or two, but sweet nonetheless.

So, a few times a week I went over to her house to play with my new friend. I liked to clean his cage, change his water, and give him treats while he sat on my shoulder. Sometimes I brought my guitar and he'd listen to me sing.

Today I decided to leave my instrument at home, because my hands were achy and the tips of my fingers were numb from overuse.

As I hopped down my front steps, my feet skidded to a stop.

The same station wagon from earlier was parked on my street. I might not have even noticed it if it hadn't been for the bumper balls. The car itself was hideous, with fake wood paneling along the sides. The paint job looked like it was maroon at some point, but now it was a faded murky brown.

Grumbling about my new view, I crossed the fifteen feet between my house and Beverly's and made my way to her backyard. I knocked on the old screen door and waited for an answer. After a minute I decided to let myself in, just like she told me to do if she wasn't home.

I lifted her stone goose statue and picked up the spare key she kept underneath it. Stepping inside, I listened for Sweet Pea loudly screeching obscenities.

I did hear something loud, but it wasn't Sweet Pea.

Jimmy Buffet's 'Cheeseburger in Paradise' blared through the house, and I followed the music to the kitchen. I wasn't sure what I would find, but as long as it wasn't my neighbor making out with *her* neighbor I was good.

Turning the corner, I stopped dead in my tracks at the sight in front of me.

It wasn't Beverly. Or Ernie.

And I most definitely *wasn't* good.

A guy wearing nothing but camo-print underwear and a peach-colored apron stood in front of the stove. He was facing away from me, and I caught sight of a large tattoo—angel wings—across the expanse of his muscular back.

Surprised, I let out a high-pitched squeak. The sound got the stranger's attention and he started to pivot in my direction.

My eyes fell to his sculpted ass, the muscles flexing as he shifted his weight from one foot to the other. He wore briefs. Not boxers or boxer-briefs—actual tighties. No guy should look good in those, but damn, he did.

His black hair was shorter on the sides and longer on top. Some of the inky strands fell over his forehead, falling to just above his bright green eyes.

His lips were parted in surprise, and something flipped in my stomach at the sight of his mouth. The bottom lip was twice the size of the top. Plump. Pouty.

Dark tattoos painted his chest and he had colorful flowers down the length of his left arm. And...

*Is that a nipple piercing?*

Because of the apron, I couldn't see his abs, but my guess was that he had a solid six-pack under there.

I opened my mouth to say something—anything.

I wanted to ask him what he was doing in Beverly's house. Or apologize for walking in on him while he was naked.

Instead, my social awkwardness presented itself full-force with the words that tumbled out of my mouth next.

"If you tried to hide in the woods, at least no one would be able to see your ass."

His emerald eyes widened. "What?"

Figuring he probably didn't hear me the first time because of the loud music, I raised my voice. "Camouflage underwear. Your butt would totally blend in with the bushes."

Looking like he was caught between laughing and being outraged, he opened his mouth to respond.

Then all hell broke loose.

# CHAPTER 5

JIMMY

After Grandma left for her date, I had the house to myself. I threw all my soiled clothes into the washer, then gave Sweet Pea one last glare as he climbed on top of his cage, happily rattling a toy as if he had nothing to be ashamed of. In fact, he seemed pretty damn proud of himself.

"Crazy-ass bird," I muttered, then went to the kitchen to search for food in nothing but my underwear.

I opened the freezer and grinned.

"Hell yeah," I whispered as I took out the pre-made hamburger patties.

One look in the fridge and pantry told me that Grandma had stocked up on all my favorite foods. The woman was a saint. A foul-mouthed saint.

Dropping three burgers into the pan, I switched on the ancient radio on the counter and turned the volume all the way up.

As the burgers sizzled, I got out the buns and set them on a plate. Next, I doused them in mustard and ketchup, then went to flip the burgers over. Something popped in the pan, spraying my chest with hot grease.

"Ow, fuck!" I hissed, stepping back from the stove. I

wiped at my reddened skin with a damp dish towel, once again cursing the bird that was responsible for my lack of clothing. If I'd had a shirt on, this wouldn't have happened.

I spotted Grandma's apron hanging on a hook by the kitchen doorway. I looked down at my unprotected torso, then back at the frilly fabric.

*So, that's what those things are for.*

After mulling it over, I knew the best option was for me to wear it. Anything was better than having first-degree burns on my nipples. After tying it on I went back to my lunch, singing along to the radio.

Once the meat was thoroughly cooked, I turned off the heat and slid the pan off the back burner. I was about to pick up the spatula when I heard a squeak behind me.

Thinking it was that damn bird again, I started to turn around, ready to tell him not to take a dump on my food.

Imagine my surprise when I ended up face to face with a girl. A gorgeous-as-fuck girl.

For about three awesome seconds we made eye contact, and my gaze dropped to her full pink lips. Her black tank top hugged her body, and the color almost matched her long dark hair. Her skin was pale—creamy. This time of year, a lot of people spent time outside in the sun. Her fair complexion told me that she either didn't have the ability to tan, or she didn't spend a lot of time outside. Either way the look suited her, the contrast stunning.

I noticed her eyes were focused on my chest, specifically the nipple that was peeking out from behind the apron—the girly apron that was barely covering my body.

Then she started rambling on about my underwear.

I didn't have time to process what was happening because a flash of bright color flew through the room. Startled, I stumbled back, knocking my plate off the counter.

Sweet Pea flew overhead and dropped a watery bird turd on my shoulder with an audible splat.

He let out a squawk as he hit the kitchen window, then knocked over an old coffee tin full of pennies my grandma always kept next to the sink. Coins scattered everywhere.

I took a step forward, attempting to catch the frantic bird, but he flew out of my reach, leaving just as fast as he came.

My foot slipped on one of the buns and I reached out to grab on to something to keep me from falling on my ass.

Unfortunately, the object closest to me was the flour container. I managed to stay upright, but the flour wasn't so lucky. An explosion of white powder filled the room as it hit the floor, covering the orange and white checkered linoleum along with the pennies.

I heard a feminine gasp and awareness hit me like a freight train.

I was practically naked. I was wearing an apron. I almost fell over while being practically naked in that apron. I had parrot shit running down my arm.

And a beautiful stranger was staring at me, with her perfect mouth hanging open in shock.

This wasn't my finest moment.

I switched off the music and the silence that followed was deafening.

"Who are you?" I barked, the question coming out harsher than I intended as I grabbed some paper towels and wiped at the mess on my skin.

"Mackenna. Beverly's neighbor," she replied, her eyes narrowing. "Who are you?"

"Jimmy." When I got a blank stare, I felt the need to elaborate. "Beverly's grandson."

"Oh." She blushed, looking away. "I thought her grand-kids were younger."

"Nope. All grown up," I said, spreading my arms, caus-ing her to glance back at me. I was reminded again of how exposed I was when she averted her eyes to the ceiling and bit her lip. She was obviously uncomfortable, and I couldn't help having a little fun with the situation—anything to dis-tract myself from the embarrassment I was feeling. "And you must be the kid who moved in next door."

"Excuse me?" she asked, her eyes cutting back to me.

"The one who knits Grandma's blankets. I take it that's you?"

"Yes, except I'm not a child, obviously." Now it was her turn to spread her arms, and her breasts strained against the material of the tight shirt.

I bit back a groan as my eyes trailed over the rest of her body. "Obviously."

There was nothing childish about her. She was above average height for a girl, probably about 5'7". Toned thighs led to soft hips. Those curves gave way to the dips in her narrow waist. And those tits. My guess was a solid c-cup. Fucking perfect.

Somewhere in the recesses of my mind, my inner gentleman was screaming at me to stop leering and estimating her bra size.

But I couldn't look away.

Her nipples were hard, which probably meant she was either cold or turned on. And it wasn't chilly in here. Grandma set her thermostat at a balmy 75 degrees, often keeping the windows cracked even though she had the air conditioning on.

Knowing this girl could be feeling the same instant attraction I was made my dick twitch. Suddenly I was very grateful for the apron, because it was hiding the stiffy I was sporting.

Mackenna huffed and started to turn away. "Well, this is awkward, and not what I had planned for today, so I'm just gonna go..."

"Wait. You're making me clean this up by myself?" I asked, stalling.

I should've wanted her to leave. She was right—this was incredibly awkward. But my desire to keep talking to her outweighed the humiliation. I still didn't know why she was here, and I wanted to find out.

Facing away from me, she paused. "Could you at least put some clothes on? That apron is ridiculous."

"My wardrobe is out of commission at the moment, so this is all I've got," I said. "Unless you want me to just take it off...?"

"No." She quickly shook her head, and I watched the long strands swish against her lower back. I didn't get a chance to admire the way her jean shorts hugged her rounded ass because she turned around with a determined look on her face.

"Do you really want me to stay?" she asked while boldly eyeing the apron, challenging me to say no.

"Yes." I didn't hesitate.

Pressing her lips together, she assessed the room then let out a resigned sigh. "Okay. I'll sweep. You get mop duty."

Her bossy, business-like attitude made me grin. I thought about arguing—just to keep her around a little longer—but decided against it. Between my wandering eyes and forcing her to clean up my mess, I had already crossed over the threshold of rude.

After grabbing the cleaning supplies from the closet, I handed her the broom and we got to work. As she swept the flour-covered pennies into a pile, I filled a bucket with hot water.

She stayed focused on the mess, doing her best to ignore me.

I didn't like it.

"What are you doing, letting yourself into my grandma's house anyway?" I asked, needing to know if this was going to be a regular occurrence. Partly hoping it would be. "Are you in the habit of breaking and entering?"

"Beverly told me I could come over anytime," she said defensively, her eyebrows furrowed. "I like Sweet Pea."

"You're kidding."

She still wouldn't look at me. "I take care of him, clean

out his cage and stuff. But if you have a problem with me coming over, then you can do it from now on."

"Oh, hell no. I want nothing to do with that bird. He's evil."

She stopped sweeping to glare at me. "He is not."

"He's an asshole," I stated flatly.

"Most parrots are assholes," she shot back.

We were only a few feet from each other, and now that she was looking at me I noticed the unique color of her eyes. They were the color of the ocean. Not clear and blue like the Caribbean.

Stormy.

Gray-blue on the outside and sandy brown around the iris.

I couldn't help feeling like I'd seen her somewhere before. "You look a little familiar. Have we met?"

"No." She bent down to gather the coins and dropped them into the coffee tin, each one falling in with a *clank*.

I crouched next to her to help, reaching for a few strays that had rolled under the table. "What's your last name?"

"Connelly," she said warily, and suddenly it clicked.

"I saw you in the news a few years ago. Your story was all over social media. You were that guy's girlfriend. What's his name... Jason or something."

She glanced away with a pinched expression. "Jaxon."

"Yeah, that's it." I snapped my fingers. "Jaxon's girlfriend."

Her head whipped back in my direction and her eyes blazed, that storm raging in their depths. "Don't call me that. Never call me that."

"Whoa. Sorry." I held up my hands, realizing I'd struck a nerve. I didn't remember much about her, just that everyone within a 30-mile radius had been talking about the breakup that ended with the guy freaking out and going to prison.

Changing the subject seemed like a good idea.

"What can I call you then?" I grinned, trying to lighten the moment. "How about Mack?"

"No." The last penny made it back into the container.

Both of us stood, and she reached around me to place it in its spot next to the sink. The kitchen was small, so she had to get closer to me. I could've moved back to make more room for her, but I didn't. I stood my ground, letting her arm brush against my stomach.

I thought she was going to leave, but instead she turned to gaze out the window over the sink. She was just a foot away from me now, and I stared at her profile. Those full pink lips stood out against her pale skin.

"How long will you be here?" she asked quietly, curiously.

"All summer," I replied and something akin to dread flashed across her face, the corners of her mouth turning down.

I was a little offended. She was the one who'd let herself into my grandma's house, uninvited. We'd barely met, but I got the distinct feeling she didn't like me much.

"Well, Mack," I taunted, deliberately using the nickname she didn't want. Leaning in close enough to smell the clean scent of her shampoo, I whispered, "Looks like we'll be seeing a lot of each other."

She sucked in a breath and stepped away. I was sure she was about to run from the room, but she didn't get the chance.

Grandma came around the corner, her purse slung around her shoulder. "I'm back. Forgot my checkbook." She glanced back and forth between Mackenna and me, then smiled wide. "Oh, good. You two have met."

"Barely," I grumped, self-consciously tugging at the hem of the apron.

Ernie was right behind Grandma, and his eyes widened under the shadow of his ballcap as he took in the condition of the room and my attire. Or lack thereof.

"Jimmy was just telling me how much he loves Sweet Pea," Mackenna piped up. "He said he wanted to clean his cage from now on, so I guess you won't need me for that anymore."

Shocked at the blatant dishonesty, I narrowed my eyes at her. "Liar."

"James Peabody Johnson," Grandma gasped, and even though Mackenna didn't smile, I saw her lips twitch at the use of my full name. "You'll be polite to our guest."

"Breaking in doesn't really make her a guest, does it?"

"Mackenna's welcome here anytime. You'd best remember that," Grandma said firmly.

The gorgeous girl shoved the broom in my direction. I took it from her, making sure our fingers brushed. The hair on my arm stood up at the contact.

Standing back, she put her hands on her hips, scowled at me one last time, then glanced at Grandma. "I need to get back home anyway. It was nice to see you, Beverly. You too, Ernie."

As she walked from the room, I could see white handprints from the flour on her waist. The sight of it was somewhat erotic, and I wished I'd been the one to put those prints there. I heard her whistle a goodbye to the parrot, then she was gone.

"Well." Ernie hitched his thumbs under the suspenders he always wore. "Gotta say, this entire situation is mighty uncomfortable. I'll go wait in the car. Great to have you here for the summer, Jimmy!"

Then it was just Grandma and me.

"Well, that was embarrassing," I said pointlessly.

Shaking her head, Grandma clucked her tongue. "Goodness. I hope you and Mackenna can work out your differences by tomorrow."

"What's tomorrow?"

"Mackenna volunteered to paint my house. I thought you could lend a hand."

I grimaced. "I think she hates me."

Grandma shrugged. "Fix it. Unless you don't want to help."

"No way in hell am I letting her do the work by herself." I may have been a lot of things, but lazy wasn't one of them. And, despite what the past few minutes might suggest, I wasn't an asshole either.

"Good answer," she said with a nod, then her face softened in the way it did when she wasn't joking around or cussing up a storm—which was hardly ever. "I mean it,

Jimmy. Be nice to that girl. I think she needs friends. Poor thing hardly ever smiles."

Feeling a mix of emotions, I glanced out the window at the house next door. I searched the windows, hoping to get a glimpse of dark hair and pale skin, but I saw nothing but closed blinds.

"She comes over to hang out with the shit machine?"

"James!" Grandma scolded, then cracked a smile. "Yes. Mackenna loves that crap factory. That girl is an enigma. I've never known anyone so kind, yet so closed off at the same time. I've tried to get her to open up to me, but it's been tough. And you know how likable I am!" Exasperated, she threw her hands in the air.

Chuckling, I nodded. "It's impossible not to like you."

"Damn straight."

"I'll try to be nice," I promised.

"Good. Be the charmer I know you are. You've got something in your hair." She gestured toward my head, then looked at the flour still covering a good portion of the kitchen. "I don't think baking is your thing. Hopefully you're better at painting." Walking out of the room, she called over her shoulder, "And by the way, you look good in peach."

Then I was alone again with no lunch, one hell of a mess, and a dick that was still slightly perked up from meeting *her*.

*Mackenna.*

I wasn't proud of myself. I'd just been a complete jerk to the hottest girl I had ever seen.

Initially, the reason for that was mostly because I was mortified, but there was something about pushing her buttons that turned me on. Her attitude was defensive, aloof, and almost dismissive. And it might've been childish but I wanted her attention, even if it was because I made her mad.

An already-interesting summer just got a lot more intriguing.

Grabbing the mop, I went back to cleaning the disaster in the kitchen and promised myself I'd make peace with Mackenna tomorrow.

# CHAPTER 6

MACKENNA

Early morning sunlight filtered through the bathroom window as pulled my hair into a messy bun. Guilt weighed on me when I thought about the way I'd snapped at Beverly's grandson the day before. He had every right to be upset with me for walking in on him like that.

It was his house, after all. Well, at least for the time being.

On my way out of Beverly's yesterday, I looked at the family picture on the wall. A much younger Jimmy sat next to a blond-haired boy in front of a Christmas tree. When she told me about her grandkids, I'd assumed that picture was recent.

It wasn't.

The last thing I expected to see in that kitchen was a solid wall of muscle, tanned skin, and tattoos.

He caught me off-guard and I reacted badly, especially when he brought up Jaxon—the one thing no one could seem to forget. Apparently, three years didn't make much of a difference in this small corner of the world. Jimmy wasn't even from this area, but he remembered.

It wasn't just that, though... I'd been shocked by the

way my body responded to the sight of those tattoos. The freaking nipple piercings. Inky black hair and green eyes.

Along with his cocky attitude, it was a lethal combination. Exactly the kind of thing that drove women nuts.

I hadn't felt true physical attraction in years, and never with that intensity. If I was being honest, that was what caught me off-guard the most.

I shouldn't be attracted to a guy like Jimmy.

He had bad news written all over him, and last time I got with a bad boy, it ended horribly to say the very least.

I didn't need temptation or distraction. One thing I certainly didn't want was heartbreak. I had a feeling Jimmy could be the trifecta of all the things I should avoid.

As far as I was concerned, he was completely off-limits. But that didn't mean I couldn't be civil toward him. Jimmy and I would need to get along if we were going to be temporary neighbors.

Or maybe I could just stay locked away in my house for a couple months.

*But what about the ice cream sandwiches?*

There was delivery for that sort of thing, right? Shaking my head, I laughed at how ridiculous I was being.

Surely, Jimmy had better things to do than hang around this sleepy town all the time. Convincing myself I probably wouldn't see him very often, I made the resolve to be nicer next time I ran into him.

After putting on raggedy gray shorts and an old white tank top, I went outside and made my way to Beverly's backyard.

My footsteps faltered at the sight in front of me.

Jimmy was there, shirtless and sweating from exertion as he spread a coat of the most obnoxious shade of green I had ever seen onto the white brick exterior of the house.

I don't know why I assumed I'd be painting alone. When Beverly mentioned the project, I offered to help, but that was before I knew about her new roommate.

Of course Jimmy would be helping. He was a strong, able-bodied man.

For a few seconds, I considered backing out. Occasionally running into Jimmy was one thing. Being forced to work together for days?

I wanted no part of that.

I could just say I wasn't feeling well and spend the rest of the day spying on him from my window. But I'd never been one to flake on my commitments. I just needed to suck it up.

Forcing my feet forward, I took the opportunity to study his body while he was unaware of my presence.

His black gym shorts hung low on his hips, and I could see the gray waistband of his briefs. The muscles of his back and arms flexed as he used the roller, going up and down in long, steady strokes. The angel wings on his back had something written within the feathers, but I wasn't close enough to see what it said.

I was so focused on finding out I didn't see the garden hose in the grass, and the toe of my flip-flop got caught on it.

Nearly stumbling to the ground, I used every core

muscle I didn't even know I had to keep from falling. Arms flailed ungracefully. Hands flapped through the air. My feet did some sort of weird dance as I struggled to stay upright.

Jimmy must have heard my scuffle because he turned just in time to see me straightening my shoulders, trying to play it off like I didn't just almost bite the dust in front of the hottest guy ever.

"Hey, Mack. Thought you weren't gonna show up." He smirked. "Thought maybe you changed your mind."

"It's Mackenna," I corrected haughtily, smoothing some loose hairs away from my face. The guilt I'd been feeling earlier was replaced with unwelcome sexual attraction and a bit of irritation. "And it's only 8:30. I didn't realize you wanted to get started at the ass crack of dawn."

"Your dear friend, Tweety Poo, woke me up at 5:00 this morning with his ungodly screeching," he said. "Figured I might as well make good use of the time."

"I'm not a morning person," I grumbled.

"That makes two of us." Jimmy laughed, and my heart did some sort of weird fluttery thing. Then he put down the roller and held out both of his fists. "Hey, pick a hand."

The sun glinted off his nipple piercings, and the temptation to gawk at them was almost too much. I kept my eyes trained on his face as I pointed at his left fist. When he turned it over and opened his hand, there was nothing there.

"Wrong," he said before opening the right hand. A Hershey kiss sat in the middle of his palm. I stared at it, not sure what his intentions were. He extended it my way, and I reared back a little when he invaded my personal space. "For you. A peace offering."

"Oh." Surprised by the random act of kindness, I picked it up, my eyes flitting from the silver-covered chocolate to Jimmy's face. "Thank you."

Unwrapping the candy, I popped it into my mouth. The chocolate melted on my tongue and my mood lifted.

Maybe Jimmy wasn't so bad after all.

I sent him a grateful look and picked up my paint brush. Starting with the trim around the windows, I purposely chose a spot several feet away and we worked in silence for a while.

My phone pinged with a text, and I smiled when I saw who it was from.

> **Krista: Mom said you're coming over this weekend!**
> **Me: That's the plan**
> **Krista: Why not today?**

I almost laughed at her impatience. I could imagine her doing the puppy-dog eyes she had down to a science.

> **Me: I'm painting my neighbor's house and trying to ignore her irritating grandson**
> **Krista: Painting and babysitting duty? Rough deal**
> **Me: Not quite. He's an adult**
> **Krista: Is he hot??**

I rolled my eyes. At fifteen years old, she was boy-crazy and too cute for her own good.

I snuck a peek at Jimmy, who seemed to be busy concentrating on his section of the house. Trying to be very discreet, I snapped a picture with my phone, then sent it to my sister.

> **Krista: Holy shit!! Please tell me you're getting some**
>
> **Me: Don't say shit. And no one is getting anything from anyone**
>
> **Krista: Boo. You're no fun. Mom and Dad won't even let me date yet**
>
> **Me: Good. Aren't you supposed to be in school right now?**
>
> **Krista: I am. It's so close to the end of the year that the teachers don't even care. Mr. Dennison is asleep**

A picture came through with the caption "Seriously", and I couldn't hold back the amused snort. The history teacher looked exactly how I remembered him. Bushy gray mustache and thick-rimmed glasses. His bald head was tilted back in his desk chair, his eyes closed and mouth open.

> **Me: My view is a lot better than yours**
>
> **Krista: No shit. Send another pic!**
>
> **Me: Don't say shit. And no**

The next message she sent me was a sticking-tongue-out emoji. I rolled my eyes again and slipped the phone back into my pocket. Then I noticed Jimmy was watching me with a sexy half-smile.

"What?" Heat crept up to my cheeks.

He paused, then shook his head. "Nothing."

Nibbling at my lip, I tried to think of something to say because I wanted to be friendlier. Small talk wasn't my strong suit, and I always ended up feeling awkward if I filled the silence with meaningless conversation.

Fortunately, Jimmy spoke up first.

"Listen." He set the roller against the house and turned toward me. "I'm sorry about yesterday. You know, when I was kind of a jerk..."

"No, I'm the one who should be sorry," I said with a shrug. "I was kind of a jerk, too."

"Truce?" He walked over and held out his hand.

"Truce." I placed my palm against his.

A spark ignited, and it felt like an electrical current ran up the length of my arm, down my belly, and into my clit.

Quickly jerking my hand away, I almost gasped.

*What the hell was that?*

Jimmy tilted his head to the side, confused at my reaction. Hell, I was confused, too. A steady throb started between my legs, wetness flooded my panties, and I had to fight the urge to rub my thighs together.

Needing to talk about anything that wasn't remotely sexual, I directed my attention back to the house. "Are you sure this color isn't a mis-tint?"

He chuckled before spreading more of the absurd hue over the bricks. "Nope. This is the color Grandma wanted. I asked her three times before she said, 'Just paint the fucking house already.'"

My lips tipped up. "When she told me about the

project last week, I thought she meant something subtle. Like sage or avocado. Not..." I waved my hand as I thought about what to call it.

"John Deere green?" Jimmy filled in.

A laugh burst out of me because that was the perfect description. I wasn't sure if Beverly was trying to make her house stick out like a sore thumb, or blend in with the cornfields surrounding Tolson. Whatever her intention was, she succeeded in both areas.

I glanced over at Jimmy to find him gaping at me, his pouty lips slightly parted.

"What?" I asked, wiping at my cheek with my forearm. "Do I have paint on my face?"

He closed the few feet between us and I held my breath as he brought his hand up to my face. Grazing my left cheek, his voice came out soft. "You have a dimple right here."

My eyes closed as I allowed myself to soak up the gentle touch. My nipples tightened and something tumbled in my stomach. Sweat trickled down my neck, and I suspected it wasn't just from the heat.

The contact didn't last long. Jimmy's hand fell away, and he gave me that sexy smirk again.

Maybe being friendly was a bad idea.

A really bad idea.

Feeling a little light-headed, I went back to painting as I reminded myself of all the reasons why I should stay away from someone like Jimmy.

# CHAPTER 7

JIMMY

I made her laugh. Grandma said Mackenna never even smiled, but *I* made her *laugh*.

That sound made my pulse speed up, made me feel out of breath.

I thought she was beautiful before, but when the grin stretched over her face and that dimple appeared...Holy fuck.

Completely awestruck, I was rendered speechless for several minutes, but not before I touched her.

I had to touch her.

It couldn't have been my imagination the way she leaned into my hand. But after the moment was over, she put as much distance between us as possible. Literally. Picked up her paint bucket and worked at the opposite end of the house.

That stung.

We didn't talk much for the rest of the morning. When I attempted to make conversation, she shut it down with short, closed-ended answers.

Frowning, I looked over at her as I refilled the paint tray.

She seemed lost in her thoughts as she tapped her foot and her head tilted from side to side, like she was listening to a song I couldn't hear. Every now and then, her lips would move. I paused several times, staying as still as I could while straining to hear her.

"Got a song stuck in your head?" I asked, my curiosity finally getting the better of me.

Without missing a beat or glancing my way, she nodded. "Uh-huh."

She was doing that thing again, her aloofness driving me crazy. The one-word responses. The lack of eye contact.

She was avoiding me. But why?

Frustration bubbled up inside me and the need to get under her skin was almost uncontrollable. I needed a reaction out of her that was anything other than indifference.

I'd prefer a scowl over an impassive expression. I wouldn't wither under her glare—I'd bask in it, if she would just look at me. Like a dog waiting for scraps under the table, I'd take anything she was willing to throw my way.

When did I become such a masochist?

I wanted to get her attention. Taunt and tease her. Stir the pot a little. Instead of giving in to that desire, I behaved myself and tried to focus on the task at hand.

I came to Tolson with a plan. No women, no partying, and no fighting. But nothing could've prepared me for Mackenna.

She made me want to get into the best kind of trouble.

The kind of trouble I knew I wouldn't regret.

And if the way her laugh affected me was any indication, I was completely and utterly fucked.

\*

Around noon, Grandma brought out an overloaded tray of ham sandwiches, potato chips, bottled water, lemonade, and snack cakes.

Setting it on the patio table in the shade, she stood back and admired the house with a satisfied sigh. "You two are doing one hell of a job. The heat's supposed to get pretty bad today. Might not be a bad idea to pack it up soon."

We thanked her before sitting down for an awkward lunch.

Mackenna noisily ripped open her bag of chips before munching away, still ignoring me. Crossing her legs and shifting away from me, everything about her body language screamed *don't talk to me*.

My eyes roamed over her face, her hair, her body. I didn't even try to hide the fact that I was checking her out.

The apples of her cheeks had a sun-kissed glow, making her appear younger, more innocent. I could tell she wasn't wearing makeup, but her eyelashes were long and dark, just like her hair. With the rat's nest on top of her head, it was obvious she hadn't gone out of her way to look good.

But she did look good.

At first glance, she was beautiful. But the longer I looked at her, the more gorgeous she became.

And even though she was trying like hell to hide it,

something told me her inner beauty outshone her good looks. Because anyone who would sacrifice their time to knit blankets for an old lady was worth getting to know.

"So why did you agree to do this?" I asked, breaking the silence. "Painting the house, I mean. Grandma said you offered to do it for free, which was really nice by the way."

She shrugged like it wasn't a big deal. "Menial tasks help to clear my head. I'm a songwriter, and sometimes my thoughts get blocked up." She gestured toward her head. "Writer's block stinks. And I like doing things like this."

"Things like knitting," I supplied, and she nodded before reaching for the bottled water. She unscrewed the cap, then took a big gulp. I watched the way her lips wrapped around it, the way her throat constricted as she swallowed.

It was like this girl had a live wire that went straight to my dick. Every little thing she did turned me on. I was so caught up in staring, I jumped a little when she continued talking.

"Knitting, driving, taking a shower..." Picking at the label on the bottle, she kept her eyes downcast. "I seem to get my best ideas when I'm doing those things. Although it kind of sucks when it happens in the car or the shower, because I can't actually write it down."

Her lips tilted up on one side. Not quite a smile, but at least she wasn't frowning.

This was the most information I'd gotten out of her yet, and I was so greedy for more. Trying to ignore the mental image of her in the shower, I continued asking questions.

"Was it one of your songs you were thinking about earlier?"

She didn't look up as she answered. "Yeah."

"What kind of songs do you write?"

That seemed to get her interest, because her face brightened a bit and she glanced my way. "Pop punk, actually. I tried country, but my style wasn't a good fit. And I'm a pretty shitty performer, so it's best for me to stay behind the scenes."

"I highly doubt that."

"It's true," she said with certainty.

"You written anything I've heard before?"

Fiddling with the plastic cap, she grinned down at her hands. That not-quite-a-smile grew wider. "Maybe. You know The Princess and the Pariah?"

"Of course," I replied. They were one of the most popular bands right now. It was almost impossible to turn on the radio and not hear something from them.

"I co-wrote 'If Only' with them."

I nearly dropped my lemonade. "You did not."

"Yep, I did," she confirmed. "It's the only reason I was able to afford this." She tipped her head to the little beige house. "It isn't much, but I like it."

Impressed, I let out a whistle. "You're really talented."

She shook her head. "I just got a lucky break."

"Talented," I insisted, not liking the fact that she downplayed her abilities. "And a home-owner. That's pretty amazing for someone as young as you. What are you, twenty?"

"Twenty-one." Her smile morphed into a smirk and my heart hammered in my chest. "What about you? From the pictures Beverly has, I thought you were a tween."

I barked out a laugh. "I'll be twenty in August."

"Nineteen? That's young. You might as well be a tween," she deadpanned with a playful glint in her eye.

She was teasing me. Maybe even flirting?

Leaning forward on my elbows, I looked her in the eye and shot her the grin that always seemed to work with the ladies. "Baby, there's nothing *tween* about me."

I could see the exact moment she shut me out again. Her eyes darted away, her expression going back to impassive. Silence settled between us again, and I internally cursed myself for coming on too strong. I should've known my usual tactics wouldn't work with her.

Taking a large bite of her sandwich, Mackenna made it clear the conversation was over.

*Damn.*

Finishing off my food, I watched Mackenna while she watched everything else: the trees, the house, the rabbit that hopped across Ernie's yard.

Had I been wrong about her flirting with me? Things were going so well and then she just totally clammed up.

"Mack."

"Hmm?" She still played with the cap on her water bottle, twisting it on then off again.

"Why won't you look at me?"

She huffed. "Why don't you ever wear a shirt?"

Relaxing back in the chair, I gave a mock frown. "Do

you have a problem with my body? Body-shaming isn't cool, you know. I could have serious insecurity issues."

Finally, she glanced over at me with an apologetic expression. "No, your body is fine."

Deliberately flexing my pecs, I grinned. "You think I'm fine?"

I needed to stop egging her on, but I couldn't help it. I'd just spent the last eight months of my life pretending to be something I wasn't, and I just wanted to be myself with Mackenna.

Her teeth closed over her bottom lip, and I swear she was trying to bite back a smile. Just when I thought I might be winning her over, she sighed and looked back at the house.

"Well." She stood up. "Ready to get back to it, or do you want to call it a day?"

"I'm up for whatever you want," I said, disappointed that our conversation was coming to an end.

Pursing her lips, she surveyed the cloudless sky. "Maybe just a little longer. I don't mind the heat, but my skin burns pretty easily."

"Let's do the north side of the house," I suggested as we cleaned up our paper plates. "We should have some shade there for at least another hour."

Mackenna walked ahead of me, and when she bent down to pick up her bucket I got an instant hard-on. The shorts she had on weren't tight, but they barely made it past her ass cheeks. They were worn and frayed. Perfect for painting on a hot day.

Also perfect for giving me a boner.

There was a tiny hole in the fabric, and I caught sight of dark purple panties—the same dark purple she had on her cute-as-fuck toes.

Her tank top left little to the imagination. When she stretched to reach higher on the house it rode up, showing a sliver of smooth, creamy skin on her flat stomach. The racer back revealed a couple freckles on her left shoulder blade, and my hands itched to move the material aside to see if she had a tan line.

Fuck me.

My loose gym shorts started to tent, and I attempted to hide it by turning away to pour more paint into the al-ready-full tray.

"So, what else do you do with your time?" I asked, hop-ing some innocent conversation would calm me down.

"I like to sew," she replied. "I make the outfits for Bev-erly's goose."

I peeked around the side of the house to take a closer look at the statue sitting outside the back door. The patri-otic dress made me laugh. It even had a matching hat. "Are you fucking with me? You made clothes for a stone goose?"

"Are you making fun of me?" She pinned me with nar-rowed eyes, making my dick stiffen even more.

"So what if I am?" I asked, pushing those buttons, watching her react.

Her nostrils flared. My cock jumped.

"I make quilts, too." She lifted her chin. "There's noth-ing wrong with sewing."

"Yeah, if you're sixty. Don't you think you're a little young to be spending your Friday nights making goose hats?" I teased. I hadn't known Mackenna long, but it was obvious she lacked a social life. "When was the last time you went on a date?"

"That's none of your business," she responded, gripping the paintbrush so hard her knuckles were white.

Part of me knew I was going too far, but this was the longest I'd held her attention yet. She wasn't looking away now, and those stormy eyes held me captive.

"Tell me... what are your other hobbies?" I continued, taking a step toward her. "Bingo nights? Drinking prune juice in the morning? Shopping for the perfect Dr. Scholl's insert?"

"You know what?" She dropped her brush into the pan, and some of the green paint splattered onto my old sneakers, "this heat isn't agreeing with me. I'm going home."

"Oh, come on," I called after her. "Don't go. I was just playing around. Mack? Mackenna. Mack-Mack..."

My pleas were ignored. She walked up the steps of her front porch, threw one last scowl my way, then disappeared inside.

Well, shit.

*So much for that truce.*

I painted for another hour by myself before I called it quits. Not only was it hot as hell, but it also wasn't as much fun without Mackenna.

As I sprayed out the roller and the tray, I felt bad about the way I'd teased her. Obviously she was sensitive, and I purposely provoked her.

The idea of Mackenna being mad all day didn't sit well with me, so I decided to go grovel for forgiveness.

After packing away all the supplies and tools into the garage, I took a quick shower and changed into clean jeans. I almost didn't put on a shirt—just to fuck with her—but I'd already pissed her off enough for today. Throwing on a gray sleeveless tee I went to the kitchen in search of Grandma, but found a note stuck to the fridge instead.

*Jimmy,*

*I've got a hot date tonight. Don't wait up.*

*-Grandma*

Shaking my head in amusement, I went out the back door and mentally rehearsed the apology Mackenna deserved. Simply telling her *I'm sorry* and *I'm not always a dick* didn't seem good enough, but it was the best I could come up with.

My plan came to a halt when I heard a voice. Her voice.

She was singing. The music carried through the window of her living room. Although the window was shut, it didn't do much to muffle the sound.

The haunting melody of 'Burning House' by Cam floated out on an acoustic guitar, and I sent up a silent thanks for poor insulation. Like a total creep, I stood outside and listened. Leaning against her siding, I let my head fall back and closed my eyes.

I didn't think it was possible to be physically affected by music. Not like this. Adrenaline rushed through my body while goosebumps spread over my skin. My chest constricted and I had to remind myself to breathe.

Mackenna had the sweetest voice I'd ever heard.

She wasn't trying to sound a certain way, wasn't conforming to what was popular. Some people tried to interject a twang or an edge in their voice when they sang, especially if the style was country or punk.

But not Mackenna.

Straightforward. Natural. Real.

So fucking sweet.

Disappointment hit me when the music stopped, but I knew I needed to move. I'd been standing here for far too long already. Just as I was about to step away from the house, she started up again.

I recognized this song, too. It was 'If Only', the one she co-wrote with The Princess and the Pariah. But Mackenna's version was so much better than the one I'd heard on the radio.

The urge to see her was too much to resist.

Moving stealthily, I peeked over the window sill. Facing slightly away, Mackenna was sitting in an armchair with a laptop in front of her on the coffee table. The guitar sat in her lap and her fingers played over the strings effortlessly.

Although I still wanted to apologize, I couldn't bring myself to interrupt her. I promised myself one more minute—just one—then I would leave.

That minute went by. And another.

I couldn't stop watching. Couldn't stop listening.

She began a new song. This one was completely unfamiliar to me, but it was the best yet. The lyrics were about being lost and life not turning out the way we expected. I could definitely relate to that.

Suddenly, as if she sensed my presence, her head turned toward the window.

I darted to the side.

She didn't stop singing, so I had to assume she didn't see me. Hoping I hadn't been caught, I flattened myself against the side of the house and inched back toward Grandma's, leaving the heavenly sound behind.

# CHAPTER 8

JIMMY

Two days. With the both of us working, it only took two days to paint the house.

I should've been proud of that.

Instead, I found myself brooding over the fact that I didn't have a reason to see Mackenna today.

Yesterday had been worse than the day before. She barely spoke three words to me, and seemed to go out of her way to work on separate areas. She'd been more covered, too, wearing a baggy pink T-shirt and old jeans. I wasn't sure if it was to ward off a sunburn or if she was trying to hide her body from me.

Leaving out the part about how I spied on her while she was singing, I'd told her I was sorry for how I acted, hoping we could make amends. She'd simply told me it was fine, and that was that.

When we were done, she stuck around to help clean up, then went inside the house to hang out with that damn parrot. While I was in the kitchen looking for something to eat, I could hear her cooing and making kissy sounds in the other room.

It made my dick so fucking hard I thought about

putting the apron back on just to hide the giant bulge in my pants.

After the visit, she left without even saying goodbye to me, and my boner deflated along with my ego.

This morning, I was woken up before 5:00 by Sweet Pea's racket, just like every other morning since I'd been here. He was starting to get on my last nerve. Fortunately, he usually stopped around 7:00 and I was able to get back to sleep.

Glancing over at the clock, I saw it was mid-morning, but made no move to get out of bed. I didn't have shit to do today and planned to spend it lazing around.

That is, until my dad called.

"Jimmy," he greeted. "I heard you finished painting already. Heard it looks great."

A grin tugged at my lips when I thought about the awful color. "Well, Grandma's house will be the talk of the town for a while, that's for sure."

"I also heard you had a helper... a lady-friend."

I huffed. "I'm pretty sure Mackenna hates me, so 'friend' isn't the right word. But, yeah, she helped. She was great. I couldn't have done it without her."

"Uh-huh," Dad said, reading me like a book because I rarely rambled. "Why don't you just ask her out?"

"I already told you." Rubbing a hand over my face, I sighed. "She hates me."

"Well, how about something to cheer you up?"

"Sure."

"I know it's only been a few days, but we're impressed

with you—the way you agreed to this and how hard you've been working." He paused. "We want you to sign up for your fall classes."

That had me bolting upright. "Seriously?"

"Now, we're not paying for them yet," he went on. "You still have to prove you can stay out of trouble. But it might be a good idea for you to get registered before they fill up."

"Thanks," I breathed out, feeling good at his words of praise. "I brought my laptop, but Grandma doesn't have internet. I guess I'll have to find somewhere with Wi-Fi."

Dad snorted. "Maybe you can try to get Grandma up to speed with technology while you're there."

"I highly doubt she'll go for it," I said with a smile. "I'll try to find an internet café or something in the next town over. Daywood might have a coffee shop."

"Alright. I'll let you get on that. Just wanted to tell you that you're doing a good job."

"That means a lot, Dad. Thanks."

After we hung up, I pulled on some jeans and a black T-shirt with cut-off sleeves. It was early enough in the day that the heat hadn't gotten too bad yet. If I left now, I had a good chance of not sweating my ass off on the way into town.

In the kitchen, I grabbed a Twinkie for breakfast and found a new note on the fridge.

> *Jimmy,*
> *I'm shacking up at Ernie's for the night. Be*
> *nice to Sweet Pea and give him a peanut.*
> *There's a bag in the pantry.*

*P.S. Don't you dare tease me about doing*
*the walk of shame in the morning.*
*-Grandma*

My face screwed up at my grandma's bluntness, and I picked up a nearby pen.

*TMI, Grandma. I don't need to know about*
*any of that... and Tweety Poo can kiss my*
*ass.*
*-Jimmy*

Grinning, I left the note where it was, and grabbed my laptop and charging cord. Before I could get out the door I turned back, picked up a handful of peanuts, and dumped them into the bird's food dish.

"I still think you're an asshole," I told him, and he squawked something that repeated my sentiment. "At least we can agree on something."

When I got out to my car I turned the key in the ignition, only to be met with silence. I tried again but nothing happened.

Just a quiet *click*.

Fucking great.

I'd have to take the car into the auto shop sooner than I thought. Blowing out a breath, I sat back and tried to think of what to do next. The morning sun rose higher in the sky, peeking over the tall trees in Grandma's yard.

Wincing at the bright light, I slid on my sunglasses. My eyes trailed over to my neighbor's house and I smiled.

Maybe I'd have a reason to see Mackenna after all.

\*

I knocked on the dark blue door and heard movement from inside the house. Shoving my hands into my pockets, I stood back and waited for Mackenna to open up, wondering what level of distain she'd have for me today.

The door swung open, but it wasn't her face that caught my attention.

She was wearing pajamas. Not just any pajamas. A fucking onesie. A zebra-striped onesie, long-john style.

I shouldn't have found it sexy—there was nothing sexy about it—but *fuck.*

Surprisingly, it turned me on. Big time. I felt my cock thicken, pressing uncomfortably against the zipper of my jeans.

And when she jutted her hip out and her hand landed on the curve there, my fists clenched inside my pockets.

Little black buttons ran all the way down the length of the ridiculous outfit and I wanted nothing more than to pop them open, one by one. With my teeth. Her feet were bare, displaying those dark purple toenails.

"Good morning," I managed, my voice gruff.

"You just can't stay away, huh?" she responded dryly, leaning against the doorframe.

*Baby, you have no idea.*

"I need a favor," I said, and she raised an eyebrow. "Two favors, actually."

"Okay..." She impatiently tapped her foot.

"I need help getting my car to the shop. It won't start."

Her lips twitched and the left side of her mouth curved up slightly. "What's wrong with the saggin' wagon?"

"The saggin' wagon?" I repeated, confused.

"The saggy testicles on your bumper," she explained with a wave of her hand. Her nose scrunched up, adorable and sexy at the same time. "That's disgusting, by the way."

Laughing, I rubbed at the stubble on my jaw. "I forgot all about that. Some friends at school put it on there as a joke…" I trailed off at her stony expression. "But I guess you don't find it very funny."

She sighed. "I'll make you a deal. Remove the bumper balls, and I'll help you."

I grinned. "You got it, Mack."

# CHAPTER 9

MACKENNA

For the past couple days, I'd accurately portrayed the personality of a stale piece of bread.

My intention was to come across so bland and boring that Jimmy would find me completely uninteresting and decide to leave me alone.

Instead, my efforts only seemed to spur him on.

He seemed to enjoy getting a rise out of me and, as much as it pissed me off, sometimes it got my heart racing—and not in a bad way.

Since ignoring him wasn't working I'd have to try a different strategy, because I wasn't sure if I could handle two months of his hotness showing up on my doorstep.

Maybe if I was super talkative, he'd become annoyed with me.

I could do talkative. I could be annoying. Having a younger sister ensured that I was refined in the art of getting on someone's nerves.

I wasn't used to having visitors, so I'd been surprised when I heard a knock at my door this morning. I didn't expect to see Jimmy standing there, looking positively lickable.

And although the sunglasses hid his eyes, I could feel his gaze on my body. It was then that I realized I was still in my PJs. The very PJs I wouldn't be caught dead in. I made him wait on the porch while I changed into rose-print leggings and a red T-shirt.

Living up to his promise, Jimmy promptly removed the bumper balls, which were currently hanging out in the glove compartment.

Now I was sitting in the driver's seat with the car in neutral as we slowly made the three-block journey to Hank's Auto Shop. It was my job to steer while Jimmy pushed it from behind.

I had no idea why I agreed to this, but I regretted it already.

Glancing in the rearview mirror, I admired the way his muscular arms were on full display, those tattoos on his left arm standing out more with the sheen of sweat on his skin.

At least he was wearing a shirt today. A small mercy for my out-of-control hormones.

As we made it to the sparse business district of Tolson, we passed the small post office on the right and two taverns on the left. And that was basically all there was to see. A couple hundred more yards down the road, and we'd be leaving town.

We neared the shop, and I turned the wheel to park the car in the gravel lot. In addition to auto repair, Hank's also offered a moving service with their transport company, but the semi-truck that normally sat at the side of the building was gone. Bright sunlight reflected off the white concrete exterior, making my head pound.

Squinting my eyes, I brought my hand up to shield against the glare. Before I knew what was happening, Jimmy was leaning through the driver's side window, placing his sunglasses on my face.

"What are you doing?" I asked, surprised by the gesture.

He shrugged. "Looked like you needed them."

Thankful, I pushed them up on my nose. "But what about you?"

"Nah, I'm okay," he said, then his lips curled up in a slow, naughty smirk. "With your reclusive tendencies, I was afraid your retinas couldn't handle the light."

I didn't bother to retort with the fact that I'd spent many hours outside with him and never went up in flames.

Because today wasn't a day for playing games.

Today was the day I would finally get Jimmy off my back.

Instead of narrowing my eyes like I wanted to, I shot him an overly-sweet smile, and the look of confusion on his face was worth the energy it took to restrain myself.

As we stepped through the open garage door at the front, Hank Evans came out from behind a small counter. Although I'd never met him, I had seen him around. His shop had been a constant presence in this town for over a decade.

He was a good-looking man for being in his mid-forties but, just like me, he was somewhat of a hermit. People in Tolson didn't know much about Hank other than the fact that he was a widower who ran a good business and didn't get out much.

"Jimmy, right?" He extended his arm and the guys shook hands.

"That's right," Jimmy replied. "I met you last Christmas at my grandma's house."

Hank patted his stomach. "I'm still thinking about her food. I hope she doesn't mind me showing up at her door again this year."

Jimmy laughed. "I'm sure she'd love it."

The older man peered over at the station wagon. "Did you push that thing all the way here?"

"It was only a few blocks." Jimmy shrugged. "The A/C stopped working a while ago, which I can live with, but it wouldn't start this morning."

Hank circled the car and rubbed a hand over his short hair. I had no idea how he wasn't overheating in the gray coveralls, but he didn't seem fazed by the weather. "Your tires seem to be in good shape. You two did a good job getting it here." His gray eyes cut to me, and he smiled. "And you're the partner in crime?"

My lips tilted up as I shook my head. "No crimes here. I'm Beverly's neighbor."

"What's your name?"

"Mackenna," I said, hoping he didn't recognize me.

"Didn't you go to school with my boys?"

Reluctantly, I nodded. "They were a year ahead of me."

I'd never had any classes with Colton Evans or Travis

Hawkins, but everyone knew they were like brothers even though they weren't related. They had already graduated when 'the incident' happened, but I was sure they'd heard about it since they stayed local to work at the shop.

Thankfully, Hank didn't bring it up. "Well, I'm glad to see you're back. Tolson needs more young folks." He turned to Jimmy. "I'll take a look at your car today. We're not too busy, so I should be able to get it fixed. Why don't you come back tomorrow morning?"

"Sounds like a plan." He handed the keys to Hank. "I just have to get something out of the back seat, and we'll be out of your hair."

After grabbing his laptop, Jimmy and I started the walk back. As we passed Buck's Tavern, I remembered my mission to bug the crap out of him, and it made me a little giddy to turn the tables.

Putting a skip in my step, I injected a cringe-worthy level of cheerfulness into my voice. "What's your favorite color?"

A little stunned by my peppy tone, he looked over at me like I'd just slapped him. "Uh, black," he replied, pointing to his shirt. "What's yours?"

"Purple. If you could listen to only one song for the rest of your life, what would it be?"

Eyebrows furrowing, he seemed confused by my randomness but answered me anyway. "That's a difficult one. I guess 'Dream On' by Aerosmith."

"Not a bad choice," I told him. "I would pick 'Barbie Girl'."

"Really?" he asked skeptically. "That's an...interesting selection."

Pressing my lips together, I suppressed a laugh. Messing with Jimmy was as much fun as I thought it would be.

"We can listen to it when we get back to my house," I suggested brightly. "That is, unless you have other things to do..."

"Nope, I'm free all day. That reminds me about the second favor," he said with a smile. "I need to use your Wi-Fi."

"What's wrong with yours?"

"Grandma doesn't have internet."

"Seriously? Talk about living in the Dark Ages."

He chuckled. "Tell me about it. She still has a landline telephone."

"Landlines are practically ancient." I snickered and pointed at his wrist. "And speaking of ancient, you still wear a watch?"

Holding up his hand, he tapped the round face a couple times. "It doesn't work anymore, unless it's 5:00. Then it's right twice a day."

"It's 5:00 somewhere, right?" I forced an obnoxious giggle.

Jimmy gave me an odd look, but started belting the chorus of 'It's Five O'clock Somewhere.' His singing was so loud, he frightened a cat that had been lounging on the front stoop of the house we passed. The orange tabby jumped at least three feet in the air, then took off into some bushes.

That time I laughed for real. "You got a thing for Jimmy Buffet? That's the second time I've caught you rocking one of his songs since I met you."

"Yeah, he's got some good ones." He smirked. "And at least I'm wearing clothes this time."

I felt a blush creep up from my chest to my cheeks at the reminder of the way his ass looked in those briefs the first time I saw him.

"So why do you wear a broken watch?" Grabbing his wrist, I tried to ignore that electric zing in my fingers when I touched his skin.

"It was my grandpa's. He gave it to me right before he passed away. Even though it stopped working a few years ago, I still like to wear it."

"Oh, I'm sorry," I said, feeling like a giant asshole. "That's a pretty good reason."

Jimmy shrugged. "I'm glad you asked."

Our eyes locked, and I was suddenly very aware of the fact that I hadn't let go of his arm yet. My eyes traveled up his skin, taking in the intricate floral design and bright colors of the tattoos.

Then I realized we were pretty much standing in the middle of Main Street, holding hands. I released the grasp I had on his arm.

"Hey, wanna hear a joke?"

He smiled. "Sure."

"What do you tell a cat when it asks you what time it is?"

"I don't know, what?"

"Right meeeoow," I answered, drawing out the cat sound.

Much to my surprise, Jimmy actually found it funny. Laughing, he rubbed at his lower lip with his thumb, drawing my attention to his mouth.

Did he have any idea how sexy the action was?

He probably had no clue. Jimmy was just one of those people who had natural, effortless sex appeal. He didn't walk—he sauntered. That was the best way for me to describe the way he moved.

"Why flowers?" I gestured to the ink running up and down his arm.

"Peonies," he responded. "They're Grandma's favorite."

And damn if that didn't warm my heart a little.

Suddenly, I felt a strong swooping sensation in my abdomen right below my sternum, and I wondered if I was having heart palpitations. I'd had this feeling several times over the past few days when Jimmy was around, and it took me a few seconds to realize what it was.

Butterflies.

Jimmy gave me butterflies.

No one had ever given me that feeling before. I'd heard about it in movies and books, but thought it wasn't real or that something was wrong with me.

There wasn't anything wrong with me.

Apparently, all I needed was Jimmy to show me that.

But this new knowledge only made me more determined to sever whatever connection we had, so I did the most incredibly awkward thing possible. I grabbed the skin on his elbow with my fingers and gave it a yank.

"Ow!" Jimmy jumped away from me while rubbing his arm. "What'd you do that for?"

"I pinched your wenis."

"My what?"

"Your wenis. It's the loose skin over your elbow," I explained, and as if that wasn't awkward enough I said the word one more time to drive the point home. "Wenis."

He threw his head back and laughed. It took him a full block to get himself under control, and the sound only exacerbated the fluttering in my chest.

Who was this guy? The rough-looking exterior and ornery attitude didn't seem to match who he was on the inside. No one got a permanent mark of their grandma's favorite flower unless they had a good heart. And his grandpa's watch? Who knew Jimmy Johnson was such a sentimental softie?

But I knew things weren't always as they seemed. Anyone could pretend to be something they weren't for a short amount of time. Some talented people could do it for years.

I wasn't sure which side of Jimmy was real.

As we stepped onto my front porch, he headed for my door.

"We can just do it out here." I stopped him, motioning to the bench swing. Having him inside my home—my sanctuary—seemed too intimate.

"I'll need a plug for my charger." He held up the black cord.

"Lucky for you, I have an outlet out here." I moved a potted fern aside and plugged it in.

He shrugged and took a seat. After getting Jimmy connected to my Wi-Fi, I sat down next to him, purposely moving into his personal space.

Looking suspicious, he gave me the side-eye. I sent him a cheerful grin. With a small smile, he shook his head and went back to clicking and typing on the keyboard.

"Whatcha doin'?" I peered over Jimmy's shoulder, blatantly invading his privacy.

He didn't seem to mind. Moving his head closer to mine, he turned the screen so I could see the website to The Ohio State University.

"Getting signed up for my fall classes. What should I take?"

I let out a scoff. "You're asking me? I wouldn't know the first thing about it."

"Sociology 101 sounds interesting, but it might be hard," he went on, scrolling down to the class description. "I'll have to take it at some point anyway, so I might as well get it over with."

"Sure." I shrugged, not having much to add to the conversation.

"Speech 101 might be cool."

I gasped. "Isn't that public speaking?"

He nodded. "Yeah. What's wrong with that?"

Giving an exaggerated shudder, I shook my head. "That's pretty much one of my biggest fears."

"No way," he said, shocked. "You performed for a living."

"I got booed off stage for a living," I corrected. "Stage fright is no joke."

His expression was soft when he glanced at me. "But I bet when you overcame it, you were awesome up there. A real force to be reckoned with."

I could tell he wasn't bullshitting. He really believed that, and his blind faith in me made my stomach do another somersault.

"Believe me, I don't belong in the limelight," I told him before changing the subject. "How many classes are you taking?"

He went back to his laptop. "Four will put me at a full schedule. I could take five to try to catch up, but I don't want to overload myself. I really need to do well this time."

"You didn't do well last time?"

Something a lot like regret flashed across his features. "No."

"Oh. That's too bad," I said quietly. "I'm sure it'll be great."

"I appreciate your vote of confidence."

"What's your major?"

"Undecided. Maybe something in business?" With a shake of his head, Jimmy made a sound of frustration. "It was so much easier when I was a kid. I thought when the time came I'd have the answer, that I'd just automatically know what I wanted to be."

"I know what you mean," I said, dropping the obnoxious act I'd been trying so hard to pull off. "I always thought I wanted to be a big star. But the idea of it was a lot different than the reality. I figured out my path, and you'll find yours."

When Jimmy looked at me, there was warmth in his eyes. "I hope so. Thanks for saying that."

"You're welcome." We smiled at each other for a few seconds before he turned back to the screen.

His fingers flew over the keyboard and I stayed quiet, letting him sign up for the rest of his classes in peace.

Since my legs were too short to reach the floorboards, I tucked my feet under my thighs. Jimmy's sneakers pushed off the porch, causing us to sway back and forth.

Sitting here with him was surprisingly calming. Closing my eyes, I enjoyed the warm breeze against my skin. I got a whiff of something pleasant. Clean and fresh. Not quite masculine like cologne. More like laundry detergent or deodorant. Breathing in deep, I let myself imagine what it would be like to bury my face in Jimmy's T-shirt and take a big sniff.

I was jarred from my shirt-smelling fantasies by the sound of the laptop shutting, and was almost disappointed when Jimmy stood up to leave.

"All done," he announced. "Thanks for letting me bum off your Wi-Fi. Saved me a trip into town."

"You can use it anytime," I offered. "You have my password now, so next time you won't have to come over."

Nodding, he shuffled his feet before walking away, and the sudden shyness was unlike him. Stopping halfway down the steps, he turned back with a smile. "I'll see you around."

"'Bye, Jimmy." I didn't believe him. After today it was safe to say he wouldn't want to see me again for a while, if ever.

Thinking I had accomplished my mission, I watched his long, steady strides until he disappeared into the house next door.

Sighing, I went inside and got a bottle of water from the fridge. As the cold liquid hit my tongue, I thought about my humiliating attempt to get my hot-as-hell neighbor to run for the hills.

I pestered him with the most annoying questions ever, made fun of his deceased grandpa's watch, told a lame joke, and molested his arm in public.

I touched his *wenis*.

He probably thought I was a complete whack-job now, and would most likely spend the rest of his time here trying to stay away from me.

I should've been happy that my plan worked, but I couldn't help feeling a little sad.

Picking up my guitar, I tried to find contentment while ignoring the hollow feeling in my chest. It was then that I realized I still had Jimmy's sunglasses on my face.

Well, crap. Maybe he'd be back sooner than I thought.

# CHAPTER 10

JIMMY

I'd never been more confused in my whole life. Mackenna had done a 180 since the day before, and I found myself on edge from the sudden change.

What the hell just happened? She'd been friendly. Perky. Chatty, even.

She fucking giggled.

Maybe we'd made some kind of breakthrough in our friendship.

Friendship? Is that what it was? Is that what I wanted?

Immediately, I knew the answer to that question was a big *hell no*. Because I wanted more than that.

Over the past few days, my feelings for her had grown way faster than I thought possible.

The first thing that caught my attention was physical attraction. The second thing that kept me on the line was how mysterious she was. But the third thing that reeled me in? Those moments when she let her guard down long enough for me to catch a glimpse of who she was on the inside.

Hook, line, and sinker—I was a goner.

I could spend the rest of the summer watching her from afar, or I could man up and do something about it.

My palms started to sweat when I thought about asking her out, and now I found myself in unfamiliar territory. Girls didn't make me nervous. My confidence level around the opposite sex had never been a problem before.

And that's how I ended up on Grandma's couch asking her for dating advice.

"So, what you're saying is, you've got a little crush?" Grandma asked with a twinkle in her eye.

"I guess so. Sometimes I get the feeling she's into me. Other times I think she hates my guts." I laughed. "I don't even know what it is about her... It's just when she's around, sometimes it feels like my heart's gonna beat right out of my chest."

"That's a crush, alright. Pesky fucking things always seem to come around when you least expect it."

I nodded. "That's the thing—I didn't plan on meeting anyone this summer. Actually, I sort of swore off women indefinitely."

"Hell, just look at me," Grandma said as Sweet Pea nibbled at some dried fruit in her palm. "I've only got a few precious years left and here I am, falling in love again."

I ignored the comment about her limited lifespan, because that wasn't something I wanted to think about. "Didn't you and Ernie date before you met Grandpa?"

"We sure did." Her eyes crinkled at the corners when she smiled. "Ernie was my first love. And now he's my last. Doesn't mean I love your grandpa any less. But if there's one thing I've learned in this life, it's that you've gotta snatch up happiness at every opportunity."

"That's some romantic shit, Grandma. You deserve to be happy."

"And so do you, Jimmy. I think you and Mackenna would make a great couple. There's nothing wrong with a good old-fashioned summer romance. But keep in mind that she lives here permanently and you don't. That's enough to make anyone wary of starting a relationship."

Leaning my elbows on my knees, I absorbed Grandma's words.

She had a good point.

Starting something with Mackenna could lead to a difficult situation since I didn't plan on staying. In August, I would be going back to school—hopefully—and she would still be here, living the life of a reclusive songwriter.

"The inner workings of a woman's mind can be complicated," Grandma went on. "I've been a woman for nearly eighty years, and some days I can't even decide what the hell I want for breakfast." She chuckled. "But I do know one thing: the heart is always constant. The problem is when the mind and the heart can't agree."

A little confused, my eyebrows furrowed. "So, if I want Mack to go out with me, I have to get her mind and heart to want the same thing?"

Throwing her head back she let out a loud cackle, and Sweet Pea mimicked the noise.

"What?" I asked defensively. "What's so funny?"

Giving me a sympathetic look, she shook her head. "Oh, good luck with that, Jimmy."

For the second time today, I found myself knocking on Mackenna's door. My plan was to thank her for helping me out, then possibly work up the courage to ask her out on a date.

To say we got off on the wrong foot was an understatement. Our first meeting hadn't been the stuff dreams are made of, and I hadn't been showing her the best side of myself.

I really wanted to change that.

If only she would give me a chance.

Hopping on the balls of my feet, I shook out my hands and cracked my neck the same way I did when I pepped myself up for a fight. When I heard the handle turn, I stood up straight and tried to exude an air of confidence I didn't quite feel.

But as soon as that door swung open, my mouth watered and it had nothing to do with the beautiful girl in front of me.

My stomach growled. "What's that smell?"

"Dinner," she replied, her voice clipped. She handed me something and I glanced down to see my sunglasses. "There you go. Thanks for letting me borrow them. 'Bye."

The door started to shut and I stopped it with my shoe. I didn't realize how hungry I was until now, and my purpose for coming over was temporarily forgotten. The aroma wafting through the air was sweet and a little spicy.

"What are we having?" I asked, craning my neck to look around her.

She moved in front of me, blocking my line of sight. "Honey mustard chicken."

"You gonna invite me in?" I asked impatiently as my stomach gave another insistent rumble.

"No." Her answer was matter of fact and honest. She wasn't trying to be coy with me—she really had no intention of letting me into her house.

There was no trace of the cheerful girl I'd gotten a glimpse of earlier. Disappointment caused something to clench in my chest and my confidence wilted. Maybe I read her wrong when I thought the attraction was mutual. Doubt crept in, and my hope that she would agree to go out with me went up in smoke.

I frowned. "Why do you hate me?"

Her eyes softened a little. "I don't hate you."

"Could've fooled me." Stuffing my hands in my pockets, I rocked back on my heels, trying to hide the fact that she'd hurt my feelings. "I just wanted to thank you for helping me out earlier. I really appreciate it."

Sighing, she glanced over her shoulder, then back at me.

My eyes fell to her lips, where she was anxiously nibbling at the pink flesh.

"I wasn't expecting company. Just give me a few minutes to pick up a little, okay?" She didn't wait for me to answer before shutting the door. I looked around, wondering if she expected me to stand outside her door like a lost puppy.

Truth was, when it came to her I felt like a lost fucking puppy. She had me tied up and twisted like no one else ever had before, and I'd wait out here for as long as it took.

Deciding to take a seat on her porch swing, I rocked back and forth as I looked out over the streets of Tolson and soaked up the sounds of summer. The gentle wind rustled the leaves of the tall oak trees, birds chirped, and the engine of a lawn mower roared in the distance.

It was peaceful, but the moment would've been ten times better with Mackenna sitting next to me.

I thought about what it felt like to have her close to me earlier—so close, I could smell her skin and hair. After I'd signed up for the last class, I took the opportunity to watch her as we swayed together. With her eyes closed behind my sunglasses, I might've thought she was asleep if it wasn't for the expression on her face.

Did she even realize she'd been smiling?

Mackenna's door creaked open and her head popped out. "You can come in now."

Grinning, I stood up. It was time for me to show her who I really was.

*

While Mackenna fixed our plates, I poked around her kitchen. Lifting a lid on the ceramic rooster cookie jar on her counter, I was disappointed to find it empty. Then I tinkered with the rooster magnets on her fridge before opening the freezer.

"Nosy much?" she said behind me.

Distracted by the four boxes of ice cream sandwiches, I didn't answer her.

"Fuck yes," I said to myself as I snagged one out of an open box, ripped off the wrapper, and took a bite.

"Um, sure. Help yourself." The look she gave the dessert in my hand was territorial and possessive.

"I just thought with the 70 million you have in there, you could spare one for your friendly neighbor. You have some sort of addiction I should be worried about?" I teased, finishing the other half in one bite.

She gave me a half-hearted glare. "I stock up on things so I don't have to make trips into town all the time. And I love ice cream sandwiches."

"Well, yeah. Who doesn't?"

"Exactly. Anyone who doesn't like them can't be trusted," she said seriously, then added, "You might as well get one for me, too."

I grabbed two more from the freezer—one for her and another for me—and sat down at her small round table. Like naughty kids, we smiled at each other while we ate our dessert before dinner.

After that, I tore into the honey mustard chicken. We didn't talk for several minutes while we ate, but it wasn't uncomfortable or awkward. The food was just really good, and I didn't want to talk with my mouth full.

Within two minutes, I'd wolfed most of it down.

"So, I have to ask," I started, taking a sip from the bottled water she'd gotten for me. "What's with all the roosters?"

I'd never seen a room take a theme quite so far. Roosters were everywhere. The wallpaper. The knobs on the cabinets. Even the salt and pepper shakers.

Mackenna shrugged. "It was already like this when I

moved in. I figured I might as well run with it. It's surprisingly popular for kitchen décor." Her face brightened a bit. "Knock-knock."

I grinned. "Who's there?"

"Cock."

"Cock who?"

"Cock-a-doodle-doo," she said with a grin.

I snickered. "I like your jokes."

Scooping up my last bite of chicken, I moaned when the flavors hit my tongue.

She smiled shyly and pointed at my plate with her fork. "You like it? It's a new recipe and I wasn't sure it would turn out."

"This is fantastic." My reply came out garbled. "If you keep cooking like this, I'll be coming over every day."

Her face fell, hurting my feelings once again. If I didn't know any better, I'd say she didn't like the idea of having me around.

*Show her you're not a dickhead.*

"Listen." Setting my fork down, I gave Mackenna my full attention. "I'm sorry if I've been rude. I think I might've given you the wrong impression of me. I never meant to make you mad."

"Really?" she asked dryly. "Because I'm pretty sure you made me mad on purpose."

Laughing, I shrugged and went with the truth. "Okay, maybe it was on purpose. It's just 'cause I think you're pretty and I like it when you talk to me, even if you are scowling."

"Oh." She blushed and self-consciously glanced away.

"Oh?" I raised my eyebrows at her shy response. "Don't you think you're pretty?"

Tracing a design on the rooster-covered tablecloth, she lifted a shoulder. "Sure, I guess. Sometimes."

"Not sometimes," I said. "All the time. You're fucking gorgeous, Mack."

I watched the pink on her cheeks deepen until it matched the color of her lips, and it made me want to kiss the fuck out of her.

Yeah, I definitely wanted more than friendship.

Now I just needed to figure out how to get her to want that, too.

# CHAPTER 11

MACKENNA

This wasn't a date. I knew that.

But it sure felt like one.

The conversation had been pleasant. Enjoyable. I was quickly realizing Jimmy wasn't anything like the asshole I'd pegged him for. And he liked ice cream sandwiches, so he had that going for him.

I was in serious danger of actually liking the guy.

There were so many reasons why that was a bad idea so, obviously, avoidance was the best option. Reaching across the small table, I brought my hand up to Jimmy's forehead.

"Are you feeling okay?" I asked, keeping my tone playful. "You're being way too nice."

His green eyes burned into mine as he gently grabbed my hand. When his thumb brushed over my palm, I felt it all the way to my core, causing a steady thrum between my thighs.

"I feel great," he replied huskily. "And I *am* nice. I just haven't shown you, and I'm sorry about that."

Snatching my arm back, I picked up the empty plates and brought them over to the sink while I tried to regulate my breathing. "I accept your apology. Thanks."

I could still feel my skin buzzing over the places he'd touched me. Needing a distraction, I turned on the faucet and started scrubbing at the dishes.

"Mackenna," Jimmy said quietly behind me, and I jumped a little at how close he was.

Something about hearing him say my full name didn't feel right. In the short amount of time I'd known him, I had gotten used to being called by the nickname he'd given me.

"You can call me Mack," I told him without turning my head.

"Is that right?" I could hear the smile in his voice.

It made me smile, too.

My smile faded away when his hands came up to rest on my shoulders. He started rubbing the tense muscles, like touching me was the most natural thing in the world.

I knew I should tell him to stop, but I couldn't find the words. It just felt too good.

So instead, I said, "Playing guitar and being hunched over a laptop isn't great for my neck, so this is...really... nice."

He hummed in agreement. The low rumble in the back of his throat was one of the sexiest sounds I'd ever heard.

I held in a moan as his thumbs worked a knot at the base of my neck. His fingers danced along my spine before his nails scraped against my scalp.

That time I did moan a little.

The plate I had been cleaning slipped from my grasp and landed in the sink with a splash.

"You know," I started, sounding a little breathless. "If this is what happens when I feed you, maybe I'll make you dinner more often."

"I like the sound of that." Jimmy's hands left my hair and slid down my neck.

Gently guiding my shoulders, he turned me around so we were facing each other. Our heads were so close I could see all the different flecks of green in his irises, and those mesmerizing orbs darted from my eyes, to my nose, to my mouth.

My lips tingled with anticipation when I wondered if he was going to kiss me, and I was shocked by how much I wanted that.

He stared for a few seconds, then his attention was drawn up to my forehead. He ran his fingertip over the half-inch scar by my hairline.

"How'd you get this?" he asked, tilting his head to the side.

And just like that, it was like a cold bucket of ice water got dumped on the moment we were having.

It was an innocent question—he was just curious. There was no way for him to know the nerve he'd hit by asking about the gruesome history behind that scar.

But that didn't matter.

Moment ruined.

I stepped away. "It's getting sort of late. You should get home."

With a wounded expression, he stepped back. Sighing, he ran a hand through his thick hair and those messy strands fell right back to the place they were before. My fingers itched to brush them off his forehead, so I linked my hands behind my back.

"Thanks for dinner." Moving toward the door Jimmy gave me a sad smile, and I found myself torn between wanting him to leave and begging him to stay.

This time as I watched him walk away, I was certain I'd scared him off for good.

# CHAPTER 12

MACKENNA

The squirrels of Tolson were fearless, vicious creatures. They had no regard for personal safety, and their lack of respect for garbage cans on trash day was appalling.

A few of the guilty rodents scurried up a tree as I got out of my car and surveyed my yard. Water bottles, leftover food, and paper plates littered the lawn. I let out a mortified squeak when I saw a few tampons among the wreckage.

Quickly grabbing a new bag from inside, I picked up everything as fast as I could while hoping none of the neighbors got an eyeful of my personal items.

This morning I'd made a trip to Walmart to get some ingredients for a new Crockpot creation I wanted to try.

I might've Googled recipes last night after Jimmy left.

Of course, it was pure coincidence that the beef stew I wanted to make happened to be on a site called 'The Way to a Man's Heart'. It had absolutely nothing to do with me hoping Jimmy would smell it and find his way back over to my house. Nope. Not at all. Pure coincidence.

After cleaning up the trash and placing it at the curb, I got my groceries from the backseat of my car. I was walking up the driveway when I noticed my mailbox door was slightly ajar. The mail usually arrived later in the day, but I decided to check anyway.

A lone envelope sat inside. No stamp. No return address. Frowning with confusion, I ripped it open to find a folded-up piece of paper.

When my eyes scanned over the typed-out letters, the blood drained from my face and the bags slipped from my fingers. A can of cream of celery soup dropped onto my big toe, but I barely felt the pain. My knees almost gave out and I had to steady myself on the mailbox as I reread the note.

With one sentence, the sanctuary I'd built for myself came crashing down.

# CHAPTER 13

JIMMY

"What do you want first? The good news or the bad news?" Hank asked, stepping up to the counter.

I frowned. Bad news? Not exactly what I wanted to hear.

"Always the good news first," I told him.

"Well, your A/C wasn't hard to fix. Spark plug issue. And we threw in a free oil change."

"Thanks," I said. "I was about due for that."

He nodded. "Now for the bad news. Your alternator was shot and had to be replaced. Fortunately, Travis was able to pick up the parts when he was passing through Champaign yesterday, but they weren't cheap."

*Fuck.* "How much is the total?"

"Two thousand dollars."

Shocked, I choked on air and started coughing. The whole damn car wasn't even worth that much.

Wild laughter erupted from Hank.

"I'm just kidding!" Bending over, he clutched his middle as he laughed some more. "That's what I call 'the shock and awe.'"

"The what?" I gasped through another cough.

"The real total is $360. Still not cheap, but doesn't seem so bad now, does it?"

Relieved, and still trying to recover from the 'shock' part, I grinned as Hank gave me a couple firm pats on the back. He was right—$360 was a lot better than $2,000.

Still, that was $360 more than I had. Now I just needed to figure out how to pay for it.

If I was the old me, I would've tried to set up a fight to earn some quick cash. Sometimes I could make $500 in one night. But that wasn't an option now.

Inwardly groaning, I tried to mentally calculate how much further that would put me in the hole. Since my credit card was maxed-out, my only choice was to ask my dad for money. Just one more thing added to the list of all the ways I inconvenienced my parents.

"Okay," I said, grabbing my phone. "I'll need a few minutes to make a call."

"Take your time," he replied, lowering his head to sift through some paperwork.

Behind him there was a 'Help Wanted' sign dangling on a rusty nail. It was crooked, faded, and had obviously been collecting dust for a while.

"You hiring?" I pointed at the sign.

He glanced over his shoulder like he'd forgotten it was there.

"We are," he confirmed. "You looking for a job?"

I scratched at my jaw as I considered it.

"Well, I hadn't planned on it since I didn't think there was much work in this town. Plus, I'm only here for a couple months." I looked down at my phone. Dad's number was pulled up and my thumb hovered over the call button. "But I'm gonna need a way to pay for the work you've done."

Looking thoughtful, Hank nodded slowly. "I might be willing to take on a temporary worker. Colton's got a fiancée and their little girl to look after. Travis is getting married next month. With the transport company, we're doing a lot of juggling around here. My boys got a lot going on this summer, so having an extra pair of hands might be a good idea."

"Listen, I want to be honest with you," I started, wanting to lay it all out there. "I don't have a ton of work experience, and I bombed pretty hard at school. I don't know a lot about mechanics, but I'd be willing to try. So, I'm interested if you're willing to take a chance on me."

Hank's face softened. "I've never even stepped foot on some fancy college campus, so you're already a step ahead of me."

"Jimmy!" a voice bellowed from somewhere in the garage, and I turned to see Hank's son walking toward me in his grease-stained coveralls. I thought my dad and I looked alike, but that was nothing compared to the striking resemblance between the father and son standing side by side. Same height, same broad-shouldered build, same buzzed haircut.

"Colton, right?" I greeted as I shook his hand.

"That's right. I was the one wearing the crazy Rudolf sweater at Beverly's last year."

My recollections of Christmas were a little hazy from all the whiskey I'd confiscated from Grandma's liquor cabinet, but I remembered a few crazy sweaters that day.

"Good to see you again," I told him with a smile.

"Dude, I found a nut sac in your glove compartment yesterday." He laughed. "Gotta say, that's a first for me on the job, and I've been doing this a long time."

I snickered. "Mackenna made me put those in there. Guess she didn't like the way they looked on my bumper."

"Oh shit, your girlfriend *literally* made you put your balls away?" Grinning, he slapped me on the shoulder. "That's classic. And Mackenna Connelly is a ball-buster for sure. Heard she moved back to the area recently."

"She's not my girlfriend," I told him, wishing it wasn't the truth. "She's my grandma's neighbor."

"She's a cool girl." Backing away, Colton wiped his hands off on a dirty rag. "I gotta get back to it, but maybe I'll see you around?"

"Well, that's likely," Hank interjected. "Because I just hired him."

My head whipped toward him, and a big smile spread over my face.

"Awesome," Colton said. "It's about time we got more help around here. Old man runs this place with an iron fist."

Hank guffawed before playfully putting his son in a headlock. Laughing, Colton broke free and threw the greasy rag at Hank's face. It was obvious that they had a great relationship, and it made me hope I hadn't messed things up too bad with my own dad.

Hank tossed me my keys. "No payment today. Can you be here tomorrow morning around 9:00?"

"You're gonna let me take my car without paying?" I asked, confused.

"Yep. I trust you," he said before turning to walk away, then called over his shoulder, "See you tomorrow!"

That feeling of hope exploded inside me again, because this was another chance to prove that I wasn't a complete screw-up.

When I got home, Grandma was on the phone—her landline telephone—and she looked distressed as she hung up. I closed the front door behind me, and she slumped down onto her couch with a huff.

"What's wrong?" I asked, sitting next to her.

"That was the mayor of Tolson. He said I can't have my house this color." Pouting, she threw her hands up. "Apparently, there are village codes or something. Fuck the codes!"

I frowned. "What does he want you to do? Change it?"

"Yes. He said some of the townspeople even offered to chip in to pay for it." Wringing her hands, she sighed. "Is it really that bad?"

Barking out a laugh, I hugged her to me and decided to be honest. "Yeah, Grandma. It really is that bad. But, hey, guess what?"

"What?"

"I got a job at Hank's Auto Shop," I said, pulling back.

Her face lit up. "Oh, that's wonderful."

"You don't mind?" I asked. "It'll mean I'm not here as much. I won't take it if you don't want me to."

"Don't be ridiculous. I think that's great. I do have a life, you know. Plus, those boys will keep you in line."

I grinned. "I have a feeling you're right about that. I start tomorrow morning."

"Can you do something for me today?"

"Anything," I replied.

"Go to Home Depot and pick out a new color? Something boring." She made a face.

I drew her in for one more hug. "I'll pick the best color they have."

"I guess this means you and Mackenna will be back at it then," she said with a shrug.

Excitement caused my heart to speed up. This new development could bode well for me, because I'd have at least two more days with the moody girl next door.

One trip to Home Depot later, I parked my station wagon on the street in front of Grandma's house and enjoyed the A/C for a couple minutes, marveling at how it worked better than ever before.

I hoped I fit in at Hank's, and not just because I needed the money. I'd had a job before, but this was the first time I was excited about it. Two summers in high school, I'd had the mind-numbing experience of being a grocery bagger. It was easy, but I didn't enjoy it.

Working at an auto shop was different. Challenging.

Being a mechanic wasn't something I'd ever considered before, but I liked the thought of fixing things and getting my hands dirty.

Speaking of fixing things and getting my hands dirty,

JAMIE SCHLOSSER

I glanced at the green monstrosity in Grandma's yard. Hauling the new gallons of paint into the garage, I set them next to the brushes and rollers.

The color I picked was still green, but a lot lighter. *Sage*, Mackenna had called it.

Then I strolled to my neighbor's house and knocked on the front door to tell her the news. There was no noise coming from inside, but I knew she was home because her car was in the driveway.

I waited a minute, then knocked again. Maybe she was taking a nap, and I held onto the hope that she'd answer the door in her PJs again.

"Mack," I called. "I know you're home."

More silence.

"I can hear you knitting in there," I teased. "Open up. Maaaack. Mack, Mack, mo Mack, banana fana fo—"

The door swung open and my amusement immediately died. Mackenna's eyes were red-rimmed and puffy. She'd been crying.

"Hey," I said softly. "I didn't mean it. I can't really hear you knitting."

"What do you want, Jimmy?" She hiccupped before her chin wobbled and fresh tears filled her eyes.

Suddenly I had the overpowering urge to hold her, to comfort her somehow. Was she upset because of something I did? If so, I was going to feel like absolute shit.

"I promise not to tease you if you let me in," I told her. "Please?"

She didn't say anything, but responded by opening the

door wider in invitation. After shutting it behind me, she flicked the deadbolt.

I followed her into the living room, which was an area of the house I hadn't gotten a good look at yet. The walls were a warm amber, reminding me of whiskey. A fluffy cream-colored carpet ran the length of the room. Mackenna's guitar was leaning against a worn blue armchair in the corner, and a brown leather couch completed the room, adding to the coziness.

It was clean, aside from several partially-full water bottles placed randomly throughout the room. I counted them and the total came to nine, which was excessive for one person. I was about to ask about it but then Mackenna sniffled, and my concern overrode my curiosity.

"Did I do something wrong?" I asked, needing to know how much groveling was in order.

"Not everything is about you," she snapped before letting out another hiccup. Blowing her nose, she sat down on the couch, then glanced up at me. Her stormy eyes were absent of their usual hardness, and her voice got softer. "Sorry. No, you didn't do anything wrong."

"Do you want to talk about it?" I sat down next to her. "I know I can be a real ass sometimes, but I'm a good listener."

She tried to smile, but it looked more like a grimace. Then I noticed a crumpled piece of paper in her right hand. Her eyes followed my line of sight, and I knew from the expression on her face that whatever was on that paper was the reason for her sadness.

Gently placing my hand on hers, I uncurled her fingers and smoothed the paper out.

*Who are you spreading your legs for, you filthy cunt?*

"What the hell is this?" I asked, confused.

Mackenna let out a laugh, but there was no humor behind it.

"A love letter," she sneered. "I thought they were supposed to tell me when he got out. Aren't they supposed to notify me or something? It was supposed to be ten years. Ten!" Her voice became borderline-frantic at the end.

Feeling the need to do something, I picked up the box of tissues from the coffee table and handed it to her.

"When who got out?" Then it clicked and I knew. "Your ex."

Nodding, she hiccupped again, and I noticed she was shaking. She wasn't just sad—she was terrified.

Rage unlike anything I'd ever felt filled my entire body. Even though I didn't remember the details about what happened years ago, it didn't take a genius to figure out it was bad. I hadn't brought up the topic of her past since that first day because it was obviously a sore subject.

But now I wondered what the hell he did to her.

"Fuck, baby," I muttered, pulling her onto my lap.

She stiffened, but didn't resist as I draped her legs sideways over mine. "What are you doing?"

"Hell if I know," I replied, wrapping my arms around her. "But I can't just do nothing when you're shaking like this."

Sniffling, she hesitated for a few seconds before awkwardly resting her head on my shoulder. I rubbed circles on her back and her body relaxed a fraction. It'd been a long time since I showed physical affection that wasn't purely sexual to a girl, but comforting her just felt right.

"Why are you here?" she asked, reminding me of the reason I came over.

I got the feeling she needed to talk about something else. Luckily, I had the perfect distraction. "We have to repaint Grandma's house. Apparently, everyone in town is upset about it. She got a call from the mayor himself."

Mackenna lifted her head and looked at me with wide eyes. "Seriously?"

"Seriously. Said he'd even pay for a new color."

That got her to smile a little. "It *is* hideous."

"A total eye-sore," I agreed.

She squinted. "Looking at it actually hurts my eyes."

I laughed. "Leave it to Grandma to give an entire town a headache."

"I mean, it's a good color for tractors. Or grass. Or leggings," she added, wiggling her thighs.

It made her ass rub against me just right. Instant wood. Apparently my cock couldn't recognize how inappropriate the timing was, and I hoped she couldn't feel it poking her leg.

"I get the feeling you have a lot of crazy leggings." My thumb ran back and forth over her knee, feeling the soft material covered in brightly-colored pineapple print.

Mackenna shifted, and I thought maybe she'd pull away from me.

She didn't.

Instead, she snuggled in closer. "Patterned leggings are very popular right now. I might as well take advantage of it while it's socially acceptable. In a few years when they're out of style, I'll just be the crazy-leggings lady at Walmart."

Grinning at the mental image, I tightened my arms around her. I rested my chin on the top of her head and looked around the room.

"Are you like that girl from the movie *Signs*?" I wondered out loud.

"Huh?" Mackenna's head popped up and she looked confused.

I pointed at the water bottles. "You know, how she's picky about the water she drinks and ends up leaving cups everywhere."

Mackenna's eyes widened as if she was just noticing the mess. "Actually, yeah. I have a thing about water that's been sitting out for too long." Seeming slightly embarrassed, she gave a half-shrug. "I can drink it if it's cold, but once it reaches room temperature it's not good anymore."

"That's...different," I said with a chuckle.

In response, another hiccup escaped and her head went back to that place on my shoulder.

"Do you want me to get you a new water?" I offered. "Might help you get rid of those hiccups."

She shook her head. "That always happens when I cry. It'll pass."

"Just let me know if there's anything I can do."

"Is it okay that I'm sitting on you like this?" Her voice was quiet. Hesitant. Unsure and sweet. "It feels nice."

I swallowed hard. "Yeah, Mack. It's okay."

Now it made sense why she was so hellbent on staying away from me. I knew what I looked like—what people saw when they looked at me. My image didn't exactly scream squeaky-clean.

And I couldn't even feel upset over the fact that she judged me, because my behavior didn't do anything to dissuade her from the first impression I gave.

As we sat silently for a few minutes, I thought about the way I'd treated her over the past few days.

The guilt that hit me was so intense I felt nauseated.

Mackenna seemed so strong and independent, but she was also skittish at times. Like an insensitive prick, I hadn't even considered the possibility that she was closed off because of something she'd been through. That maybe she wasn't unfriendly—she was scared.

I even made fun of her for not dating.

"I'm so sorry," I whispered into her hair.

"What for?" she asked, and her warm breath tickled my neck. "It's not your fault my ex is a psycho."

"For everything. God, I'm such a shitbag. You've obviously been through some serious stuff and I've been a complete dick."

"It's okay," she responded automatically.

"No, it's not," I said adamantly, shaking my head. "And I like it that you knit and sew. It's cute."

She sighed. "I haven't exactly made things easy for you, Jimmy. I know it doesn't seem like it, but I *can* take a joke."

"Speaking of jokes, why did the fisherman sail the ocean?"

She paused to think. "I don't know, why?"

"For the halibut."

Mackenna let out a snort. That snort turned into a laugh.

Clutching my shirt, she buried her face in my shoulder while she giggled uncontrollably. The sound was infectious. Right there on her couch we lost our shit together, laughing over something that wasn't even very funny in the first place.

Once she got herself under control she lifted her head, and the smile she wore reached her eyes. "That was a terrible joke."

"I know." I smiled, fighting the sudden urge to kiss her. "Hey, what are you doing tonight?"

She just shrugged, her movement restricted by my arms that were still around her.

"Well, first, you should report this letter to the police. If he just got out he's probably on probation, and this needs to be on record in case..." I trailed off, not wanting to voice my concern.

Her body trembled as she finished the sentence. "In case he comes back."

"Yeah." I nodded. "And after that, you're going to have some fun for once. Grandma's got a hot tub." I waggled my eyebrows at her. Then my face got serious. "And maybe you can tell me about what happened?"

"It's such a long story." Sighing, she looked away.

"I've got time. And I need to know if he's going to be a problem."

Glancing back my way, she scoffed. "Why? What are you going to do about it?"

"Anything I have to," I said, the need to protect her overwhelming.

I was afraid she was going to argue with me, so I was surprised when she didn't protest.

Obviously she found some comfort in my presence, or else she wouldn't be sitting on my lap. Mackenna's fingers absentmindedly played with a rogue string around my cut-off sleeve as she thought it over.

When she finally spoke, her voice came out a little happier. Playful even. "I might need a little liquid courage first, but all I have is half a bottle of Boon's Farm."

Snickering, I hugged her tighter. "Now *that* I can help with."

# CHAPTER 14

MACKENNA

The sun had fully set and the stars were popping up in the darkening sky. Fireflies lit up the yard. The sound of cicadas filled the air.

It was the perfect summer evening.

Or, at least, it would've been if I wasn't scared for my life.

The warm water felt soothing as I sank down into the hot tub, taking the seat across from Jimmy. The motion detector light on the side of the garage turned on, bathing the backyard in a calming yellow glow.

I hadn't gone swimming in ages. The floral-print one-piece swimsuit I found at the bottom of one of my unpacked boxes still had the tags on when I dug it out. Tugging at the halter straps, I tried to relax but it wasn't easy.

Tension and fear remained at the forefront of my mind.

There wasn't much the police could do since there was no way for me to prove the note was from Jaxon. Basically, they said they would look into it. They could question him, but he could deny it. If I really wanted to take it a step further, I could apply for a restraining order.

All of it sounded like one big headache.

Water splashed as Jimmy stood up and leaned over the side of the hot tub. I admired the way the wet black swim trunks molded to his ass. When he turned back toward me, he had both arms behind his back.

"Pick a hand." Grinning, he hopped up and down a little, causing rivulets of water to run down his chest. One of the drops disappeared into his belly button, and I imagined myself licking him there. My gaze drifted down, following the dark trail of hair into the waistband of his shorts.

My eyes darted up to his, and I wondered if he caught me checking him out. From the smirk on his face, I concluded the answer to that was yes.

"Come on, pick one," he insisted, and I pointed to the right side. He revealed an empty hand. "You're not very good at this game."

With a sigh I shrugged, and Jimmy showed me his left, which held a stainless-steel flask. He passed it to me.

"What's this?" I asked, screwing off the cap and bringing it to my nose.

"Liquid courage."

My face scrunched up at the smell of the whiskey, but I tipped it back anyway. Coughing because of the way it burned on the way down, I wiped at my mouth and handed it back to him.

He gave me an expectant look as he took a swig. I knew what he wanted to talk about, but I wasn't ready yet.

Taking the flask back, I did two shots in a row. Jimmy raised his eyebrows in surprise, but didn't say anything as he waited for me to spill my history.

"Where did you get alcohol?" I asked, delaying the inevitable conversation. "You're not old enough."

"My grandma keeps a bottle of Jack on hand for 'medicinal purposes'," he said, putting air-quotes around the words.

I giggled, feeling warm from the effects of the alcohol already. I'd always been a light-weight, and I hadn't eaten much for dinner. My appetite was gone after getting that note.

The anxiety that consumed me earlier returned, and Jimmy must have been able to see it on my face. With his eyes on the house, he started humming 'John Deere Green' by Joe Diffie.

Effectively distracted, I let out a laugh that sounded more like a snort. He went all the way through the chorus, singing a word here and there.

"Not bad, James Peabody," I teased, and he scowled at the name. "You can actually carry a tune."

"So can you."

I narrowed my eyes suspiciously. "And how do you know that?"

He took a sip. "I heard you the other day. Your window doesn't do much to muffle sound."

"Oh," I said awkwardly. "Guess it's time to have my windows replaced."

Jimmy's eyes met mine. "It was the most beautiful thing I've ever heard."

"Thanks." I played with some of the bubbles on the surface of the water. "But for the record, I don't sing in front of people anymore unless it's for songwriting purposes."

"Not even your friends?"

"I don't really have any."

Giving me a look, Jimmy raised his hand and pointed at himself.

I laughed. "Well, if we're going to be friends, I feel like I need to come clean about something."

"What's that?"

"I lied about 'Barbie Girl'," I confessed. "While that song does have an appropriate time and place, it wouldn't be my first pick if I had to choose a forever-song."

"You don't say," he responded sarcastically. "So, what is it then?"

"'Crash' by Dave Matthews Band," I told him. "It brings back good memories because it was the first song I taught myself on the guitar."

"How old were you when you learned to play?" he asked.

"Twelve."

He grinned. "That's awesome. It's great that you found your calling so young."

"So, what are your talents?" I asked, switching the conversation back to him.

A flicker of insecurity crossed his face, and he looked down at the water. "Still trying to figure that out. Apparently, being able to do a 55-second keg stand doesn't count for much. I guess I don't have a lot going for me right now."

I frowned at his self-deprecating comments. "I bet that's not true. And by the way, 'Dream On' is an excellent song choice."

"Yeah?" He smiled.

"Yeah." I smiled back.

"So," he started, his usual cockiness returning. "Are there any more requirements for our friendship?"

"Yes, actually. You have to tell me about your back tattoo."

Smirking, he stood up in the water and angled his back toward the light. The angel wings spanned his entire upper back. As I looked closer, I was finally able to read the words woven into the intricate feathers.

I raised my hand, wanting to trace the lines.

"You can touch it," he said as if he could sense my fingers hovering over his skin.

I gave in to the desire and lightly trailed my fingers over the left side. The seven deadly sins.

>*Pride.*
>*Greed.*
>*Lust.*
>*Envy.*
>*Gluttony.*
>*Wrath.*
>*Sloth.*
>And on the right side were the seven virtues.
>*Humility.*
>*Charity.*
>*Chastity.*
>*Kindness.*
>*Temperance.*

*Patience.*

*Diligence.*

When my fingers were done with their thorough inspection, I stepped away and sat down into the water.

"Why?" I gestured toward him, referring to the tattoo.

He settled back into his spot across from me. "To remind myself that even though people have faults, there's a flipside. Redemption is obtainable for anyone who wants it."

"Wow," I said, impressed. "That's really beautiful."

The conversation stalled. I took the flask from Jimmy and managed to swallow a huge gulp. When I gave it back, he drained the rest and tossed the container onto the grass. I was momentarily disappointed that the alcohol was gone, but then he bent over the side again and came back with two beers.

"I think I owe you an apology," I admitted as he handed me one of the bottles. "I haven't been myself with you. After the way I've acted, you must think I have, like, zero sense of humor."

"Sometimes I'm not very funny." His body bobbed up and down in the water, and his nipple piercings peeked out.

Refusing to be distracted, I continued. "I knew you were just teasing, but I didn't want to like it."

"But you did like it?"

"Yeah, sometimes."

"And that's a bad thing because...?"

"Because you're hot," I blurted out.

He laughed. "Is that a problem?"

"Yeah," I said, the buzz helping me to be more straightforward. "It's a big problem."

"I like it when you're honest."

I tilted my head to the side. "Because I tell you you're hot?"

"Well, yeah," he smirked cockily. "But also because I want to know you. Here's the deal." He sat up straighter, squaring his muscular shoulders. "Let's have a give-me-your-shit conversation."

"What the hell is that?"

"That's where we tell each other our secrets—the things we're afraid to say. No judgment, just honesty. Lay it all out there."

"All of it?"

"As much as you're willing to say. I'll even go first."

"Okay…" I agreed reluctantly.

"Remember how I said I didn't do well at school? Well, I went to college with a plan and when things didn't go the way I thought they should, I kinda lost my shit. After my high school girlfriend broke up with me, I fell into some bad habits."

I took a second to process his confession. "So you were heartbroken?"

"Yes and no. I'm not sure how deep my feelings for her really went, but being dumped sucked," he said. "My way of dealing with it was to party. I drank a lot. Slept around a little. Neither fixed anything."

"By slept around, you mean…?"

"A few casual hook-ups. It wasn't hard to find girls who were just looking for a good time." Biting his lip, he seemed to be holding back.

"Come on, Jimmy. All of it," I reminded him.

Blowing out a breath, he raked a wet hand through his hair. The dampness caused it to stick up in certain places, and I liked the way it looked out of place.

"Guys are supposed to like that sort of thing, you know? It was easy. No feelings involved. But in the morning, I always just ended up feeling sort of empty. And that loneliness made me want to fill the void with more partying, more girls. It was a destructive cycle. And that's how I failed my freshman year of college," he finished with a shrug.

I was taken aback by his honesty. "Well, hey, at least you're owning it and not making excuses for yourself."

"Yeah, I guess that's one way of looking at it. I'm trying to turn things around, get my priorities straight." Playfully splashing water at me, he said, "Now it's your turn."

Taking a deep breath, I tried to think of where to start. The truth was, my story didn't begin with Jaxon.

"When I was younger, I was the chubby kid with glasses and bad hair. I didn't have a lot of friends. I wasn't athletic and I wasn't super smart, so I felt like I didn't fit in anywhere," I explained. "The summer before my junior year I dropped fifteen pounds and grew a couple inches. Mom said I was a late bloomer. I got contacts and new clothes. I changed so much that some people thought I was a new kid when school started back up. I was shy, naïve, and completely inexperienced when it came to boys. I was the perfect target for someone like Jaxon. He was intense, obsessive, predatory. I just didn't know enough at the time to be able to recognize how dangerous he was."

"How old were you?"

"Sixteen. He was the first person to ever show interest in dating me, and I jumped at the chance. I just wanted a boyfriend." I huffed out a humorless laugh at how pathetic that sounded. "He was nice for the first few weeks, then his true colors came through. He was abusive in pretty much every way. Physically, emotionally, sexually."

The silence that stretched between us was beyond uncomfortable, and I wondered if I'd said too much.

"Did he rape you?" Jimmy's voice came out quiet and raspy, like he was afraid to know the answer.

I stared at the bright green house as I thought about how the sexual abuse started right away. All the times Jaxon wouldn't listen when I said *no*. How angry he would get, and how that anger turned into physical force.

"I didn't see it like that at the time... I mean, he was my *boyfriend*, you know? We went on dates and stuff. I finally had someone to take me to the homecoming dance," I said, recalling how exciting it was at first. "And after he pushed me into doing things I wasn't ready for, he'd just tell me he couldn't help himself. That he loved me too much to stop."

"That's bullshit," Jimmy growled. "That's not love."

"I know that now." Familiar shame washed over me. "And I think part of me knew it then, too. But I didn't tell anyone. I was too ashamed, and he banked on that. I ended up shutting out my family and friends until he was the only person I had left."

"So what happened the night he went to jail? I could look it up, but I'd rather hear it from you."

"Long story short? He broke into my house with the plan to kill me, then himself," I stated, matter-of-factly. "I shot him. He didn't plan on me defending myself. The trial was pretty cut and dried. The voicemails, the texts, and the 9-1-1 call made his intentions clear." I shuddered at reliving the details. "Plus, he was armed with a baseball bat and his stepfather's hunting knife."

"Motherfucker," Jimmy cursed through gritted teeth.

"And to make matters worse, when shit hit the fan it was like the whole town turned against me," I added.

"Who turned against you?" he asked, sounding angry on my behalf.

"Basically the entire school. I guess it's an exaggeration to say the whole town, but when you're in high school it feels that way. The end of my senior year was me just trying to lay low and keep my head down until graduation."

I went on to tell him about the harassment, egging, and vandalism on my locker. I didn't leave any details out. He wanted the truth and I gave it to him. When I was done, his mouth pressed into a thin line.

"I can't believe you went through that alone."

I huffed. "I can't believe I was such a doormat."

"Hey." His voice was firm, yet gentle at the same time. "You were sixteen, Mack. There's a difference between being young and being a doormat. He took advantage of you. You are not a doormat."

"Not anymore," I agreed. "And I'm not a damsel in distress either. I shot him once and I'd do it again."

"Have you been able to date since then?" he asked, shifting from one uncomfortable subject to another.

When I thought about the one relationship I had a couple years ago—if you could even call it a relationship—I felt embarrassment mixed with a little regret. "I dated a guy in Nashville. He was nice."

"Nice?"

"Yeah. Normal and nice."

"And did you...uh..." Jimmy didn't have to finish the sentence for me to know what he was asking.

I gave a sharp nod. "I tried. The sex was...okay. It only happened a few times before we both decided we were better off as friends."

"So, he was *nice* and the sex was *okay*."

Grimacing, I took another drink. "I tried so hard to be normal because I just wanted to feel something. But I had a bit of an issue..."

"What issue?" Jimmy tipped his bottle back, like maybe he needed some liquid courage, too.

"I can't believe I'm telling you this," I muttered. I blew out a breath before continuing. "I would kind of freak out if I wasn't the one on top. Needless to say, that made things awkward."

I inwardly cringed when I thought about the panic attack that followed my first attempt at intimacy since

Jaxon. Talk about a way to ruin the mood. Jeremy was a bass guitarist I'd met at an open mic night. He was quiet, kind of shy, and he was in the business for the right reason—he loved making music. We bonded over the common interest, but the physical chemistry between us had been lacking and I was never able to feel comfortable with him.

"You needed to feel like you were the one in control," Jimmy concluded. "That makes sense."

Feeling exposed, I looked away. "You can be honest. You must think I'm pretty messed up, huh?"

"Anyone would be messed up after that," he replied.

He didn't completely answer my question, but at least he didn't try to deny it that he thought I was messed up. This was supposed to be an honest conversation, after all.

I chugged the rest of my beer and glanced over to find Jimmy watching me.

"Please stop looking at me like that." My voice came out small.

"Like what?"

"Like you feel sorry for me."

His jaw clenched. "I could kill him for what he did to you."

"I already tried that," I said in a sing-song voice, my intoxication level going from tipsy to full-on drunk.

"Have you talked to someone about it?" Jimmy asked. "Like a doctor or something?"

I nodded. "Yep. I went to therapy for a year when I moved down to Nashville. It was the one thing my parents asked me to do when I left. I even attended a support group for a while."

"Did it help?"

"Not really." I pinned him with my gaze, wanting to appear strong. "Yes, the experience changed me, but I'm not ruined."

"I don't think you're ruined," he said sincerely. "I like you just the way you are."

Pushing off the wall, Jimmy floated over to me, closing the four-foot gap between us. He took the empty beer from my hand and placed the bottles outside the hot tub.

Then he sat next to me.

My breathing hitched when he linked his pinky finger with mine underneath the water.

A gesture of support. How could such a small action make me feel so safe?

I could feel his eyes on me but I didn't dare look his way. Instead, I tightened my finger around his and relaxed back into the water. We sat that way for several minutes in silence as I soaked up the physical contact.

We'd been still for so long that the motion detector light turned off. Jimmy's finger rubbed against mine and it made me wish for something *more*.

If I tried hard enough, I could almost imagine that I was just a normal twenty-one-year old girl sitting next to a guy I was crushing on.

Jimmy shifted toward me like he was preparing to say something, but I broke the silence first.

"So, the friends with benefits thing. That's something you've done before?"

He took several seconds to respond and his answer was short. "Yeah."

Feeling bold from the alcohol, I made a desperate suggestion. "Could we do that? Be friends with benefits, I mean."

"No," he responded quickly, as if the very idea of being with me like that was out of the question.

Ouch.

My cheeks flamed, and I was glad it was too dark for him to see it. Humiliation from the rejection was a total buzzkill.

Suddenly, I felt ridiculous for throwing myself at Jimmy. Here I'd been thinking we were on the same page, and he was just trying to be a friend.

"Okay." I stood up on shaky legs, causing the water to splash around me. The light came back on and I tried to climb out of the hot tub without slipping on my ass. Grabbing a towel off the patio chair, I hastily wrapped it around my waist. "You're right. That was a really bad idea. 'Bye, Jimmy."

Turning quickly, I started back toward my house.

"Mack, wait!" I heard splashing behind me and I walked faster, determined to end this awkward-as-hell night.

"Goodnight," I called without stopping.

I heard an "oh shit" followed by a thud, and I turned to see Jimmy sprawled out on the lawn.

Fantastic.

He was wasted.

And that meant I couldn't even seduce a drunk guy.

But despite how embarrassed I was, I couldn't just leave him there.

Trudging back over, I nudged his shoulder with my foot. "Hey." Nothing. I did it again. "Hey." Still no response. Bending down, I shook him with my hand. "Jim—"

My word turned into a screech because he grabbed me, pulled me on top of him, then rolled us until we were laying side by side. It took me a moment to focus on Jimmy's face.

He grinned. "Fooled you."

# CHAPTER 15

JIMMY

The cool grass felt good on my heated skin as Mackenna fumed.

"That's not funny, James *Peabody* Johnson," she snapped, trying to push away from me.

Laughing, I held on tight. "Yeah, it is."

Giving up, she stopped wiggling and let out a sad sigh. "I can't blame you for not wanting to sleep with me."

The hurt in her voice caused an echoing ache in my chest. Her eyes stayed focused on some spot on my shoulder, and even without much light I could see the blush on her cheeks.

After what I learned tonight, things became a lot more complicated. I wasn't dealing with a girl who simply didn't like me—that was something I could work with. No, this was someone who'd been traumatized.

This wasn't a matter of winning her over with my charm but a matter of gaining her trust, which presented a completely different obstacle. A much more difficult obstacle.

I wasn't deterred, though.

We just needed to get to know each other. People said

the best relationships started out with a foundation of friendship.

I'd be the best fucking friend she'd ever had.

What she was offering was every guy's dream—a summer fling with a hot girl who lived two states away.

But I wanted more than that from Mackenna. If I agreed to her offer, I'd be settling.

I needed her to know my reasons for saying no.

"Do you want to know why I really came over to your house yesterday?" It was a rhetorical question, so I didn't wait for her to answer. "I wanted to ask you out."

"On a date?" she asked incredulously, her eyebrows nearly hitting her hairline. "But you don't even like me."

Grinning, I tucked some of the damp hair behind her ear.

"You're so wrong about that. The truth is, I want you so bad it hurts. And I'm not just talking about my dick, even though you've been the cause of blue balls for me constantly since we met." Her eyes widened at my candor, and I continued before she got too freaked out and ran away. "But I won't do casual with you. It's all or nothing."

"I can't believe you're turning down no-strings-attached sex," she said, shocked.

I laughed. "Neither can I. Honestly, though...I can't have sex with you if you don't trust me, if you don't feel safe. Don't you see how messed up that would be? You deserve better than that." I paused. "And so do I."

"Okay, I see your point," she said with a slight pout.

Suddenly, I wanted to kiss that scar on her forehead.

Then I recalled the way she freaked out when I asked about it. Dread formed in the pit of my stomach when it occurred to me how she might've gotten that injury.

"Did he do that?"

"Do what?"

I answered her by placing my lips over the mark, giving it a light kiss.

Sucking in a breath, she nodded. "We went hiking one day. He came on to me and I said no—not because I didn't want to have sex outside, but because I didn't want to at all. And I told him that. He got mad and pushed me. I hit my head on a rock."

My fists clenched behind her back. "How many stiches did you need?"

"Four."

I'd never had the desire to kill anyone before, and it was a weird feeling. Sure, I'd been in fights, but I never really wanted to hurt anyone. That wasn't the case now.

I wanted to find this guy. I wanted blood.

"Do you really think he's going to come after you?" I pulled back a little to look her in the eye.

Her lips pressed together. "I don't know. The scariest part is not knowing what he's thinking or what his intentions are. It's been such a long time. Honestly, I thought he would've forgotten about me by now."

"This is the same guy you shot, right? I'd say that would make you pretty memorable," I joked, trying to lighten the situation. "And totally badass, by the way."

My comment didn't make her laugh. Instead, her

fingers tightened on my shoulder and her voice came out in a whisper. "What if he's here? Like, right now... What if he's watching me?"

I understood her concern. A small part of me hoped he was watching. Because if he was nearby, that meant I could get my hands on him. And if I could get my hands on him, I'd make sure he never harassed Mackenna again.

But I kept those thoughts to myself.

"I'm staying at your house tonight," I told her, making sure my tone left no room for argument.

"I thought you said you weren't gonna sleep with me," she shot back, her slurred words giving away her level of intoxication.

"I'm not. I'll sleep on the couch."

"You don't have to do that. It's not big enough for you anyway." Her argument came out stilted and half-hearted. From the way some of the tension left her body, I could tell she felt safe with me.

"It's either that or I sleep on your porch," I told her. "Your call."

Letting out a cute huff, she sent me a sexy smirk that went straight to my dick. "Are you going to be my bodyguard or something? 'Cause that'd be kinda hot."

"Yes," I said seriously.

"Do you have any more beer?" she asked.

I smiled at the random change of subject. "Sorry, no."

"That's okay." She sat up, holding onto the pink towel around her waist. "Let's go finish off my Boon's Farm."

Jumping up, she ran toward her house, and I had no choice but to follow.

*

The leggings Mackenna changed into were purple, decorated with yellow starfish. When I realized I didn't have anything to wear except my wet swim trunks, she ran upstairs and came back down with a pair of gray sweatpants. They were a little short, the ankles hugging me mid-calf, but the waist fit.

She offered to find me a T-shirt, too, but when I told her I was good without one, she rolled her eyes and muttered something under her breath about *hot nipples*.

Between the whiskey, beer, and wine, I knew Mackenna had to be pretty drunk. Which is exactly why I asked her to sing for me.

Even three sheets to the wind, I thought I'd get an argument from her, so I was surprised when she picked up her guitar. Settling into the blue chair, she clamped a small triangle pick between her teeth while she plucked at the strings and adjusted the tuning knobs.

Once she seemed satisfied with the tinkering, she turned to me. "Okay. What are you in the mood for?"

"Something of yours."

She groaned. "Seriously? Which one?"

"The one you were playing the other day."

"'If Only'?"

I shook my head. "It was about being lost or something."

Her eyes widened to the point of comical. "You heard me play 'Weak'?"

"If that's what it's called, yeah."

"No," she said, furiously shaking her head back and forth. "That's, like, the most personal song I've ever written. I wrote it when I was eighteen, right before I left for Nashville. No one's ever heard it."

"But I heard it."

"You weren't supposed to." She glared with unfocused eyes.

I sent her a charming grin.

Swaying a bit, she absentmindedly strummed the strings, as if her instrument was an extension of her own body.

For a second, I envied the passion she had for her career.

At her age most people were still in college, getting buried in student debt or working a dead-end job living paycheck to paycheck. Some people went their entire lives without finding *their thing*—the thing they were put on this earth to do.

One of my biggest fears was that I would end up being one of those unfortunate people.

But this amazing girl in front of me already had it figured out. She had talent, perseverance, and luck on her side. I knew she was lonely, though. Because of her past, she'd gotten used to shutting people out.

I wanted her to let me in.

"That song is too depressing," she continued, still plucking random notes. "People want hopeful words, especially when it's about something so serious. They want a song that will make them feel like there's a way out. Like everything is going to be okay."

"And the song isn't about that?"

"No. It's the opposite, actually. The way it feels when you're in a dark time."

"I want to hear it again. Please?"

Glancing up at the ceiling, she let out a cute growl before emptying her wine glass.

"Don't think this is going to be a regular thing," she slurred. "I can't even feel my face right now."

I started cracking up, but my laughter was cut short when she began to sing.

> *I got your message, God,*
> *I read it clear and loud,*
> *This isn't the way I ever*
> *thought things would turn out,*
> *I'm a fucked-up mess of chances,*
> *In this fucked-up life I live,*
> *Here's to a second chance,*
> *That left me here for dead,*
> *Here's to the world I know,*
> *We have driven this road hard,*
> *And packed the gravel down...*
> *We are the weak,*
> *We are the lost,*
> *We are the sick and tired of being left alone,*
> *Being left alone...*
> *Maybe I can't find the words,*

*This isn't the first time*
*I've been down and out,*
*This is a tightrope walk,*
*With the blinders on...*

As she started the chorus again, singing about being weak and lost, I knew I was getting a glimpse of something personal, something deep inside her no one else had ever seen.

This was the eighteen-year-old version of Mackenna—broken and alone—baring her soul in the form of song lyrics. Lyrics she'd kept all to herself.

In that moment, I felt more connected to her than I ever had to anyone. And I'd only known her for a few days. How was it possible for me to see inside someone's heart so soon? Someone who was so determined to keep me out?

And after those last chords rang out, she gave me a lopsided smile. That dimple appeared and I was speechless.

I was such a lucky motherfucker. Not just because I got to hear her sing, but because I had the opportunity to know her.

And I needed to tread lightly so I didn't mess it up.

When she leaned over to set her guitar on its stand, she lost her balance.

"Whoa." Reaching out, I caught her around the waist before she could hit the floor. "I think we should get you to bed."

"The room is spinning," she grumped.

Kneeling in front of her, I placed my hands on each side of her face. "I need you to tell me the truth. What are the chances you're going to throw up?"

"None." She wrinkled her nose, then a burp bubbled up. "I think."

"Come on," I said, scooping her up into my arms.

"What the hell do you think you're doing?" she asked, though there was no heat behind her words. Looping her arms around my neck, she didn't seem to mind having me hold her. Just like on the couch earlier, her body relaxed and she rested her head on my shoulder.

"Carrying you up the stairs," I replied. "Which one is your room?"

As I reached the top step, she pointed to the right. I kicked the door open before flipping the light switch with my elbow. The room stayed dark.

I looked up at the ceiling fan. "Your lightbulb burn out?"

"No. My lamp." Waving her arm at the small lamp on her nightstand, she snickered. "It's a touch lamp. Like magic. Seriously, just touch it and it turns on. Ohh, that sounded dirty."

I laughed, enjoying her drunk rambling as my feet padded across the hardwood floors. "I'll be sure to touch it."

She giggled as I gently placed her onto the bed. "Won't Beverly wonder where you are?"

I shook my head. "She spends most nights at Ernie's anyway. If I get back early enough, she won't even know I was gone."

"Such a troublemaker," she taunted, falling backwards and closing her eyes.

Bringing my hand to the light, I tapped it once and dim light filled the room. The lamp looked old, with shiny brass and glass plates that were decorated with a floral design.

Glancing over at a silent Mackenna, I thought she might be passed out, but she was staring at me with heavy-lidded eyes.

"How are you feeling?" I sat down next to her.

"I think I have a crush on you," she rushed out, the words running together.

I chuckled, lying back so we were side by side. "Oh yeah?"

"Well, I can't be sure, but I think this is what it's supposed to feel like."

Puzzled, I raised an eyebrow. "You've never had a crush before?"

"Of course I have. I mean, when I was younger, there were some boys in school I thought were cute. But it was different then."

"How so?"

"Well, for starters, I didn't think about them naked."

Fuck. I loved it when she was transparent with me, but her honesty was seriously testing my resolve to keep my hands to myself.

Grunting, I threw an arm over my face. "You've gotta stop saying stuff like that."

"I thought you wanted me to be honest."

"I did. I do." My words came out muffled. "*Fuck.*"

She giggled again and I felt the mattress dip. Letting

my arm fall to the mattress, I looked over to find Mackenna propped up on her elbow, seeming a little more sober now.

"I want a compromise," she said in that bossy, business-like tone I liked so much.

"Oh, this is gonna be good." I laughed. She was tenacious.

"We do the friends with benefits thing—" She cut off my attempt to argue by holding up her hand. "You want me to trust you if we have sex, right? Show me how. I want to know what that feels like. Please?"

She was begging—fucking begging—me to have sex with her. My thoughts went wild, trying to figure out a way to give her what she wanted, while also getting what I wanted, too.

Conflicted, I rubbed a hand over my jaw. "I don't know, Mack..."

"Please, Jimmy," she pleaded, obliterating my self-control.

"Do you have any idea how hard it is to say no to you?" I asked quietly, feeling vulnerable.

Playfully poking me in the chest, she grinned. "Then don't say no."

"Okay, I'll humor you. What do I get out of this?"

"Well, there's the sex part," she pointed out. "Plus, if we're having sex, then we won't be arguing. That's a win-win."

"Unless it's angry sex," I added with a wink. "That could be fun."

Mackenna rolled her eyes. "We'd need to lay some ground rules, though."

"What is it with you women and your rules?"

"It's important to have boundaries."

"Alright." I sighed. "Let's hear it."

"Rule number one—you can't buy me flowers," she said. I must've looked confused because she explained, "Flowers are a waste of money. If you're going to spend money on something, at least let it be useful. Like guitar picks."

"Guitar picks," I repeated, amused.

"Now it's your turn." She made a 'go ahead' gesture with her hand.

Shrugging, I toyed with a strand of her hair. "Don't have any."

"Not even one rule?"

"Nope. I don't play by the rules anyway."

She gave my shoulder a shove. "I'm serious."

I laughed.

"Okay, okay. Geez." Pausing to think, I tried to think of something I wanted from her that she wouldn't normally agree to. I snapped my fingers when it came to me. "You have to sing to me every day."

She gasped. "No way."

"You said I get a rule. That's rule number two."

"Once a week," she bargained.

"Twice a week," I countered.

"Fine." She huffed, and I smiled because I got my way.

"What's rule three?" I asked, distracted by the way her fingers explored the tattoos on my forearm.

"Obviously, we can't fall in love with each other, but I don't think that should be a problem since we can't go more than one day without pissing each other off."

"Next," I said, purposely avoiding any agreement to rule three.

"Your turn again," she told me.

Then a brilliant idea came to me. "You're mine for as long as I'm here. One hundred percent exclusive."

Her face screwed up, causing an adorable wrinkle between her eyebrows. "That's not really friends with benefits then. Doesn't that mean we're dating?"

I shrugged. "Pretty much. I refuse to share you, so, no dating anyone else."

"Okay," she gave in, and I had to restrain myself from doing a fist pump in the air.

"I can't believe I'm dating Mackenna Connelly," I said teasingly, and she scoffed. "One of your songs is on the radio, and here you are, hanging out with a bum like me."

"Hey," she said softly, her fingers traveling up to my bicep. "You're not a bum."

"And you're not as unfriendly as you want people to think you are."

Her lips turned down. "And you don't know me as well as you think you do."

"But I'd like to."

"What do you want from me?" she asked, apprehensively biting her lip.

"A lot of things," I answered honestly.

She sighed and the next words came out sluggish.

"Today's been a weird day."

"Maybe it's time to sleep it off," I suggested. "You'll probably be dealing with one hell of a hangover tomorrow."

"Okay. But first, I have to pee." Staggering to her feet, she made it across the room, and I heard the bathroom door shut in the hall.

I fell back onto her pillows and closed my eyes. Her sheets smelled good. Clean and something that was distinctly *Mackenna*. I didn't want to move. I wanted to stay right here. With her.

When I heard her shuffle back into the room, I made a split decision. Keeping my eyes closed, I stayed still and tried to even out my breathing.

"Jimmy?" She poked me a couple times in the chest. "Jimmy."

I feigned a snore.

It took a lot more than a few shots and a beer to get me pass-out drunk, but she didn't know that.

I was a bastard for pretending to be asleep. Ultimately, I was forcing her to make a choice: stay here with me or go sleep on the couch. My intentions were completely innocent, though. I just wanted to be next to her. Feel her warmth and watch her sleep.

And yeah, I knew how creepy that sounded.

But also, my instincts told me to stay as close to her as possible. If anything happened, it would be a lot harder to keep her safe if I was in a different room.

Staying completely still, I waited. I could almost hear Mackenna's inner thoughts as she debated what to do.

When she let out a resigned sigh and dropped her head onto the pillow next to mine, it took everything I had not to wrap my arms around her.

This night had taken an interesting turn.

I'd gotten Mackenna to agree to date me. Exclusively. Technically, we were in a relationship.

For now.

It was a giant victory and I gladly accepted it.

# CHAPTER 16

JIMMY

Mackenna was a bed hog. Correction: she was a fucking starfish, just like the ones on her leggings.

Those memes about co-sleeping parents with children who can take up an entire bed, despite being tiny? Yeah. It was like that. Only Mackenna wasn't toddler-sized.

Somehow I'd ended up lying on my back in the middle, and Mackenna was sprawled out on top of me, arms and legs spanning the width of the mattress. Her head was tucked below my chin, her lips resting against my neck. Every puff of her warm breath on my skin sent a jolt straight to my dick.

My hard-as-hell dick, which was nestled right against her pussy.

Even through the sweatpants, I could feel the heat coming off her center. My balls ached with the need for release and I knew I'd be rubbing one out in the shower later.

Every now and then, she would sigh and wiggle a little.

It was torture.

Really good torture.

To distract myself, I thought about my first day on the

job at Hank's. Nervousness took over as I wondered what tasks I'd be doing and if I would even be good at it.

Would I fail at this, too?

I'd been straightforward with Hank when I told him I had no experience with cars. When I was younger, I went through a phase where I liked to put together those model cars, but that wasn't the same as working on actual vehicles.

From the pinkish glow coming through the window, I estimated it was almost 7:00, but I didn't want to leave yet. I allowed myself several more minutes of feeling Mackenna on top of me. And when I couldn't hold back any longer, I wrapped my arms around her, placing one hand on the small of her back and the other by her neck.

Brushing the hair away from her face, I ran my hands through the silky strands a few times. She shifted up my body, which was a small relief for my dick, but it put my face right by the place where her neck met her shoulder.

Running my nose along her skin, I inhaled. The smell of the water from the hot tub still lingered, but there was something else.

Slightly sweet. *Her.*

"Mack," I whispered, my lips grazing her collarbone.

"Hhmmff?"

"I gotta get back home to get ready for work."

Quickly sitting up, she looked incredibly adorable in her sleepy, rumpled state.

"I'm so sorry. Did I make you late? What time is it?" she babbled, rubbing her eyes.

I chuckled. "No, I'm not late, but I thought I should get back before Grandma realizes I'm gone."

Nodding, she made a sound of agreement. But she was still straddling me, anchoring me to the bed.

Unable to stop myself, I rubbed my hands up her thighs. "Baby, as much as I love seeing you like this—and I really, really love seeing you like this—you're gonna have to get off me so I can leave."

Her eyes widened before she squeaked and ungracefully fell to the other side of the bed. Leaning her back against the wall, she covered her face with her hands.

"Oh, my God." Her voice came out muffled. "I'm so sorry for molesting you."

I threw my head back and laughed.

"I'm not complaining." Grabbing her ankle, I dragged her back over to me and placed her leg over my lap. "Text me today to let me know you're okay. I'll be over as soon as I get off work."

"You worried about me, James Peabody Johnson?" she teased with a smile.

I decided to let her get away with calling me by my full name, because it was sexy when she was playful.

Throughout my life, the unfortunate middle name had been a source of embarrassment. Dad always went on about how it was a family name and how I should be proud to have it. Honestly, it didn't sound so bad passing through Mackenna's lips. And if it gave her a reason to flirt with me, she could say it all day long.

"Yeah, I'm worried," I told her honestly. "Lock your doors. Stay by your phone."

"You're kind of cute when you're bossy."

"I'll remember you said that." I gave her knee a squeeze before reluctantly moving off the bed. "You should go back to sleep. There's no reason for both of us to be up this early."

Mackenna seemed to agree, because she collapsed back into the pillows and pulled her purple comforter up to her shoulders.

Fighting the urge to crawl back into bed, I forced my feet to move. Stopping in the doorway, I looked back at her. With a flick of her fingers, she gave me a cute wave before burrowing further under the covers.

\*

Hot water ran down my back as I braced my hand on the pink-tiled shower wall. My other hand went to my erection, stroking from base to tip.

I ran my thumb over the barbell piercing just below the head and hissed when my balls drew up tight.

This wasn't going to take long, which was a good thing since I didn't have much time.

Closing my eyes, I let my mind go to a place it hadn't gone yet. While Mackenna had occupied many of my thoughts since meeting her, I hadn't allowed myself to give in to the fantasy of being with her.

Now I couldn't stop myself from imagining what it would feel like to have her touch me.

The hand on my cock wasn't mine anymore—it was hers.

She was kneeling before me, her lips parted. Her delicate hand moved up and down as she stared at my dick with fascination and hunger.

Stroking faster, I envisioned Mackenna taking me into her mouth, applying just the right amount of suction. Her tongue flicked over the piercing. She moaned, and I imagined feeling the vibrations in my shaft.

The muscles of my abdomen and thighs tensed as I got closer to release.

She bobbed up and down while keeping a firm grip on the base, moving her hand in time with her head. Water ran down between the valley of her breasts, her nipples stiff and pink.

She took me in deeper, faster, her lips stretching wide to accommodate my girth.

When those big stormy eyes looked up at me, it pushed me over the edge.

"Fuuuuuck," I groaned, the orgasm hitting me fast and hard.

I kept my eyes shut for a second, trying to hold onto the fantasy of filling Mackenna's mouth with my cum. I wanted her to take it all. Every last drop.

The pulsing of my cock subsided and my hand slowed. I gave my dick one more tug before leaning back against the wall as I tried to catch my breath.

Holy shit.

If a simple figment of my imagination was that intense, what would the real thing be like?

Hank didn't waste any time getting me right into the dirty work. After giving me one of Travis's spare coveralls, he passed me off to Colton and told me to have fun.

First thing Colton had me do was shadow him on an oil change. He gave straightforward instructions, being sure to tell me how many quarts of oil to put in and how to check for leaks the customer might not know about.

Then he rambled on for a good ten minutes about different kinds of oil for different vehicle models, and my head started to spin.

I rolled up my sleeves and reached underneath the hood of the SUV we were working on next.

"You should remove your watch," Colton spoke up. "Getting it caught on something is a good way to get injured. Plus, you don't want to break it."

Unbuckling the leather strap, I shrugged. "It's already broken anyway."

"I bet my dad could try to fix it for you," he offered. "He loves to tinker around with that kind of stuff."

"Seriously?" I asked. "That'd be cool."

"Yo, Dad!" Colton hollered and Hank's head popped out of the office. "Jimmy's got a broken watch."

Hank's face lit up and he hurried over to us. Colton wasn't joking—the guy was really excited.

"Lemme see here." Getting out a pair of bifocals, he inspected the watch in my palm. "Can I?" he asked, as if he could sense it was important to me.

I nodded and let him take it.

Flipping it over, his eyes bounced to me over the rim of his glasses. "I can try to get it working again if you want."

"Sure. It's not like you can break it twice."

There was an extra hop in his step as he retreated to his office with my watch.

Colton and I went back to work, and after we were done with another oil change, he showed me how to fill out the invoices for customers. Meanwhile, Travis replaced brake pads on a Ford pickup truck.

"Is that something I'll learn how to do, too?" I asked Colton, curious about the process.

Grinning at my eagerness, he nodded. "In time." Then he glanced at the clock on the wall. "Dad said you can leave at noon. It's not very often that Travis and I are here at the same time. We thought we'd go over to Buck's Tavern for lunch. You in?"

I took a second to consider it because I was antsy to get back to Mackenna's house, but I also got the feeling she'd been getting annoyed with all my 'well-check' texts.

"Sure. I'll just let Mackenna know I'll be a little later."

Colton laughed and shook his head as he muttered, "Ball-buster, for sure."

> **Me: You okay?**
> **Mack: For the 75th time, YES**
> **Me: What kind of leggings are you wearing?**
> **Mack: I thought you said you were only going to text me if it was**

**important**

**Me: This is important**

A picture came through. Flamingo leggings. I was grinning so hard my face hurt. I shot off a text, letting her know my lunch plans with the guys, then met Colton and Travis in front of the shop.

We crossed the street to Buck's, and as soon as we got inside, the smell of fried food made my stomach growl. The tavern was long and narrow, with a sleek wooden bar off to the right and about a dozen square tables in the dining area on the left. We chose to sit by the front window.

"What kind of food do they have here?" I asked, looking at the old laminated card on the table that listed burgers and fries as the Friday special.

"If it's fried, they probably have it." Colton pointed at the tiny menu. "Taco Tuesdays are pretty popular. I would avoid Wednesday, though."

"What's on Wednesday?"

"The only day my ex works here," he replied seriously.

Travis started cracking up. "That's only half of the truth. The other reason is Buck started experimenting with Chinese food. Let's just say it's not his forte."

I grinned. "Noted."

Like me, Travis's hair was longer on top, but his fell past his eyebrows. He raked a grease-coated hand through the brown strands. Neither of the guys seemed fazed by the grime a hard day's work left behind. I'd tried my best to get my hands clean, but there was only so much a bar of soap could do. I would need to invest in a scrubbing tool.

Or maybe not. Maybe in time, I wouldn't be bothered by the dirt either.

A waitress came by, placing ice waters in front of us. After she took our orders, I turned the conversation back to work.

"So, what's my schedule gonna be like? I'll be there as much as you need me."

"Monday through Friday, 9am to whenever the work is finished. We usually close up around 4:00 on busy days. No weekends at the shop, but sometimes we have transport deliveries," Colton informed me.

"Sounds great. You guys have an awesome business," I told him. "Must feel pretty good to own such a successful company."

"It hasn't been without struggles," he said, looking serious. "Travis and I started helping out when we were fifteen, and there were times when Dad couldn't afford to pay us. Thought he'd have to close up for good at one point."

"I'm not putting you guys in a bind, am I?" I asked, wondering if Hank's generosity was putting him in a tough spot financially.

"No way," Travis chimed in. "We're glad to have the extra help. A few years ago, we opened the truck testing lane to increase revenue. Then we added the transport company. I'm on the road a lot." He hiked a thumb toward Colton. "Him, too."

"Did you always know you wanted to be mechanics?"

They both nodded, then Colton added, "Growing up, it's what I knew. I've always loved it."

"My favorite part is trucking," Travis said. "I can't imagine doing anything else."

Then his face lit up and he glanced over at Colton. For a few seconds, they seemed to have some kind of telepathic conversation.

Turning toward me, Colton leaned his elbows on the tabletop. "Hey, what do you think of truck driving?"

I shrugged. "Guess I've never thought about it before."

"You should consider it," Travis said. "The power behind a semi. Life on the open road. There's nothing like it. And we could use another driver."

At twenty-two, Travis and Colton weren't that much older than me. When they talked about their careers, I could hear how much they loved it. Just like Mackenna, they'd found their calling. And again, I was both impressed and a little jealous.

"It does sound pretty great," I said honestly. "But I'm only here until August."

"Oh." Travis looked disappointed.

"Well it's great to have you, even for a short time." Colton elbowed Travis. "Especially with this guy's wedding coming up. They're taking a two-week honeymoon."

"That's right. Hank said you were getting married. Congrats, man," I said to Travis.

"Thanks." He had a goofy grin on his face. "And you're invited."

Although I appreciated it, I shook my head. "Don't feel obligated to invite me. You guys don't know me that well."

Travis made a dismissive sound. "The whole town gets

an open invitation. Literally. Angel decided to have it the same day as the summer festival because she wants everyone to be there. I heard you're dating Mackenna Connelly. You should bring her, too."

I smiled because I didn't have to correct him on my relationship status.

Our burgers and fries showed up, effectively ending all talk of weddings, auto shops, and semi-trucks.

It was too early for me to tell if I would be good at my new job, but I knew one thing—I looked forward to finding out.

# CHAPTER 17

MACKENNA

I had officially thrown in the towel on thinking I could get Jimmy to go away.

It didn't matter if I was grumpy or annoyingly cheerful. Whether I was slinging insults his way or drunkenly throwing myself at him.

He seemed to enjoy all of it.

I was completely baffled.

And if I was being honest, I enjoyed his company, too.

It also didn't hurt that his protective side was sexy as hell. He was totally hovering and I couldn't even argue with him about it because, as much as I hated relying on someone, I felt safe when Jimmy was around.

It'd been a long time since I let someone be there for me. And right now, I needed him.

This morning, waking up to the sound of Jimmy's strong heartbeat had been one of the best things ever until I realized I'd attached myself to him like a leech. That was embarrassing.

He was the only person I'd ever done that to. I'd shared a bed with my sister countless times throughout our lives and never attacked her like that. Usually I liked my own space when I slept, but for some reason I was drawn to Jimmy.

All day long, he'd been sending concerned text messages, and from the last one I knew he should be here any minute.

I rarely put makeup on. Most days I didn't even brush my hair.

Now I found myself running back and forth from my bedroom to the bathroom, trying to find all the girly supplies I hadn't unpacked yet.

"Aha!" I let out a triumphant shout when I found my makeup bag in the cardboard box labeled 'not important'.

Dumping all the contents onto the granite countertop, I searched for my foundation, blush, and eyeliner. I probably didn't have time to do the works, but something was better than nothing.

I glanced at myself in the mirror over the sink and noticed a pink tinge on my cheeks. I wasn't sure if it was from excitement or the sun exposure while painting, but it looked good.

I threw the blush back into the bag and got the bronzer instead. After I was satisfied with the half-assed job I did on my face, I ran my fingers through my hair. I debated whether I should change my clothes. In the end, I decided to stick with the leggings because Jimmy seemed to like them.

After trading my oversized T-shirt for a fitted black tank top, I was ready for our date.

Was it a date? According to the conversation we had last night, it was.

If Jimmy really wanted to call it dating, then that was fine with me. The chance of me being interested in another guy was less than zero, so it wasn't difficult to agree to those temporary terms. Surprisingly, I felt immense relief at knowing he wouldn't be with anyone else either.

As I sat in my comfy chair and waited, the sound of the ticking clock on the mantel only fueled my anxiousness. My face felt hot, and my hands were cold and clammy.

When that soft knock came at my door, a foreign kind of giddiness buzzed through my body.

I peered through the peep hole. Jimmy was there, looking every bit the part of hot mechanic. His unzipped coveralls hung around his waist, exposing the black T-shirt he wore underneath. I admired the way it hugged his arms and chest just right.

I may have been intimidated by his tattoos at first, but that wasn't the case at all now. He owned those tattoos. He was meant to have that ink on his body.

"Mack? You okay?" Jimmy's muffled voice came through the door, and I realized I'd just been standing there ogling him through the peep hole.

Like a complete psycho.

Awesome.

After letting him in, I turned toward the living room and he followed.

"I came straight here," he said, gesturing to the grease staining his clothes. "Sorry I'm so dirty. Just wanted to check on you first."

There was a smudge on his forehead. Before I could

second-guess what I was doing, I reached up and wiped it away with my thumb until the mark was gone. He smelled like sweat, motor oil, and sunshine. He smelled like a man. A hard-working man. And it was wonderful.

Grabbing a hold of his forearm, I tugged him down onto the couch with me.

He sat stiffly, holding his arms away from the leather. "I'm gonna get your couch dirty."

"I don't care," I responded, not at all bothered by the mess.

"If you say so." Shrugging, he relaxed into the cushions.

Curious about how his first day went, I asked him what he'd done and how he liked it.

Jimmy's face lit up, and his hands slashed animatedly through the air as he told me about different types of oil and other things he learned on the job. I never knew someone could be so excited about car parts, but seeing him so fired up made those butterflies come alive again, ricocheting inside my abdomen.

"What?" he stopped mid-sentence when he was saying something about tires. "Why are you smiling like that?"

Bringing my hand up to my face, I realized I was grinning like a loon for no reason.

"I just—" I tried to think of how to explain it. "—you're so happy. I guess it's just contagious?"

Reflecting my smile, Jimmy brought his forehead to mine and brushed my cheek with his thumb.

"So, what are we going to do today?" I asked as sudden nervousness hit me. I had no idea how to do this. With no wall of liquid courage to hide behind, the brave, horny girl from last night was gone.

Would we jump right into ripping each other's clothes off? Would there be foreplay? Most importantly, would I freak out or would I be able to keep my shit together?

My heart sped up at the thought of feeling all his tattoos. And the nipple piercings. And his lips on mine.

Equal parts anxiety and desire battled it out as I waited for his answer.

"Hold hands," Jimmy replied.

Narrowing my eyes, I tried to figure out if he was serious. "You're joking, right?"

"Nope." He leaned back. "We're gonna sit on this couch, watch a movie, and hold hands."

"That's it?" I asked, relief and disappointment simultaneously flooding my system.

Nodding, he held out his hand and I gave him mine. Linking our fingers, he pressed our palms together and my heart did that fluttery thing again.

I looked down at our hands, admiring the contrast. His were darker, rougher. I could tell he'd attempted to wash off the grease from the shop, but some remained in the crevices of his skin and under his fingernails. Something about it was incredibly sexy.

He rubbed his thumb over my knuckles. "You didn't get to do this stuff, did you?"

"What stuff?"

"The innocent stuff," he said. "The things you do when you're not thinking about sex, when you're just happy to be on a date sitting next to someone you like."

I swallowed hard. The truth of his statement hit home, because that was a necessary step I'd been forced to skip.

Giving him a small smile, I nodded. "That sounds really nice, actually."

"But first, I need a shower." He leaned in close and pressed a kiss to my scar, just like he did last night.

Before I could read too much into it, he was walking toward the door, telling me to lock it behind him.

Jimmy had only been gone for ten minutes when he came back wearing black, low-sitting sweatpants and a plain gray T-shirt. The dark, damp hair on his head was in disarray, like he'd simply scrubbed a towel over it.

Sticking to his word, he held my hand all evening. It wasn't boring, though.

I had no idea there were so many different types of hand-holding.

Sometimes he brushed the inside of my wrist with his thumb. Other times he idly played with my fingers while we watched the movies he borrowed from Beverly. He earned big brownie points when he massaged my palms, applying the right amount of pressure over every inch of my hands and fingers, soothing the stiffness from hours of playing guitar.

And when my palm ended up sweaty from nerves and constant contact, I shyly wiped it off on my leggings while muttering an apology. Jimmy just laughed before slinging an arm around me. Then he twirled my hair around his finger for a good twenty minutes.

He managed to touch me at all times, while keeping it completely innocent.

It was thrilling and new.

By the time we made it into my bed—for sleep only—my body was a jittery mess of hormones. The place between my thighs was wet, hot, and achy.

I'd never been more turned on in my life.

Who knew hand-holding could be such amazing foreplay?

# CHAPTER 18

MACKENNA

"This color is one hundred times better," I said to Jimmy as I covered the bright green bricks with the new paint.

"You pretty much picked it out," he told me with a grin. I gave him a questioning look and he laughed. "I went to Home Depot and asked for sage green. I'd never heard of it before you said it that day. Seems like it was a good choice, though."

I was surprised that he even remembered such an insignificant conversation. "It's a popular color because it's subtle. I think the mayor will approve."

He moved by me to roll paint on the other side of the window I was trimming around. "As long as it doesn't rain, we should be able to finish this weekend."

"Oh, that reminds me. I'm staying at my parents' house tonight, so you're off babysitting duty," I joked. "But I'll be back tomorrow morning."

Jimmy stopped rolling and frowned. "You're not doing that because you think you're a burden or anything, right? Because I don't mind. Your bed is a hell of a lot more comfortable than mine anyway."

I shook my head. "I've been planning it for a while. I

feel kind of guilty because I don't visit them as much as I should. Plus, I miss my sister."

A half-smile appeared on Jimmy's face. "I didn't realize you have a sister."

Pulling up the most recent picture on my phone, I turned it toward him. Krista and I were on the couch at my parents' house, our heads pressed together as we took a selfie.

"She's fifteen, and it's like she completely skipped the awkward teenager phase and went straight to being cute as a button."

"I love it when you smile," Jimmy said, peering closer. "I thought you two would look more alike. But then again, my brother and I couldn't be more different."

"We have some similarities, but her hair is lighter and her eyes are darker. She'll probably end up being taller than me, too. How old is your brother?" I asked, slipping my phone into the back pocket of my shorts.

"Ezra's a year younger," he said before telling me about his brother's limp, how shy he was, and how he would be spending the summer at a physical therapy camp. There was so much affection in his voice when he added, "He's the coolest kid I know."

"Cooler than you?"

He grinned. "Way cooler."

Most of the morning had been spent with Jimmy and me working silently side by side. Only this time, the lack of conversation wasn't intentional on my part. It was just comfortable.

Every now and then, we exchanged smiles and flirty glances.

Sometimes I caught him staring at my mouth, and the need to feel his lips on mine was so intense that it became a physical ache. My nipples tightened to the point of painful. I throbbed between my thighs. I licked my lips, which felt hot and tingly.

Jimmy hadn't shaved for a couple days, and I yearned to feel the dark scruff scrape against my cheeks, my chin, my neck. But just when I thought he was finally going to give in, he'd turn away and go back to painting.

It frustrated the hell out of me.

In less than a week, I'd gone from recoiling at the idea of being intimate with someone to feeling like I had to physically restrain myself from launching my body at him like a spider monkey.

Of course, he was shirtless again. Jimmy seemed to be in a permanent state of half-dressed 90% of the time, which only added fuel to the fire.

Being a temptress wasn't my expertise. I knew nothing about the art of seduction.

But all I wanted was a damn kiss.

So far, my efforts to get him to make a move weren't successful. I'd purposely left my paint bucket next to his so I would have a reason to get close to him. A few times I let my arm touch him in some way—his stomach or his chest—but he seemed to remain unaffected.

By coincidence, Jimmy ended up bending down to refill my bucket at the same time I went to dip the brush.

This resulted in me smearing paint down the side of his face.

I giggled, and he shot me an amused look. Then I decided to take full advantage of the situation.

"Here," I said, whipping my T-shirt over my head, leaving me in a black sports bra.

Pressing my body against his, I leaned up to wipe off the mess. Jimmy's hands fell to my waist. His fingers clenched against my bare skin, like he couldn't decide if he wanted to pull me closer or push me away.

"Mack," he rasped.

"Hmm?" I said innocently while dabbing at his jaw.

"Are you pushing me on purpose?" His voice was low and husky.

Our eyes locked. All I could do was nod as I wiped the last of the paint away.

The sound he responded with was tortured as he briefly leaned his forehead against mine. "I'm trying to go slow with you, but you're making it really difficult."

"Turtles are slow. Snails are even slower. Then there's you," I teased.

His jaw tensed. "What do you want?"

"A kiss would be nice," I answered honestly.

Jimmy walked me backwards, until I was flush against the side of the house. I was fully aware that the paint was still wet and I probably had brick print all over my backside.

Strong arms caged me in as he placed a hand on each side of my head. I waited to feel that old familiar panic build inside of me, but it never came. Instead of feeling trapped, I felt safe.

"Jimmy... Do you want to kiss me?"

Licking his lips, he didn't take his eyes off my mouth as he nodded.

"They why don't you just do it already?" I challenged, my voice barely above a whisper.

He leaned in closer until our faces were just inches apart.

"Because I feel like if I do this, things will change," he replied. "And I'm not sure you're ready for it."

I shook my head, confused. "What will change?"

"Everything," he breathed out before closing the distance.

Soft lips met mine and I gasped at the gentleness of it. I thought Jimmy's kiss would be rough and demanding, but it was slow. Deliberate. Unbelievably sensual.

My eyes closed as our mouths moved together.

That plump, pouty bottom lip. It did things to me. I wanted to suck it into my mouth. I wanted to bite it, then lick the sting away.

But just as quickly as the kiss started, it ended.

A sexy sound rumbled in Jimmy's throat as he reluctantly pulled back. Before he could get too far, I wrapped my hand around the back of his neck.

"More. Please," I pleaded against his mouth. "Please don't stop yet."

"Damn." Jimmy gave me what I wanted as he dove back in.

He cupped my face, the large span of his hand covering my cheek and the side of my neck. I could feel the sticky paint transfer from his fingers to my skin.

The gentle kisses continued, but I wanted more. Deeper. Harder.

Hesitantly, my tongue swept out, tasting the seam of his lips. Jimmy must have taken that as a green light, because his mouth opened wider and he let me in. Our tongues melded together in perfect rhythm, and his stubble rubbed against my skin.

Wanting to get closer I grabbed at his chest, but there was no shirt to hold on to. His skin was warm and smooth under my fingertips. Curiously, I ran my thumbs over the barbells through his nipples.

The restraint he was holding on to finally snapped.

Groaning, he wrapped an arm around my waist and pushed us away from the house. His other hand landed on my ass as he picked me up. My legs automatically wrapped around him, and I whimpered when he sucked on my tongue.

He slammed us up against the house again, his arm taking the brunt of the impact.

"Shit," he panted between frantic kisses. "Tell me if it's too much. Do you want me to stop?"

I was too worked up to answer. Needing friction, I shifted slightly, grinding my pelvis against his.

He growled.

"I'm serious, Mackenna. Fuck," he whispered, moving his mouth down to my neck. "What are you doing to me?"

"Kissing you?" It came out sounding like a question.

"No." He shook his head. "I've kissed girls. It never felt like this before."

"Violating you against the side of your grandma's house?"

He laughed against my collarbone. "That's definitely a first for me."

Sliding his hand down my thigh, he released the hold he had on my body. Once my feet were back on solid ground, a wave of embarrassment hit me.

I just attacked Jimmy in broad daylight. In his grandma's yard. We had neighbors, and anyone could've gotten an eyeful. I bet the old lady gossip chain was going right now. Landlines all over town were probably occupied.

"Oh, no you don't," Jimmy said, pointing at my face. "You don't get to regret what we just did."

I wanted to respond, but all I could think about was the way his lips felt against mine. He must have taken my silence as a bad thing.

He frowned. "Do you, though? Regret it, I mean."

"No. I want to do it again," I told him before reaching out to feel his chest.

He jumped away. "Keep touching me like that and I'm gonna need a cold shower."

Getting an idea, I grinned and picked up the nearby garden hose.

"I can help you out with that," I said, squeezing the nozzle.

A powerful jet of water shot out, spraying Jimmy's

stomach. The look of shock on his face was so hilarious, I couldn't stop the giggles coming out of my mouth. Without saying a word, he stalked toward me.

"Jimmy," I warned through another fit of giggles. "I'll spray you again."

He gave me an evil grin.

I backed up until there was no length left on the hose, then I really let him have it. He didn't even flinch as I soaked his skin and shorts.

When he reached me, I let out a squeak and abandoned ship. Dropping the hose, I turned to run.

"I don't think so, baby." Jimmy laughed as he hooked an arm around my waist. Pulling my back against his wet front, I felt a hard bulge against my lower back. He lowered his head until his mouth was right by my ear. "The cold shower didn't work."

He pressed his lips to the side of my neck and I shivered.

"What are the chances you aren't going to retaliate with the hose?" I squirmed in his hold.

"Zero," he replied before spraying the top of my head.

Screeching, I spun away from him. Then I realized my mistake when all it did was give him better access to spray me.

The best solution I could come up with was to launch myself at him. He had no choice but to drop the hose and catch me. I wrapped my arms around his neck and my legs around his waist.

We were both breathless and laughing as we stared at each other for several long seconds.

I was still smiling when I brought my lips to his. This time, there was no hesitation to the kiss. Open-mouthed, tangling tongues. Hunger. Desperation. Passion.

It was all-consuming, and the rest of the world fell away along with any concern I had about the neighbors watching. The magic of the moment chipped away at my self-consciousness, and in its place I gained a sense of freedom.

I nipped at Jimmy's bottom lip, then gave him one last peck. When we parted, our foreheads rested together and his fingers flexed on my thighs.

"What are you doing to me?" he asked for the second time.

I didn't overthink my answer. "The same thing you're doing to me?"

He nodded, his nose rubbing against my cheek before he placed a kiss over my dimple. "I sure as hell hope so."

# CHAPTER 19

MACKENNA

My phone vibrated with a text and I looked down into my lap to read it.

**Krista: Did you take any more pics of Hot Guy for me?**

Smiling at her across the table, I rolled my eyes.

**Me: No. Get your mind out of the gutter**

The gutter is exactly where my mind went when I thought about what happened earlier today.

My first kiss with Jimmy. It was so different than anything I'd experienced before—so much better—that it almost felt like my first kiss ever.

When I got home after painting, I barely recognized the girl looking back at me in the mirror. Bright eyes, flushed cheeks, and swollen lips.

My body was covered in sage green smears and handprints left behind by Jimmy. I liked seeing the evidence of his hands on me. As I ran my fingers over the streaks on the side of my neck, I refused to think of the last time a man left his mark there. Because these marks were different. They were done with affection and gentleness. They were wanted.

Another text interrupted my daydreaming.

**Krista: Are you staying the whole night?**

"No phones at the dinner table, girls," my dad cut in before taking a sip of his iced tea.

"Pookie started it," I goaded, using the nickname I gave her when she was a little kid, which I knew for a fact she hated.

She let out a huff before taking a bite of her steak.

I changed her name in my phone to Pookie, then took a screen shot. Snickering, I sent it to her. Krista's brown eyes glared at me.

"Phones," Dad reminded with a wave of his fork.

"Ryan," Mom said under her breath, shooting him a look. "Let the girls have their fun. It's been a long time since Mackenna's been home."

Reluctantly he agreed, and Krista and I went back to having text wars under the table.

**Me: Yep**

**Pookie: Squeeeee!**

**Me: What is that? Squeee??**

**Pookie: It means I'm excited, Butt Face**

**Me: Whatever you say, Pookie**

She sent an angry-looking emoji and I snorted.

**Pookie: Will you stay in my room tonight? Just like we used to?**

Since my parents moved to the new house, I'd only spent one night here. They had a simple guest room set up for me with a twin-size bed. Krista and I were probably too old for sleepovers but I had to admit that sleeping on her queen mattress sounded better, even if she did steal the covers.

She was growing up too fast. The long light brown hair she used to tie into braids was now a shoulder-length bob. I still remembered the day she came home from the hospital, all tiny, pink, and bald. It was love at first sight. And when she got a little bigger, I used to carry her around and call her my sack of sugar.

**Me: As long as we can braid each other's hair and talk about boys**
**Pookie: Obviously**

After dinner, Krista went outside with Dad to water the garden and I helped Mom rinse off the dishes.

She wasn't going to take the news about Jaxon well.

Part of me wanted to keep it from her because I didn't want her to worry. But years ago, I made a promise to myself and to my family that I would never let someone like Jaxon keep me silent ever again.

"Mom," I started, passing her a plate. "Jaxon is out."

Startled, she dropped the plate and it landed in the dishwasher with a loud clatter.

"What do you mean, *he's out*? Out of jail?" she asked. Clearly horrified, her blue eyes held so much fear behind the thick fringe of her dark bangs.

Continuing to rinse out some cups, I nodded.

"He left a note at my house. I reported it to the police but I'm not sure how much they can do about it." I glanced over to find an expression of pure fear on her face. "I'm not telling you this to scare you. I just wanted to let you know. Communication is important—"

"I'm glad you told me," she cut in, placing her hand on my arm. "Really. Thank you for telling me."

"I want to be honest with you. I'm scared," I admitted. "According to public records he's been out for almost a month, and I didn't even know it."

"Honey, if you want to move home you're always welcome here."

"You know I have the means to protect myself," I told her, referring to the gun I owned. Then I added, "And I have nice neighbors. Maybe I could even get a dog."

The gun wasn't the only defense on my side—and I didn't mean Jimmy either. While it was nice to have a big, strong guy looking out for me, I was capable of taking on an attacker. Not only was I trained in self-defense, but I'd also spent a lot of time practicing at the shooting range down in Tennessee.

Three years ago, I couldn't hit a bullseye from five feet away. That wasn't true anymore.

"We knew this was going to happen someday. It's a little sooner than I expected, but I'll be okay." Handing my mom another plate, I gave her a reassuring smile.

She smiled back. "Something's different."

"What do you mean?"

"I don't know what's changed, but it's something. You just seem... alive," she tried to explain.

"I *am* alive," I said defensively.

"I know." She sounded choked up, and I suspected she was about to cry. "Years ago, I lost my little girl. I don't mean you simply grew up—I mean, something in you stopped existing when you dated that boy. You used to smile all the time. You loved life. And that all stopped when..."

Before she could get too emotional, I hugged her. "Mom, I'm still here."

"You haven't been the same since then," she whispered shakily. "But something is different today. You look happy. I don't know the reason for it, but whatever it is, I'm thankful."

The last of the dirty silverware made it into the dishwasher. With a loving pat to my cheek, Mom tossed the dish towel over the side of the sink and left the kitchen.

I didn't have to think very hard about what had changed. I'd always thought of myself as the type of girl who didn't need a guy to be happy, and I still believed that was true.

But it wasn't just any guy who'd made the difference.

It was Jimmy.

# CHAPTER 20

JIMMY

Damn it. Maybe kissing Mackenna had been a mistake.

No. That wasn't true at all.

It was the best thing ever. That kiss was everything.

I hadn't expected her to respond to me that way. Feeling her mouth open for me. Listening to that quiet moan of satisfaction. Watching her melt under my touch.

It put me on a high that was better than being drunk, more fun than any party, and more intense than the adrenaline rush I got after a fight.

And when she begged me to kiss her again? In that moment she totally owned me, and I loved every second of it.

Problem was, now that I'd had a taste I wanted more. A lot more.

I thought having a night apart might be a good idea. Knowing Mackenna was safe at her parents' house gave me peace of mind, and it gave us some distance to think about the past several days.

But I wasn't used to this feeling—missing someone so much it made me restless—and I didn't like it.

"What are you brooding about over there?" Grandma's

question cut into my thoughts. "*Wedding Crashers* is supposed to be funny. You look downright depressed."

"I'm not brooding," I lied. "My favorite part is coming up."

"Ah, the motorboatin' quotes. Those are the best. Vince Vaughn is a fine piece of ass. I'll spare you the details of my fantasies about that man."

Cringing, I laughed. "You're not right in the head, you know that?"

She pointed a finger at me. "But I got you to laugh. Does this have to do with a certain next door neighbor?"

There was no point in trying to deny it.

"Yeah," I sighed.

"Why aren't you spending the night over there tonight?" she asked, and my eyes widened at being called out. I thought I'd been sneaky enough that she wouldn't notice my absence the past couple nights. "Oh, you thought I didn't know? I might be old but I'm not senile. I made your bed two days ago. Can't help noticing it's still the way I left it."

"How do you know I didn't make it?"

She shot me a look. "Jimmy, I hate to be the one to tell you this, but your bed-making skills are absolute shit."

I barked out a laugh and held up my hands. "Alright. Yeah, I've been staying over there but I've got a good reason for it."

"You don't need my permission to spend the night elsewhere. You're an adult and I'm a lousy babysitter anyhow. Things certainly moved fast with you two—not that I'm judging."

"It's not what you're thinking," I told her, then paused. "How much do you know about what happened to Mackenna a few years ago? With her ex?"

"This is Tolson. I know everything."

"I thought so. Why didn't you tell me?"

She shrugged. "Figured that's Mackenna's story to tell. Besides, a first-hand account is a lot different than rumors or news reports."

I nodded in agreement. "Well, her ex recently got out of jail. He left a threatening letter at her house. She's pretty shaken up about it and I'm worried about her."

"Ah, the knight in shining armor." She smiled. "If that's not a way to get a girl to fall for you, I don't know what is."

"It's not even about that. I just want to be there for her," I explained before admitting my true feelings. "I care about her. A lot."

Grandma beamed. "Even better."

*

When I got into bed, I looked at the clock on my phone. It wasn't even 10:00 yet. As I scrolled through my contacts, I brought up Mackenna's number and fought the urge to hear her voice.

For some reason, the thought of calling her made me nervous. What if she didn't pick up? What if I was coming on too strong?

Never in my life had I second-guessed calling a girl. If I was being honest, they usually contacted me first. Like a chicken-shit, I opted for sending her a text instead.

I typed out 'Hey beautiful' then immediately deleted it. Way too lame.

Then I typed out 'Hi', but changed my mind again. Way too short.

I thought about earlier when I walked her home. I bet she had no clue about how disheveled she'd looked.

I grinned as my fingers flew over the keys.

> **Me: How long did it take you to scrub off my handprints today?**

I stared at my phone for a minute before setting it down on the nightstand. I told myself to play it cool. But as soon as that ping sounded, I snatched my phone with lightning speed.

> **Mack: A while. Next time it will be your responsibility to clean it off**

Images of her in the shower flashed through my mind. All soaped up and naked. Part of me hoped she meant it, while the other half wanted her to stop saying shit like that. My willpower was hanging by a thread.

> **Me: I might take you up on that challenge. There's always tomorrow**
>
> **Mack: ;)**

A fucking wink face. What I wouldn't give to see her wink at me for real.

> **Me: I want to see you. Send a pic**
>
> **Mack: I don't think you want that right now. My sister and I are doing the whole girl sleepover thing.**
>
> **Me: What's the definition of that**

**exactly?**

**Mack: Braided hair, painted nails, and face masks**

**Me: Now you definitely have to send a pic**

About a minute later, a picture of Mackenna and her sister came through. I grinned. Their faces were covered with green goop, and messy pigtails stuck out at weird angles.

She was gorgeous.

**Me: Hideous**

**Mack: Hey! You were warned**

**Me: I'm just kidding. You're beautiful, even when you look like an alien**

**Mack: Thanks, I think**

**Me: So what else is on the agenda tonight?**

**Mack: Probably sleep soon. I'm having a great time. I think I needed this**

**Me: I'm glad. That makes missing you a little bit easier**

I wondered if I was being too honest, but fuck it. I was done playing games. Holding my breath, I waited as I saw those dots appear. Then they stopped. Then they started again.

**Mack: You miss me?**

**Me: Like crazy**

**Mack: Good. Because I miss you too**

Her confession caused a grin to pull at my lips.

**Me: I'll let you get back to your sis. I can't wait to see you tomorrow**

**Mack: Looking forward to it. Good-night Jimmy**

**Me: Night Mack**

I stared at the picture she sent for longer than I should have. I loved seeing her happy, seeing her having fun with her sister.

It made me miss my brother. This was the first summer of my life we weren't spending together. As if he could read my thoughts from two states away, a text from him appeared.

**Ezra: Hey. How many laws did you and Grandma break this week? Do I even want to know?**

I laughed.

**Me: I've been keeping her in line. I was just about to text you. What are you up to this weekend?**

**Ezra: Went to a graduation party tonight**

**Me: Oh that's fun**

**Ezra: Eh. Not really**

**Me: Did something happen?**

Concern caused my heartrate to pick up. It wasn't like Ezra to go to a party in the first place. When he didn't respond right away, I lost patience and called him instead.

He answered on the second ring. "Hey."

"What's wrong? Did someone fuck with you?" I didn't waste any time getting straight to the point.

Ezra sighed. "No. It wasn't anything like that. It was just lame and, well, I'm sort of confused about something that happened."

"What is it?"

"That girl I like... She tried to kiss me."

I chuckled. "Isn't that a good thing?"

"Not when she has a boyfriend," he replied, sounding miserable.

I frowned. "Oh. Yeah, that's not good."

"I wish I'd just done it," he said, exasperated. "I should've let her do it."

"Nah, you don't want to mess around with someone who's taken. Not cool."

"Yeah, I guess. I mean, I know you're right." He paused. "It's just that it would've been my first kiss. And I really wanted it to be her."

It wasn't news to me that Ezra hadn't even kissed anyone before. I had a feeling that when he finally gave his heart to someone, that person would have it forever. But that meant the girl on the receiving end of his love needed to be worthy of it.

"Don't sell yourself short, okay? You deserve better than being runner-up," I said confidently. "But, hey, at least you've got some game, huh? You've got committed girls throwing themselves at you."

"That's one way to look at it," he grumbled before changing the subject. "Hey, you're coming back for my graduation next weekend, right? Mom and Dad want you to bring Grandma."

"So I get to add chauffer to the list of my duties, too? No problem," I said with humor.

That humor disappeared when I realized I'd be leaving Mackenna in Tolson for two days. The thought of her being here alone made me uneasy.

Then I had an idea.

"I might bring someone. A girl," I added.

Ezra's laughter was so loud I had to pull the phone away from my ear. When he finally calmed down, he said, "I thought you were done with women."

"So did I. Mackenna's different, though." There was no need to hold anything back with my brother, so I spilled my guts. "It's been less than a week and I'm crazy about her. I am so completely fucked."

"Well, shit. If she's got you by the balls already, I definitely need to meet her."

I thought about the bumper testicles and laughed, because that wasn't the first time someone referred to my balls when it came to Mackenna. It was literally and figuratively correct.

Now I just needed to get her to agree to come home with me. I had a feeling that was easier said than done.

# CHAPTER 21

MACKENNA

The second day of painting—which was technically the fourth in total—ended much like the day before. I was covered in sage green marks in the shape of Jimmy's hands. And he was covered in mine. The teasing, playing, and kissing had been foreplay of the best kind.

I'd been waiting for this moment—the moment when my desire for Jimmy became bigger than my fear of intimacy.

As soon as the front door shut behind us, I mauled him. Wrapping my legs around his waist, I connected our lips while running my hands over his pecs. I was beginning to love the fact that he hated wearing shirts.

"Mack," he panted. "Mack, wait. Baby, slow down."

"Don't want to," I mumbled against his neck before sucking on a spot under his ear.

He groaned as he fell back against the wall. "What do you want? Because, God help me, whatever it is I'm going to give it to you."

"Not sex," I said, knowing I wasn't ready for that step yet. "But everything else would be fantastic."

Pulling back, Jimmy looked me in the eye before leaning in to tenderly kiss the corner of my mouth.

"Okay, here's the deal. First, you and I are both going to take showers—separately." He attempted to give me a stern look and I smiled. "Then we're going to talk about you coming to Ohio with me next weekend for my brother's graduation."

"Wait, w-what—" I stuttered.

"Then we'll get to the 'everything else' stuff."

Letting go of the hold I had on him, I planted my feet on the floor.

"Back up a second. You want me to come with you to your parents' house?" I asked, and he nodded. I raised my eyebrows. "For an event that's reserved only for family?"

Grinning, he nodded again.

I sighed. "Listen, I realize you feel like you need to protect me or whatever, and I appreciate your concern. But I'm a big girl. Unfortunately, this is something I might be dealing with for a long time. I'm not your responsibility."

"Do you like me?" he asked, then added, "I mean, in a more-than-friends, you-want-to-jump-my-bones kind of way."

My lips tipped up. "I guess that's one way of putting it."

"Well, I like you a helluva lot. Yeah, I'd worry about you while I'm gone," he confessed. "But I'm also being selfish because I'd miss you. And I found out last night that I don't like missing you, so I'd rather not if I don't have to."

Well, crap.

What's a girl supposed to say to that?

It was tempting, the thought of seeing him with his family and meeting the brother he loved so much. But I knew my social awkwardness would somehow end up making me look like a weirdo. Meeting the family was a big step in any relationship. How would we explain that we were friends-with-benefits, but also sort of dating for now?

"I'll think about it," I told him. "It would just be weird because I don't know anyone that well, including you."

I playfully poked his chest and he grabbed my hand before placing a kiss on my palm. "I'd say you're getting to know me pretty well. And Grandma's coming, too. You've known her for over a month."

I feigned concern as I thought of my way out. "But what about Sweet Pea? That poor bird can't be all alone for days. Who would clean up his poop?" I gave a mock pout. "I'll make the sacrifice and stay behind."

"Nice try." Jimmy's grin stretched wide. "Ernie's doing it."

"I'll think about it," I said again.

And I did think about it. As I took my shower, I thought about the way my heart pitter-pattered when Jimmy said he'd missed me. I thought about how fun it might be to go on a road trip with him and Beverly.

But it was too soon. Wasn't it?

As I rinsed the conditioner from my hair, I tried to come up with a way to let Jimmy down easy.

# CHAPTER 22

JIMMY

Mackenna had the most comfortable mattress I'd ever had the pleasure of lying on. Growing up, I'd always had a twin-size bed. And at college, that was the only choice in the dorms.

This bed, though... It was so massive, it took up most of the room. It conformed to the shape of my body so that every position felt perfect. The only thing that made it more perfect was having Mackenna next to me, underneath me, on top of me.

And I wasn't even talking about sexual positions. That was just sleeping.

But now I had her looking at me with lust in her eyes. Her toes grazed my ankle as our limbs tangled together. My thumb rubbed over her knee, tracing the flower print on her leggings. The clean scent from her shampoo mingled in the air between us.

"So," I started, toying with her slightly damp hair, "about my brother's graduation..."

With an apologetic expression, she glanced away. "I don't think so, Jimmy."

"Give me one good reason."

"My fern might die," she tried, and I laughed at her feeble excuse.

"Ernie can water it."

"What will I do without my ice cream sandwiches?"

"I'll get some for you. Gotta feed that addiction." I tweaked her on the nose.

She sighed. "It's not that I don't want to go. But I would be imposing."

I knew there was a good chance she was going to give me a hard time on the invitation to my hometown, and I was prepared to fight dirty.

Instead of arguing with her, I tilted her face toward me. Brushing my mouth over hers, I pushed my tongue past her lips. I kissed her slow and deep, and she let out a quiet moan in the back of her throat.

When she tried to reciprocate by sucking on my bottom lip, I pulled back a little until I was just out of her reach.

She chased.

I moved to the side and pecked her cheek.

Again, she followed. I chuckled when she missed and ended up biting my chin.

"What the hell, Jimmy?" She huffed impatiently. "Kiss me."

I placed my head on the pillow next to hers. "Say you'll come with me next weekend."

"Oh, so it's like that?" she asked breathlessly, her voice full of the snarky tone I liked so much.

My teeth scraped over her collarbone before I worked my mouth up to her jaw, then rubbed my nose over hers.

"Please?" I whispered against her lips.

"You don't play fair," she whispered back.

"I know. Say yes."

She let out an exasperated sigh. "Oh, my God. Okay! Okay. Just put me out of my misery already."

"Misery? Is making out with me that awful?" I teased.

"Jimmy," she whined, her fingers curling against my back. "I'm, like, in actual pain here."

Her voice was quiet and hesitant, like she was telling me a secret. Like she was telling me something she didn't fully understand, and I was reminded again of how innocent she was.

"You ever felt like this before?" I asked, even though I knew the answer.

She shook her head. I knew what she needed.

"Where does it hurt, baby?" I moved my hand to her breast. "Here?"

Running my thumb over her nipple, I felt how hard it was through the fabric of her shirt.

Nodding, she moaned and arched her back.

"And here?" I slowly trailed to the other breast and repeated the action.

When I glanced up at her face, she gazed back at me with heavy-lidded eyes. Her chest rose and fell with quick breaths, and she licked her lips. Seeing her respond to me and knowing how much I was affecting her made my cock throb.

I could relate to the ache she was referring to because I felt it, too.

She wasn't the only one in pain.

But this wasn't about me.

"Where else?" My fingers went to the waistband of her leggings, but I made no move to go further. I dragged my fingertips back and forth against her smooth skin, from one hipbone to the other.

Her stomach quivered.

Mackenna's hand landed on top of mine. Taking a deep breath, she paused before pushing both of our hands into her pants. Letting her guide me, I felt a small patch of hair before my fingers slid through her wetness.

We both moaned.

"Holy fucking shit, babe." Resting my forehead on her shoulder, I took a second to get myself under control.

It was hard not to think about what it would feel like to push into her slick heat, and the throbbing in my dick intensified.

"What do you want?" I placed an open-mouthed kiss on her neck. "I need you to say it."

Mackenna shivered and pressed down on my hand.

"I want you to touch me," she replied, giving me the permission I needed.

I circled her clit and she gasped.

"There," she breathed out. "It hurts there."

"I'll make it better," I promised, continuing to slide my fingers over her slick pussy.

Moving her hand in tandem with mine, I let her set the pace, let her show me how hard and fast she wanted it.

Her eyes screwed shut and her lips parted. "That feels good."

Then her arm pulled away and it was up to me to finish the job.

When I moved to her opening to collect more of her wetness, she tensed. It was almost unnoticeable, but I felt the slight jolt in her body and the way her breathing hitched.

"Watch me," I whispered, and she opened her eyes. "It's just me. You tell me to stop and I'll stop."

"Don't stop." She shook her head. "Keep going."

"I'm gonna get you off this way." Applying more pressure, I rubbed her swollen clit faster, and her body started to shake. "Keep your eyes on me."

"Okay," she panted. "Okay."

"Better than okay?"

She nodded. "Yes. So much better."

My erection pressed insistently on the outside of her thigh and I resisted the urge to thrust against her.

Against my own will, my hips started moving. The head of my dick slipped through the opening in my briefs, and the piercing below my sensitive tip rubbed against the nylon of my gym shorts, causing relief and torment at the same time.

Getting the piercing had been at the beginning of my self-imposed celibacy. Because of the healing time, I knew I wouldn't be able to be sexually active anyway.

All healed up now.

And the new sensations were almost too much. Too good.

The girl beneath me was too beautiful. Too sexy.

My feelings for her were too deep. Too unexpected.

For the first time ever, I was going to come inside my pants.

Mackenna's body shuddered and writhed as she spread her legs wider. I wanted to peel the leggings off her so I could see the perfect pussy I was touching, but I could tell she was close.

Her hand gripped the pillow under her head and she gasped.

"Jimmy," she whimpered. "I'm about to—I'm gonna—"

A moan ripped from her throat as her body bowed off the bed. A gush of wetness soaked my fingers and I continued making circles over her clit as she rode out the orgasm.

She canted her hips, the movement causing her body to rub against the tip of my dick.

My balls drew up tight and I couldn't hold it back any longer.

With a groan, I pressed myself up against her thigh as my cock pulsed and warm cum coated the inside of my shorts.

For several minutes, neither of us said a word as we basked in the moment. Our breathing evened out, our hearts slowed.

My fingers still cupped her hot, wet center and she jolted from oversensitivity when I slid my hand out of her leggings.

When I glanced at her face, Mackenna wore a lazy smile.

"What am I supposed to say now?" Her tone was light and a little playful. "Is thank you an appropriate response?"

I chuckled. "You can say whatever you want." I placed a kiss on her forehead. "And I feel like I should be the one saying thank you. That was the hottest experience of my life."

"But I didn't even take my clothes off. And you didn't get to…" she finished with a wave of her hand.

"Ahh… I sort of did," I said, a little embarrassed.

Propping herself up on her elbows, she raised her eyebrows. "Did what?"

"I need to change my shorts," I stated flatly.

Shocked, her mouth dropped open, her lips making a perfect 'O'.

Then a slow smile spread over her face, and she pointed to the dresser. "The gray pants you wore last time are in the top drawer."

I gave her a quick kiss before hopping up to change.

When I got back, I pulled her close.

"So, my brother's graduation…" I started again.

Mackenna's eyes narrowed. "You tricked me."

"I did not. You agreed of your own free will."

"I was coerced."

"No takebacks."

Frustrated, she blew out a breath. "Fine. Tell me about our trip."

Grinning because I got my way, I gave her the rundown. "We leave early Saturday morning. It's about a five-hour drive and the ceremony is that afternoon. We'll stay the night, then come back Sunday."

The more I talked about the trip, the more excited I got. I wanted to show Mackenna everything. My town, my family, my old high school.

If I wanted to get her to know me, this was the perfect opportunity.

# CHAPTER 23

MACKENNA

And here it was. The unavoidable family awkwardness I'd been dreading.

"I don't need that big fancy hotel room," Beverly insisted. "Let Jimmy and Mackenna have it."

Jimmy threw his hands up. "I don't know why we can't all stay at the house."

"There isn't enough room," Matthew, Jimmy's dad, who I'd just been introduced to ten minutes earlier, argued. "I'm not making Grandma or Mackenna sleep on the couch, and you won't fit."

Trying to sink further into the very couch they were talking about, my eyes volleyed from one person to another as they discussed the sleeping arrangements.

"The hotel has a two-room suite," Linda, Jimmy's mom, interjected. "Both Mackenna and Grandma can stay there; very comfortably, I might add."

"I'm not going to separate the lovebirds," Beverly said, motioning between Jimmy and me.

I didn't have to look in a mirror to know my face was bright red.

When I'd heard Jimmy on the phone with his dad

earlier in the week, he simply told him he was bringing a friend. And now Beverly might as well have told everyone that Jimmy and I were banging like rabbits—even though we weren't.

"Listen," I finally spoke up. "I have a solution. I'll get my own room."

"Like hell you will," Beverly exclaimed at the same time Jimmy said, "Absolutely not."

I looked from Linda to Matthew. "I don't want to be the reason you have to pay for a hotel."

"We would've had to get the hotel room either way." Linda smiled at me, then pointed at Jimmy and Beverly. "These two are just stubborn."

"Fine," Jimmy said before tossing an arm over my shoulder. "Mack and I will take the room. Grandma, you can have my old bed."

Clearly pleased, Beverly smiled.

But Matthew didn't seem so happy. "Hang on a second now. I'm not sure it's appropriate for you two to be staying the night together. No offense, Mackenna."

"None taken," I said, deciding it was best not to announce the fact that Jimmy and I had already slept in the same bed multiple times. "I'm fine with whatever you decide."

It wasn't a secret that Jimmy and I hadn't known each other long, and I couldn't blame his dad for feeling the way he did.

Apparently, Jimmy didn't agree.

"I'm an adult, Dad. And I'd like to stay with my girlfriend."

Jaw dropping, my head snapped toward him. Did he just say girlfriend?

I wasn't the only one surprised by his statement, because four pairs of shocked eyes landed on us.

"I'm not—he's not—we're not—" I stuttered, completely lost for words because the term implied a certain level of commitment.

"Well, it's settled then!" Beverly clapped her hands together and headed toward the kitchen. "Matthew, do you have any whiskey in this house?"

Seeming concerned, Jimmy's dad chased after her. Linda hid a smile behind her hand, and Ezra spoke up for the first time since introductions were made.

"Thanks for coming to my graduation," he said shyly, fidgeting in the green recliner in the corner of the living room. "I don't have a ton of friends coming to see me walk across that stage... So it means a lot to me that you came all this way."

And just like that, my heart melted.

I thought *I* was awkward, but Ezra took it to a whole new level. It was endearing, though. The way his cheeks flushed just from meeting someone new. The floppy mess of blond curls that fell over his forehead. He was exactly how Jimmy described him.

"Thanks for wanting me here," I responded sincerely.

"You're always welcome," Linda said before brushing her own blonde curls out of her eyes. "Now, if you'll excuse me, I have to make sure Beverly isn't raiding the liquor cabinet."

Something shifted during dinner after the graduation ceremony. As we sat around the dining room table, eating Linda's meatloaf, I felt the world tilt a little.

Something had changed, but I couldn't put my finger on it—probably because it wasn't just one thing.

My heart felt lighter at the sound of Jimmy laughing with his brother as they argued about who knew all the songs to '90s boy bands and who was better at chess. Ezra proudly claimed the knowledge to the Backstreet Boys lyrics and, apparently, Jimmy was chess champion of the house.

When I told them I was terrible at chess, and would be staying far away from Jimmy during a tournament, his hand caressed my knee under the table and my heart soared in a completely new way.

Pride welled up in my chest when his family asked about my career and seemed genuinely impressed at my accomplishments.

"So you can just work from home?" Linda asked. "You never even have to leave the house?"

"Basically, yes. There will be times when I have to travel to the band for collaborations," I explained. "But I can record at home and send them the demos. Plus, we can do a lot of our meetings over Skype."

"That's so cool," Ezra chimed in, seeming to be more comfortable around me by the minute. "Can you get autographed posters? And tickets to concerts?"

"Ezra," Matthew scolded. "You can't just demand stuff from our guest."

I laughed. "Actually, you can. Someone might as well enjoy the perks to my job. Yes to both of those things."

The shy boy from earlier completely disappeared as his face lit up. "Thank you so much." He pointed his fork at Jimmy. "Keep her."

Before either of us could respond Beverly asked for another whiskey on the rocks, and her request was denied. She pouted, but I wasn't oblivious to Jimmy discretely passing her his flask under the table when Matthew and Linda went into the kitchen to get dessert.

They brought out an ice cream cake, which was pretty much a glorified ice cream sandwich. My eyes shot to Jimmy, wondering if he'd requested it on my behalf. He gave me a knowing look and I hid my goofy smile behind my napkin.

My mouth watered as they passed me a slice. It was perfect, with an Oreo cookie crust on the bottom, a layer of mint chocolate chip ice cream, and whipped cream on top.

Heaven.

Then Jimmy's parents switched to the topic of his classes in the fall, and my heart did a nosedive, plummeting to the pit of my stomach. The fluttery feeling I'd gotten so used to morphed into a sick, churning sensation below my sternum.

My appetite suddenly disappeared and I placed my fork down on the plate while staring at the half-eaten dessert.

I'd known all along Jimmy didn't intend to stay in Tolson, so the dread I felt was unexpected. And unpleasant.

As they talked about the college campus and dorms versus apartments, reality hit home.

There would be a time, in the near future, when I would be alone in my house. Alone in my bed. Just... alone.

Two weeks ago, that was all I'd wanted.

So why did it make me so sad?

# CHAPTER 24

JIMMY

Pacing from one end of the hotel room to the other, I took a few deep breaths and shook out my hands. I pulled open the mini fridge and uncapped a water before taking a long drink as I listened to the shower running behind the bathroom door.

I was extremely wound up—probably from holding myself back with Mackenna all week. Although we made out like teenagers and were almost always touching in some way, we hadn't gone further than kissing since last Sunday.

Mackenna hadn't asked for it, and I hadn't pushed.

But I could feel it—soon one of us was going to lose control. In this battle of wills, one of us would break first.

And I needed it to be her. She had to be the one to make a move.

There was something extremely erotic about that fact that I'd gotten her off, but I hadn't seen her naked yet. Not even a nipple.

There was also something sexy about being in a hotel room. Maybe because it was unfamiliar. Away from reality. Kind of like being on vacation.

I heard the water shut off, and when Mackenna came out I felt like the wind was knocked out of me. Not because she looked any different than usual—but because she looked the same.

And everything about her was perfect.

Long, damp hair around her shoulders. Pink cheeks and lips stood out against her pale skin. Loose white T-shirt. And those crazy leggings. This pair was decorated in roosters, just like her ridiculous kitchen.

Feeling a little weak in the knees, I sat down on the edge of the bed.

When she got close enough, I grabbed her by the thighs and dragged her over between my legs. From where I was sitting, it put me at the right height to kiss her stomach. I nuzzled the soft material of her shirt with my nose and let out a happy sigh.

"Jimmy," she whispered. I looked up at her troubled eyes and immediately knew something was wrong. "What are we doing?"

"Um, we'll probably watch TV or something. We could order a movie—"

"That's not what I'm talking about and you know it," she interrupted softly.

Placing another kiss over her belly button, I wrapped my arms around her. She squeaked when I pulled us down onto the mattress so we were lying side by side.

Anxiously twisting her fingers together, she continued. "We're together all the time. Sometimes you look at me like I'm—" She paused as she searched for the right word. "—important. You called me your girlfriend."

"That's what a relationship is, Mack." I brushed a strand of hair out of her face. "And I'm proud of you. Proud to tell people you're mine."

"This wasn't supposed to be a relationship. It was supposed to be fun."

I frowned. "You're not having fun?"

"I am," she admitted, absentmindedly tracing the tribal tattoo on my chest. "But it seems like more than that, too."

"I want more than casual with you. I was pretty clear about that from the beginning."

Her eyebrows pinched together. "I just didn't realize it was going to feel like this."

"Like what?"

Those stormy eyes connected with mine, and she didn't need to say the words for me to know what she meant. She was having feelings for me. Feelings she'd never had before.

"You're not alone in this," I told her. "The feeling is mutual."

"You're someone to be proud of, too," she said, affectionately rubbing her thumb over my bottom lip. She smiled a little, but her eyes were sad. "But this won't last. You know that, right? You're leaving at the end of the summer."

She wasn't telling me anything I didn't already know, but there were other options we hadn't discussed. "What about long-distance? Would you be willing to do that?"

"No," she replied with certainty.

"No?" Rubbing at the spot over my heart, I tried to lessen the ache I felt at the thought of ending things with her when I went back to school. "We could try. People do it all the time."

"No," she said again with a quick shake of her head. "I'm not cut out for long-distance relationships. Missing you would be terrible. I'd always wonder what you're doing. Who you're doing it with..."

"You don't trust me." It wasn't a question.

"Don't take it personally." Twisting her lips into a wry grin, she attempted to lighten the mood as her hands went back to exploring my body. "It's not like we've known each other for a long time, Jimmy."

"Well, that's something I can work on," I told her. "We've still got time."

Her fingers stopped their perusal of my chest, and her face turned skeptical. "We don't have to decide anything today."

Like hell we didn't. She might've been unsure about us, but I wasn't.

But she didn't need to know that right now. The last thing I wanted was to scare her away.

"Your brother is the biggest sweetheart in the world," she said, switching gears on the conversation. "In fact, your whole family is great."

I smiled. "Ezra's the best person I know. I'd be lucky to be half as good as him someday."

"You don't give yourself enough credit. You ended up being way better than I originally thought," she joked before her face got serious. "I judged you. I'm sorry about that."

"I didn't exactly give you the best first impression."

She smirked at the reminder. "Speaking of that, your undies? Those little briefs you wear? Hot as fuck."

I laughed and groaned at the same time.

"Undies? Little briefs? I have no idea how you can talk about it that way and still turn me on, but damn. Say fuck again," I requested, burying my face in her neck. I playfully nipped at her until she giggled.

"I thought most guys wore boxers."

"Most guys don't have a dick the size of mine," I blurted without thinking, and the look of surprise on her face was almost comical. "I'm not trying to sound like a cocky prick. There's a practical reason I wear them. They help support things. Plus, I have a piercing. I like to know everything is staying in the right place."

Mackenna's eyebrows shot up. "A piercing? On your *penis*?"

Snickering at the fact that she whispered penis like it was a bad word, I nodded. Her mouth opened and closed a few times, but no words came out. Then her eyes bounced down to my crotch and lingered there as if she was trying to have x-ray vision.

"Hey, my eyes are up here," I teased.

She blushed, obviously embarrassed at being called out. If she kept staring at my dick like that, the willpower I was trying to keep firmly in place would definitely unravel.

Scooting up on the bed, I piled the pillows up so we had

a place to sit, grabbed the remote, and opened my arms in invitation. Mackenna didn't hesitate as she crawled up next to me.

We spent the rest of the evening watching bad reality shows and cuddling in bed.

And when she fell asleep, her ear was right over my heart—the heart that was becoming a little less mine and a little more hers every day.

# CHAPTER 25

JIMMY

Over the next week, Mackenna and I spent every minute of our free time together.

She insisted on helping with the chores around Grandma's, and we were a good team. She made everything more fun—yard work, laundry, even cleaning the toilets. My girl wasn't afraid to get her hands dirty.

The rest of the time, we hung out at her house. Mackenna liked to knit with her legs draped over my lap while we watched movies. We talked, told each other bad jokes, and sometimes she'd sing to me.

I learned more of her quirks. Like the fact that she ate at least one ice cream sandwich a day, usually before dinner. And she was obsessed with Crockpot recipes, but rarely followed through with them. She'd tacked at least ten recipes to her fridge, but so far I'd only had the pleasure of eating the honey mustard chicken and beef stew. Both were off-the-charts awesome.

Then after dinner we'd make out until my balls were blue, but I wasn't complaining.

I'd never been happier.

I was addicted to her smiles, the ones she seemed

to save just for me. The sexy lift of her mouth when she smirked. The naughty tilt of her lips when she teased me. And the full-on laugh when that dimple on her left cheek appeared—that one was my favorite.

And she was starting to get comfortable around me.

How could I tell? Water bottles.

Little by little, she was letting her guard down. Letting those water bottles pile up. Caring more about my company and less about the way her house looked.

If I went downstairs, I knew I'd see three on the coffee table, a couple next to her chair, two on the mantel, and one on the front windowsill. There was no rhyme or reason to the oddly-placed ones, but when she was in writing-mode she got a little scatterbrained.

Sometimes Mackenna's face would light up with an idea, and she'd sprint to her laptop or grab the nearest notebook to write it down. Other times she was so lost in her own thoughts that she'd drop everything she was doing, and vacantly stare into space while her lips moved to a song I couldn't hear. Even if she didn't have her guitar, her fingers would twitch and wiggle.

It was fucking adorable.

Last night, she Skyped with her manager and sent out a few new demos for the punk band. I loved the fact that she let me witness her writing process.

The mornings were my favorite time.

Every day I woke up with her wrapped around me. I loved the warmth of her body, the scent of her hair, and the fact that it seemed like she couldn't get close enough.

Mackenna didn't know it, but sometimes I set my alarm a little early just so I could enjoy being with her for a while.

She was still sleeping when my phone pinged on the nightstand. I picked it up and when I saw the name on the screen, I gently untangled myself from the starfish and quietly left the bed.

**Jay: Got some info you might want**

Jay Langston was a local who was my age. We met years ago when I was visiting Grandma, and we used to get together during the times when I was in town.

Over the past couple years, he'd gotten into some sketchy stuff. I suspected it was drugs, but I didn't know for sure. He didn't have a job, and he didn't come from a wealthy family, but always seemed to have money.

Last fall, Jay came to visit me at college and witnessed one of my street fights. He'd told me about an under-ground fighting ring in this area, and at the time I really hadn't thought much of it.

Until recently, I'd purposely avoided him. I didn't want to get tangled up in whatever illegal activity he was a part of, but he had a knack for finding things out. Personal information. And not just rumors—facts.

I had no idea what his methods were, but I thought he might be able to tell me something about Mackenna's ex. More specifically, his whereabouts.

There hadn't been any more mysterious letters, but I knew Mackenna was on edge.

After taking a seat on the couch, I dialed Jay's number.

"Hey, man," he answered, sounding way too awake for

6:00 in the morning. Never one to beat around the bush, he cut right to the chase. "Here's what I got. Jaxon has been bumming around some trailer park in Brenton, but it seems like he's been laying low. And you're not gonna believe this, but he's been trying to break into the fighting rings."

"No shit?" I flexed my hands at the thought of pummeling that motherfucker's face.

"Yeah. He's got a good chance. I mean, everyone wants to bet on the beefed-up guy who just got out of the pen."

"Can you set me up?"

"I can try." He paused. "I thought you told me you were out of the fighting scene."

"I was, but I'm willing to make an exception for this one."

Jay let out a whistle. "Man, don't let anyone hear you talk like that, or else they won't let you fight. They don't do grudge matches. You're not even supposed to know each other."

"Well, that's good because I've never met him."

"Do I even want to know what this is about?"

"No," I told him honestly. "It's probably best if you don't."

"Are you sure about this?" he asked. "Just say the word and I'll see what I can do."

Scratching at the two-day stubble on my jaw, I weighed the pros and cons.

I wanted the chance to give that son of a bitch the beating he deserved, but I also needed to be smart about it.

Setting up a fight would guarantee a meeting on neutral ground where that could happen.

But the last thing I needed was to get into trouble. Plus, I had a feeling Mackenna wouldn't want me getting involved this way.

"Give me some time to think about it," I said. "I'll let you know."

After we hung up, I decided to go to Grandma's for a shower before I got ready for work.

I didn't get very far.

As soon as I walked out the front door, I stopped dead in my tracks at the sight in front of me.

I experienced a mix of emotions as I took in the garbage scattered over Mackenna's driveway. The metal trashcan was on its side next to her car. The windshield had been shattered.

I approached the vehicle, doing my best to keep my temper in check. However, it was the word that had been keyed into the dark blue paint on the hood that pushed me over the edge of anger.

Blowing out a breath, I ran my hands through my hair as I paced the yard a few times.

Mackenna was going to be pissed. Devastated. Terrified.

I hadn't even delivered the news yet and the remorse I felt over the fact that I had to be the messenger was killing me. I gave myself about five minutes to calm down, then I went back into her house, toed off my shoes by the door, and quietly made my way up the stairs.

Sitting down next to Mackenna on the bed, I studied her peaceful expression for a minute before her day was ruined.

I wished I could shield her from this. Wished I could lie to her and somehow hide the evidence and magically fix her car before she found out. More than anything, I wished it was possible to turn back time so I could catch that fucker in the act.

It didn't take a genius to figure out who did it. Jaxon had vandalized her property right under our noses while we were asleep.

"Mack." I gently rubbed her arm. "Wake up, baby."

"Hmm?" She rolled onto her back but didn't open her eyes.

"I'm sorry, but you need to come see something." Taking her hand in mine, I rubbed her palm with my thumb.

"What is it?" she mumbled sleepily.

"Your trashcan... Um, the driveway is a mess... Your car..." I tried to explain, and failed miserably.

A half-smile appeared on her face and she pulled the covers up to her chin. "It's just the squirrels. Don't worry about it."

"Baby, this wasn't squirrels," I said regretfully.

Something in my voice must've conveyed that this was serious because her eyes shot open and she sat up.

She pawed at her hair, trying to tame the messy strands with her fingers. "What's going on?"

"I'll show you." Linking our fingers, I helped her out of bed, then pressed a kiss to her forehead.

Still a bit disoriented, she followed me down the stairs.

When we got outside, she ran to the driveway. She stood there, completely still, for a good minute while she looked at the damage. I wanted to ask her if she was okay, but I knew that was a stupid question.

She finally lost it when she traced the letters carved into the hood.

*CUNT*

Wrapping her arms around herself, she let out a sob, and I couldn't stand back anymore. Coming up behind her, I rubbed my hands up and down her arms, then hugged her to me while she cried.

Just like her laughter made its way straight to my heart, so did her tears.

In that moment, her pain was mine. And as much as that pain wanted to turn into anger, I needed to be strong for her. I pushed down my temper as I buried my nose in her hair.

Mackenna's sobs subsided and hiccups took over.

"Mack," I said quietly. "Go inside while I clean this up."

"That son of a bitch ruined my car!" she growled angrily, radiating a level of rage I'd never seen from her before. It would've been cute if it wasn't so fucking scary. She turned toward me. "Why does he have to be so fucking ominous about it?" she asked, slashing her hand through the air. "Why doesn't he just show up at my damn door? Oh yeah, because I'd shoot his ass!"

Yep, my girl had claws. She was ferocious if she had to be, and I was glad for that.

"Hey, I'm gonna fix it." I gave her a reassuring smile. "Good thing your boyfriend works at an auto shop."

"Boyfriend," she repeated, like testing out that word was weird for her. Although I'd called her my girlfriend several times already, it was the first time I'd heard her say the term when she was referring to me.

I liked it.

"Yeah. We're dating, so I'm your boyfriend," I told her with another megawatt smile. "Hey, what did one race car say to the other race car?"

She sniffled, but her lips tilted up. "I don't know. What?"

"I'm Audi here."

A hiccup mingled with a laugh. "That's a good one."

"Ten minutes," I said while guiding her up to the house. "Go do something that makes you happy for ten minutes and I'll take care of this. Play some music. Eat an ice cream sandwich or five."

"Okay." She tossed another pained look at her vehicle, then with one more hiccup she went inside.

The smile I'd been trying so hard to keep on my face dropped as I pulled out my phone. Jaxon didn't realize it, but he'd just made my decision very easy. One text to Jay sealed his fate.

**Me: Set it up**

# CHAPTER 26

MACKENNA

It was Wednesday, which meant three things.

One, I was spending the morning at Beverly's. I'd started hanging out with her and Sweet Pea a couple days a week while Jimmy was at work. I made the excuse that I didn't want them to be lonely, but the truth was I found myself seeking out the company when I didn't have work to do.

Two, I was supposed to get my car back tomorrow. I hadn't seen it yet, but Jimmy's texts assured me it would be as good as new. I reported the vandalism and property damage, but the police said there wasn't much they could do when it came to finding the suspect because there were no witnesses. Despite my protests, Jimmy had gone to every neighbor on our block to ask if they'd noticed any suspicious activity in the area, but no one had seen the attack on my car.

And three, it had been exactly seventeen days since Jimmy and I had gone past first base—and, yes, I was counting. Sexually frustrated didn't even scratch the surface of how I was feeling.

Learning that Jimmy was well-endowed along with the

mention of the piercing piqued my curiosity. During our make-out sessions, I'd felt his hardness pressing against me, and I thought having an erection for hours on end was enough to make any guy break.

Just from the looks of Jimmy, you'd never know he had so much self-control, but the guy seemed to have it in spades.

I kept waiting for him to take things further, but then at night he'd just give me one last kiss and we'd go to sleep. He was a perfect gentleman.

It was sweet. It was romantic.

It was becoming a problem.

If I had to spend one more night next to him in bed without actually doing anything, I suspected I might die. Death by sexual frustration. That could be a real thing.

I didn't know how to be sexually assertive, but I was willing to try. Maybe I needed to catch him off-guard in some way.

"Oh, no you don't!"

I jumped guiltily at the sound of Beverly's voice, wondering if I'd spoken my dirty thoughts about her grandson out loud.

Then I saw her chasing after Sweet Pea as he flew across the living room toward the cracked window. Waving her hands wildly, she cut him off just in time. Missing his intended target, he ended up tangled in her curtain. His tiny toes got caught in the wispy material and he flapped helplessly while letting out a pathetic-sounding "*fuck.*"

Beverly huffed as she helped the bird out of the

predicament he'd gotten himself into. "He's ruining all my curtains."

"Have you thought about getting his wings clipped?" I asked before taking a sip of my lemonade.

She looked horrified. "Of course not. That's like chopping a man's dick off."

Stunned by her statement, I inhaled some of the liquid and began coughing violently. I shouldn't have been surprised by anything Beverly said—I was quickly learning that she didn't have much of a filter.

"I don't think that's the same thing," I said through a wheeze. "You don't want him to escape again."

"He was born with wings, he should have wings." Beverly shrugged before giving him some peanuts to snack on. "Never thought I'd love a parrot, but he's part of the family now." She sat down on the couch next to me and picked up a Twinkie from the plate on the coffee table. "So anyway, do you want to go?"

My eyebrows pinched together in confusion. I hadn't been listening to a word she'd been saying earlier. "Go where?"

"To the dress fitting tomorrow. We can make a girls' day of it. Angel's going to be such a beautiful bride."

"Oh," I said before an awkward pause ensued. "I really don't feel like I should be going to that. I've never even met her."

"I'm the matron of honor," Beverly said, proudly straightening her shoulders. "I'm sure she wouldn't mind if I brought you along. Besides, Angel is one of the sweetest people you'll ever meet." Her face lit up like she had the best idea ever. "You two should be friends. She only lives a few blocks from us."

According to Beverly, her best friend was actually younger than me—younger than Jimmy, even. It was odd, but I guess there was no age limit on friendship. From the brief history she'd given me, I learned Angel showed up as a runaway in Tolson over a year ago, with no intentions of staying. But this town and its residents made an impression on her heart. Apparently, Travis Hawkins was one of those people.

I couldn't blame her for falling for him. If my memory of him in high school was correct, he was a really nice guy. Not bad on the eyes either. With brown hair, hazel eyes, and dimples, he'd had more than one girl at Daywood High swooning over him.

Now that Travis and Jimmy were coworkers, I felt like my worlds were slowly colliding—which was typical in small towns—but I was surprised to find that I didn't hate it.

In fact, I kind of liked the idea of being part of a circle of friends. Maybe it was time for my antisocial streak to come to an end.

"You know what?" I smiled at Beverly. "I think I'd like to come tomorrow."

Clapping her hands, she beamed. "Wonderful."

She went back to talking about the wedding, and I tried to pay attention as she went on about dresses, flowers, and cake.

But I couldn't stop my mind from going back to fantasies about Jimmy.

# CHAPTER 27

JIMMY

"Jimmy!" Travis shouted from the back of the garage. He strolled over to me at the front counter where I was filling out the invoices. "What do you say we break outta here tomorrow?"

"What?" I laughed.

"I have to take the rig down to southern Illinois to pick up the trailer. Thought maybe you'd like to ride along and see how things work on the road."

"Yeah," I replied, excited. "That would be awesome."

He grinned. "I already cleared it with Hank, so you're good to go. We'll leave here around 8:00 in the morning and probably won't get back until 5:00 or so."

"Sounds great," I responded, and he gave me a clap on the back before turning to walk away.

While I loved working in the shop, there was something intriguing about truck driving, and I'd hoped for this opportunity.

Now I'd get my chance to find out what all the fuss was about.

"Hey, Travis," I called out before he could get too far.

Tossing a greasy rag from hand to hand, he came back over. "What's up?"

I lowered my voice. "Is there a boxing gym somewhere in the area?"

Pressing his lips together, he thought for a few seconds. "Not that I know of. There might be one in Champaign. How come?"

"My dad and I used to spar with each other. I miss it," I told him. It was a half-truth. While I did miss boxing with my dad, that wasn't the real reason I wanted to brush up on my skills. But I wasn't about to come right out and tell Travis I was training for a fight.

"There's a gym in Daywood," he said. "Colton and I go there together on Saturdays sometimes. It's small, but they have a few punching bags. Would that work?"

I nodded. "It's better than nothing."

"Hey, maybe we could even spar with you," he suggested. "It just can't be before this weekend, because if I show up to my wedding with a black eye I'm pretty sure Angel will kill me."

We both laughed.

"Yeah, we can plan on it," I said before going back to the last invoice.

Then it was time for my favorite part of everyday—going home to Mackenna.

When I got to her house, I was hit with the aroma of my favorite dinner. Honey mustard chicken.

She spoiled me, and I told her that as I hugged her from behind while she got our plates ready.

She was quiet as we ate. Unusually quiet.

Every time I asked her if something was wrong she'd

force a smile and tell me everything was fine, but I could tell something was off.

We stuck with our normal routine—watch TV, hold hands, then make out until I thought I might come in my pants.

Her kisses were different tonight. More aggressive. Needy.

Hot as fuck.

But instead of acting on the impulse to rip her clothes off, I resisted. After we got into bed, I gazed down at her face before placing a kiss on her perfect lips.

Then I tapped the touch lamp twice. Darkness engulfed the room and I pulled her close.

Usually Mackenna went right to sleep, so when she fidgeted for several minutes, I knew something was up. Just as I was about to ask her what was wrong—again—she spoke.

"Jimmy?"

"Yeah?"

There was a long pause. "Nothing."

I shifted away to look at her, even though I couldn't see anything in the dark. "What's up?"

"It's nothing."

"Did something else happen? Something with your ex?" I asked, concerned.

"No." Another pause. "I, um, forgot to tell you I'm going with Beverly to Angel's dress fitting tomorrow."

Among the many things I'd learned about Mackenna in the time I'd known her, one of them was that she was a terrible liar. She was holding something back from me, but I didn't want to push. Another thing I'd learned was that she had to do things in her own time. Sometimes it was frustrating because I wasn't a patient guy.

I swallowed back the urge to interrogate her.

"That sounds fun," I responded. "And pretty perfect, too, because I'm going on a ride in the semi tomorrow down to southern Illinois. I won't get back until evening."

She propped herself up on an elbow.

"That's exciting." I could tell she was smiling. "Why didn't you tell me earlier?"

I chuckled. "Well, I was going to, but it was a little difficult with your tongue down my throat."

A pillow smacked me in the face.

Growling, I pounced on her. My lips found her neck. Her jaw. The shell of her ear.

She giggled, and her fingers curled against my back.

Ignoring the insistent erection straining against the cotton of my briefs, I forced myself to pull back. "Guess we've both got a lot going on tomorrow. Let's get some sleep. Unless there was something else you wanted to tell me?"

She sighed. "No. Goodnight, Jimmy."

"'Night, Mack."

*

When I woke up, I was disoriented because it was still dark in the room. Also, Mackenna was on top of me—which was the norm—but she was awake. Either that, or she was having one hell of a dream.

Her lips landed on my chest, placing a light kiss there before her tongue flicked over my skin.

"Mack," I rasped.

"Jimmy," she responded, amusement in her voice.

Okay. So she wasn't asleep.

Moving her hips slightly, she rubbed her pussy over my cock—my cock that was already wide awake and ready for action.

My hands landed on her waist, torn between pulling her off or pushing down to grind her against me harder.

Then I noticed something else that was different. Very different.

She was naked. My hands moved down, sliding over her hips to her thighs. Not one bit of clothing. Only smooth, warm skin.

Yep. Definitely naked.

I groaned. "What are you doing?"

She leaned down until our chests were touching. Skin to skin. Her nipples rubbed against me.

Closing her teeth over my bottom lip, she tugged, then licked the abused spot.

*Fuck. Fuck. Fuck.*

I loved it when she did that and she knew it.

Her head dipped down and her tongue flicked over my nipple, then she gently sucked on the barbell. My dick jumped.

I gasped. "Baby... I don't know if this is a good idea."

Deciding to do the right thing, I tried to roll her to the side, but the starfish wouldn't budge.

Somehow, Mackenna had managed to attach herself to my body so fully that I couldn't get her off me. Her legs were hooked behind my knees, her arms wedged underneath my shoulder blades.

It was absolutely ridiculous.

Even though I was incredibly turned on, I couldn't help finding humor in the situation and started to laugh uncontrollably.

I laughed so hard my stomach muscles screamed in protest.

Mackenna sat up. "Is my attempt to seduce you really so funny?"

I felt her pull up on the comforter and wrap it around herself. Reaching out blindly, I hit the lamp, lighting up the room with the dim glow.

Looking down at me, Mackenna had a pained expression on her face.

Shit.

I didn't mean to hurt her feelings.

She started to climb off me, but I stopped her by putting my hands on her thighs. Glancing away shyly, she pulled the purple blanket tighter around her chest.

My hand went to her face and I caressed her cheek.

"You wanna know how I really feel? I want you more than I've ever wanted anything. I spend most of my time thinking about being inside you and the other small percent desperately trying not to think about being inside you. You've got me by the balls, Mack." I let out a humorless laugh. "But I can only hold myself back for so long."

"So stop holding back." Letting out an exasperated sigh, she reached over me and tapped the lamp twice, cloaking the room in darkness once again.

Then she jumped off the bed and I heard her shuffling around the room.

"What are you doing?"

"Getting dressed," she snapped.

I hit the touch lamp again. Mackenna had her back to me, and she'd managed to slip on her zebra onesie. I wondered if she'd worn it on purpose to just drive me insane.

She was still buttoning up the front when I grabbed her from behind and pulled her onto my lap. Pushing her hair to the side, I kissed the side of her neck.

"What do you want?" I whispered.

She huffed. "I want you to stop treating me like I'm broken."

I flipped us so I was on top and didn't hesitate when I started to undo the black buttons.

"Like this?" My eyes challenged her—begged her—to stop me, but she didn't.

With unsteady fingers, I made it down to her belly button.

My cock got impossibly harder as I stared at the sliver of pale skin. All I needed to do was push the material to the side and I would finally see her breasts. Sensing my hesitation, Mackenna sat up a little and shrugged it off her shoulders, slipping her arms out.

As she reclined onto the pillows, I swallowed hard at the sight of her.

Topless.

Submissive.

Innocent.

Trusting. For some reason, the fact that she trusted me turned me on more than her nudity. And it was a great sight.

Pink nipples stood out against pale skin—the same pink as her lips. My eyes followed the swell of her tits, down her flat stomach, to the curve of her hips.

The rest of her was hidden by the pajamas.

I needed to change that.

But first, I cupped both breasts, loving the way they filled my hands. Using my thumbs, I circled her stiff peaks.

At the sound of her tiny gasp, I glanced up to find her heavy-lidded eyes staring at the way my hands held her tits.

Without looking away from her face, I slid my palms down, gathering the black and white material along the way. I tugged it off and by the time I made it to her ankles, the shaking in my hands intensified along with the throbbing in my dick.

Tossing the outfit behind me, my eyes roamed her body.

She had faint tan lines from our time painting together, and I traced the outlines around her upper thigh with my fingertip. My hand was just inches away from her pussy. There was a small patch of hair at the apex of her thighs, and if she spread her legs I'd get to see everything.

"What do you want now?" I asked huskily.

Her head tilted to the side. "You're letting me call the shots?"

"Yep," I told her before my hand fell away from her leg.

"Okay, um—" She paused awkwardly, and I knew giving these orders was a completely new experience for her. "Take off your shorts. And those hot as fuck undies, too."

Smirking, I stood up and I hooked my thumbs under the waistband. My erection bobbed impatiently in front of me as I pushed off my clothes.

The way Mackenna looked at my dick was a mixture of impressed and apprehensive. Mouth gaping, she sat up to get a closer look. My cock twitched at the way her tits swayed when she leaned forward.

"It doesn't bite," I joked.

"Are you sure?" Her eyes flitted up to my face and she started to ramble. "One year my mom got these, like, hybrid cucumbers for her garden. They were ginormous, and she even won some pickle contest with her garden club." Her eyes fell back down to my dick. "You're bigger than her prize-winning mutant pickle."

I laughed so hard I had to sit down. Mackenna laughed, too, and she rested her forehead between my shoulder blades. Never in my life had I lost my shit—buck naked—with a hot girl, but that's how things were with Mackenna. Sexy one minute, hilarious the next.

And I wouldn't have wanted it any other way.

Turning slightly, I cupped her face. "You're awesome, you know that?"

"Did I ruin the mood?"

"You wanna see for yourself?" I glanced down.

Lust filled her eyes and her smiled faded. "Yes."

# CHAPTER 28

MACKENNA

Jimmy shifted as he sat on the side of my bed and my gaze fell to his erection. His massive erection. It was thick, straight, and long. The barbell piercing just below the tip matched the ones in his nipples.

"You need to tell me what to do," he said, drawing my attention up to his face. "You call the shots, remember?"

I nodded, eager to have free rein over his body. "Lie down on the bed."

He did as I said, and his heavy dick rested against his stomach. When I wrapped my hand around it, he let out a quiet hiss. I was transfixed by the velvety softness of it.

But feeling it with my hand wasn't enough.

Crawling up Jimmy's body, I straddled him, and I didn't hesitate as I started rubbing myself on his smooth shaft. My wetness coated his length, making it extra slick.

I moved my hips over him, loving the slide of skin on skin. Back and forth. Back and forth. Back and forth.

With every pass, my sensitive sex hit every ridge of his cock, and that piercing under his thick head rubbed my clit just right.

My body quivered, a familiar tension building in my

core. Needing something to hold on to, my hands landed on Jimmy's chest and my fingernails dug into his skin.

He let out a sexy growl. "Fuck, babe. I could get off this way."

"So could I." I gasped when his hips started moving with mine. "But I want the real thing."

He froze. "I don't have a condom."

"What?" I asked, shocked. "How do you not have condoms?"

"Uh..." He let out a laugh. "I kinda didn't plan on this happening today. Or any time soon, actually. Remember how I told you I wasn't into casual sex anymore? Well, I meant it."

"But this isn't casual, is it?" As I asked the question, I wasn't sure what I wanted the answer to be. This arrangement may have started because I wanted to be friends with benefits, but somewhere along the way my feelings for Jimmy had become stronger than that.

His green eyes burned into mine when he said, "No, it's not."

"Have you been tested?" I asked, nibbling at my lip.

"Yeah," he nodded. "And I've never gone without a condom."

"Can you pull out?" I suggested, desperate to feel him inside me.

"Yeah, I can do that. You trust me?"

"Yes." I let out a relieved sigh.

The truth was that I did trust him. In the past few weeks, Jimmy had shown me over and over what it meant to be respected and cared for. He'd also shown me what it was like to want to have sex so badly I couldn't see straight.

"How do you want it?" he asked, his hands sliding up my thighs to my stomach.

"I want you on top."

His hands halted. "Are you sure?"

Nodding, I swung my leg over so I was kneeling next to him. He sat up and cupped my face, running his thumb over my dimple.

"You call the shots," he whispered again.

Grabbing his shoulders, I brought him on top of me as I fell back onto the pillows, and he positioned himself between my thighs.

With his arms on either side of my head, his large frame bracketed me in. The tip of his cock was poised at my entrance.

There was no panic. No fear. No anxiety. Just his warmth surrounding me, the weight of his body over mine feeling like a security blanket.

"Okay. Are you ready?" he asked, his voice raspy.

Making some sound of agreement, I spread my legs wider. I felt delicious pressure as his head slipped inside.

And when he started gently pumping his hips, my mouth fell open at the way he stretched me, the way that piercing rubbed against my inner walls.

He was barely inside and it felt so good already.

Dipping his head toward mine, Jimmy kissed me slowly as his body stilled. I noticed his shoulders were trembling.

"You're shaking," I whispered, running my hands up and down his muscular back.

He huffed out a laugh. "I'm trying really hard not to bury myself in you right now."

"Do it," I begged.

"Gotta go slow." His voice was strained. "Don't want to hurt you."

Wiggling my hips, I encouraged him to sink into me, to quell the ache in my center.

With a deep groan, he moved his hips forward, slipping in a fraction more. Slowly inching deeper. Looking down at where we were joined, I noticed he was only about halfway in.

"Holy shit, Jimmy."

I reached between us to feel his cock. My fingers explored the length that was still exposed. Curiously, I circled the place where he filled me, feeling the wetness there, marveling at the way part of his body disappeared into mine.

Jimmy patiently waited for me to be done with my assessment. When I glanced back up him, his eyes held so much tenderness.

"Okay?" he asked quietly.

I nodded. "Okay."

He smirked. "Gimme a minute, and you're gonna be saying words a lot better than okay."

"You're such a cocky ahh—" My insult was cut off when he pushed all the way in, filling me in ways that had never been done before.

The throbbing I felt turned into a new kind of pain. A good pain.

Jimmy held himself there, unmoving.

"Fuuuuck." He dropped his forehead to mine, his breathing ragged. "Am I hurting you?"

I let out whimper as my body got used to his size.

"It does hurt," I admitted. "But it feels really good, too."

"Good," he grunted. "Because you feel amazing."

A bit of self-consciousness seeped in. Jimmy said I was in charge, but there was one problem with that.

"I don't know what to do next," I confessed in a whisper.

"You don't have to do anything," he told me. "Just let me show you how good it can be. Let me show you what it's supposed to feel like. Keep your eyes open. Watch me. It's just me."

"I'll always know it's you," I responded, rubbing my thumb over his bottom lip.

Mouth parting, Jimmy sucked in a breath as he looked down at me with an indescribable expression. Something close to awe. Then his tongue slipped out and licked the tip of my thumb.

I surrendered to him, putting my hands up by my head on the pillow. He kissed the corner of my mouth, before linking his hands with mine.

We were as connected as two people could be, but for some reason it didn't feel like enough. I wanted more.

I greedily squeezed his hands as I rocked my body under his. Jimmy's responding groan was my reward.

"You love to make me lose control, don't you," he accused, his lips brushing against mine with every word.

Nodding, I smiled against his mouth.

Then he began to move.

His tongue stroked against mine in time with the gentle rhythm of his hips. I let out a long, shuddering moan.

I never thought I would describe sex as magical, but that's what this was. Pure magic.

Sex with Jimmy was an out-of-body experience. I could almost see myself there, pinned beneath his weight, his body like a shelter to my storm. Thoughts of lurking dangers and fears of intimacy scattered like those coins in Beverly's kitchen the day we met.

Only, I didn't need to pick up these pieces; I didn't want them back.

Instead, I let Jimmy replace the vacant space with something that felt a lot like love.

With every thrust, he filled me up, hitting some spot deep inside of me. Every push and pull of his cock ignited nerve endings I didn't even know I had. The barbell dragged over my inner walls, massaging places I never would've been able to reach with my own fingers.

My already-wet center gushed around him, making the slide of skin on skin slicker. Smoother. Even better.

His lips grazed over mine—not quite a kiss—and I caught his lip between my teeth and tugged. He moaned as the motion of his hips faltered.

"You feel so fucking good." His voice was shaky. "So.

Fucking. Good." Punctuating each word with a thrust, he buried himself deeper.

I tried to keep my eyes open to watch him, but sensation won out and I gave in to it.

I'd never felt more safe in my life than I did right now. Right here. With Jimmy.

Which meant I wasn't damaged beyond repair. For a long time, I feared that I would never be able to truly enjoy sex. The immense relief over the realization that I wasn't broken made me emotional.

Much to my horror, I started to cry.

Tears streamed from my eyes, sliding down my temples into my hair. I gasped out a sob, which turned into a hiccup.

"Mack?" Jimmy asked, slowing to a stop. "Shit. I'm sorry, baby."

His hands left mine and I grabbed his shoulders to keep him from pulling away. "Don't. Please don't go. I'm not crying because I'm upset."

His face softened because he understood what I meant. "You don't want to stop?"

Shaking my head, I suppressed another hiccup. "No. It feels really good."

"Better than okay?" he grinned.

I grinned back through watery eyes. "Way better. Sorry I'm such a mess."

"You're perfect. Hiccups and all." He kissed the tip of my nose. "Tell me what to do now."

From the slightly pained expression on Jimmy's face, I

could see how hard he was trying to restrain himself while he waited for my command.

"Don't hold back," I demanded.

Bracing one hand on the headboard above me, he nodded his agreement.

Then he really let me have it—the uninhibited Jimmy.

His lips went to mine and his tongue fucked my mouth in time with hard, deep thrusts. A surprised shout left me at the power of it.

He didn't let up this time, didn't hold anything back as he pounded into me over and over again. The sensations were so intense I squirmed, almost trying to get away from it. But if I moved, he moved with me. If I shifted away, he followed.

He was relentless, in the best way possible.

His hand snaked between us and he put pressure on my clit with the pad of his thumb. Sweat slicked our bodies and I couldn't tell if it was his or mine. Didn't matter.

I felt something winding up in my center, building, tightening. My legs began to shake. My hands clawed at the sheets. My breaths came out in a series of staggered pants and whimpers.

Heat flooded my cheeks. Not a flush of embarrassment. I was aroused. Needy. *So* close to getting off.

"Jimmy," I moaned. "It's happening."

He groaned and pushed deeper. "Let me have it, baby."

His hand went to my hip, anchoring me to the bed as I thrashed under him.

I imagined his cum shooting off inside me, filling me

with warmth. I knew it wasn't rational or responsible, but it turned me on.

I cried out as tremors wracked my body, and I gripped his cock in an orgasm so strong my vision became spotty. I was slightly aware of how loud I was being, but I couldn't bring myself to care.

As the blinding spasms tapered off to erratic flutters, my body went limp and I let out one more moan.

Jimmy gave two more hard thrusts before pulling out.

With a throaty groan, he stroked his dick, spilling jets of cum onto my stomach. Watching him jack himself off made my core clench with another mini-orgasm.

A stillness came over the room, the only sound our ragged panting and pounding hearts.

Our eyes locked.

Both of us wore goofy smiles as Jimmy rested his forehead against mine and we tried to catch our breath. When he leaned over the side of the bed, he came back with his T-shirt and used it to wipe off my belly.

Once I was cleaned up, he tossed it to the floor and fell next to me. "Holy fucking fuck."

"Uh-huh," I agreed, still breathless.

Wrapping an arm around my middle, he pulled me flush against his body, then rested his head on my chest. I ran my fingers through his hair as my pulse slowed.

It was a peaceful moment. The most peaceful moment I'd had in years. It was strange how sex—such a mature act—could make me feel innocent again, but it did.

A crack inside my heart had been healed.

At the beginning of the summer I thought I knew what home and happiness felt like, but I was wrong.

Jimmy felt like home now.

And as scary as that realization was, I pushed all fear away because uncertainty didn't belong here tonight.

Even if this happiness was a temporary reprieve from my solitary existence, I would revel in it for as long as possible.

# CHAPTER 29

JIMMY

Loss of sleep had my feet dragging on the walk to work the next day, but I had zero fucks to give. The bright blue sky and the crisp morning air perfectly reflected my sunny mood.

Last night was the best night of my life.

I'd suffered a lot of hangovers in the past, but none of them were worth it. The high of a great party always came with a low the following day.

Regret. Remorse. Repeat.

But the high of being with Mackenna? It stayed with me and gave me something to look forward to.

I couldn't wait to see her tonight.

But for now, I had something else to look forward to. Truck driving.

As I approached the shop, I saw the rig sitting out front. Without the trailer attached, it looked a lot smaller. Travis was wiping down the shiny red exterior of the driver's side, right over the black and white company logo on the door.

*Hank and Sons Transport.*

Travis finished up just as I made it to the garage. He eyed my coveralls. "You got clothes on under there?"

"Jeans and a T-shirt," I replied. "Why?"

"You don't need to wear the uniform on the haul. Gets hot in the truck sometimes. You can hang it up in the office. That's where we keep the extras."

Unzipping the front, I shrugged out of the material, then went into the office. Hank was there, punching some numbers into a calculator.

"Where should I put this?" I held up the coveralls.

"Any hook on the wall over there will do."

I hung it up in between spares belonging to Colton and Hank.

"When you come back tonight—" Hank reached under his desk and slid out a square cardboard box. "—you can use this one from now on."

When he opened the lid, he pulled out a pair of identical coveralls—all except for the nametag. I swallowed hard at the sight of the embroidery over the left breast pocket.

*Jimmy.*

I coughed and tried to man up because I wasn't about to get misty over a damn nametag.

"You didn't have to do this," I told him, running my finger over the lettering. "Don't get me wrong. This means a lot to me, but I hate to make you invest in this when I'm not here for very long."

Waving his hand, he made a dismissive sound. "You deserve to have one of your own, even if you're not in it for the long haul. Plus, you've been doing one hell of a job. You've shouldered a lot of the responsibilities around here. Made my life easier. I'm proud of you, son."

Ah, shit.

Was the old man trying to makc me cry? He was the one who gave me a job when I desperately needed it, and here he was making it seem like I was the one doing him a favor.

Hank made me feel something I hadn't felt in a long time.

Pride. The kind of pride that made you feel like a better version of yourself. For the first time in a while, I wasn't the guy who failed.

"Thanks," I managed gruffly.

"That's not all I've got for you." He pulled open the top drawer to his desk and grabbed my watch. "Good as new. Sorry it took me a while to get it back to you. It took a lot of tinkering, but I got it to work."

The time was set correctly and the hands moved around the face. Holding it up to my ear, I listened to the old familiar ticking. A comforting sound.

"This is awesome." I smiled as I strapped it to my wrist. "Guess I know who to come to if it gives out on me again."

"I hope you do. I'd love it if you came back to see us, even after you're a big-shot college student."

The mention of my impending school year didn't cause excitement like it used to. In fact, I was surprised when my stomach tightened with dread at the thought of leaving this town, this job, and Mackenna. I shook it off, blaming the weird mood on lack of sleep.

"Oh, by the way," Hank said, pulling an envelope from the back pocket of his coveralls. "Your paycheck."

I couldn't contain the smile on my face as I folded it and stuffed it into my jeans. I was still grinning like a fool when I hopped up into the semi where Travis was waiting.

He looked over at me from the driver's seat. "Buckle up, Jimmy. Your life's about to change."

With a loud rumble, the rig roared to life. Travis was right about the semi having power. I could feel the roaring engine all around me through the seat, through the floorboard.

As we drove away from Tolson, I discreetly pulled the envelope out of my pocket. My first paycheck. There wasn't a ton left over after Hank deducted what I owed him for my car, but it was more money than I had before.

It was enough to do something that was long overdue—take Mackenna on a real date.

I'd wanted to cover the damages on her car, too, but she wouldn't let me. Luckily, when I mentioned what happened to Hank, he said it was 'on the house' as long as I put in the labor. Said it'd be good practice for me.

And it was good practice. Not only that, but it helped me put my energy into fixing what had been done, instead of having murderous thoughts about some asshole I'd never met.

Memories of the night before flashed through my mind as we made it out onto the interstate. The way it felt to be inside of Mackenna bare was mind-blowing and intense. Sex had never felt like that, and it wasn't just because we didn't use a condom.

I could pinpoint the exact moment I fell in love with her. When lust turned into something deeper.

*I'll always know it's you*, she'd said, then she brushed her thumb over my bottom lip.

That one touch.

I felt it all the way to my soul.

If I hadn't been lying down, it would've brought me to my fucking knees.

I wanted to tell her, and I almost blurted out those three words. But telling Mackenna I loved her the first time my dick was inside her seemed like an asshole thing to do.

So I kept my mouth shut and tried to show her instead.

As I moved on top of her, I looked into her eyes and swore I saw the same love reflected back at me.

I was pulled from my daydreaming when some static came through the CB radio, and I went back to appreciating the experience of riding in a semi for the first time.

The four-hour drive flew by as Travis and I listened to music, and talked about everything from our hometowns to our women. He was excited about his wedding and having babies with his wife. Apparently, they planned to start growing their family right away.

Before I knew it, we were at our destination, and Travis was hooking the trailer back up to the rig. He walked me through the process, saying terms like *fifth wheel* and *kingpin*. In less than twenty minutes, we were back on the road.

When we stopped at a truck stop down in Effingham, I used the restroom while Travis paid for the fuel. After I came out, I grabbed a Dr. Pepper and a bag of chips from the back of the store.

I was waiting in line to pay when my eyes zeroed in on a small rotating display on the counter. More specifically, a necklace dangling among a wide assortment of jewelry. It caught my attention because it immediately reminded me of Mackenna.

When it was my turn to pay, I toyed with the little purple starfish on the silver chain.

If I bought this for her, was I breaking rule number one? Mackenna said not to get her flowers because it was a waste of money. Did that apply to necklaces, too?

Fuck it.

I just knew she had to have this.

Decision made, I plucked it off the stand and slid it toward the cashier with my soda. Then I pointed at the box of Magnums behind the counter. "Those, too."

Maybe tonight's date wouldn't be a total crapshoot after all.

# CHAPTER 30

MACKENNA

On the way to the dress fitting, Beverly gave me a quick rundown of everyone who would be there.

Brielle was a bridesmaid and she was engaged to Colton, who was Travis's best man. Ava, Brielle's daughter, was the flower girl. Travis's mom, Karen, wasn't in the wedding party, but she was getting fitted for a special 'mother of the groom' dress. Hank was also a groomsman, and Ernie would be walking Angel down the aisle, but they weren't allowed to come today—because, girls only.

And Beverly was the very proud matron of honor; she reminded me three times during the twenty-five-minute trip.

As soon as I stepped through the door of the small bridal shop, I was bombarded with all the new faces.

Brielle was attractive, with dark hair and brown eyes. She greeted me with a handshake before introducing the equally beautiful four-year-old at her side. In matching pink sundresses, Ava was Brielle's mini-me.

When Brielle told me how much Colton liked Jimmy, and how things had been easier for Hank and the gang since he started on at the shop, I felt happy and proud.

Because that was my *boyfriend*.

Ava tugged on my hand and I glanced down at big blue eyes. "Did you know I get to wear a princess dress two times?" She held up two fingers. "One time with Angel, and one time with my mom."

Brielle mouthed behind her hand, "Flower girl."

I laughed.

Then I was ambushed by a hug. Wavy blonde hair covered half my face, and I had no other choice but to return the embrace of the affectionate stranger.

When she pulled back, I could only conclude that this was Angel. Her name was fitting. With a cherub-like face, she had large blue eyes and slightly rounded pink cheeks.

"It's so great to meet you," she said, bouncing a little from excitement, and her enthusiasm made me grin.

"You too," I told her. "Beverly has nothing but great things to say about you. In fact, I think she's trying to set us up right now."

"Damn straight, I am," Beverly confirmed. "You two should be friends."

Angel nodded. "I agree."

Karen simply introduced herself as 'the mom' before putting an arm around Angel, like she was claiming her as her own.

Then Angel clapped her hands. "Everyone is here. Now, who wants to see my dress?"

*

A chorus of squeals erupted in the area outside the dressing room as Angel emerged from behind the curtain. Stepping up on a pedestal, she smiled as everyone fawned over her dress.

It was gorgeous and she looked perfect. The cream-colored fabric had an overlay of lace, giving it an antique feel. The shop assistant came up behind her and loosely pinned her hair up, then finished off the outfit with a wide, light-blue ribbon around her waist.

Angel pivoted in front of the three-way mirror. Her hands skimmed over the lace and some of the pearl beading around the sweetheart neckline.

When she turned back around, her eyes were red-rimmed and brimming with tears.

"Angel, dear," Beverly said as she pulled a pack of tissues from her purse. "What's wrong? You don't like it?"

"I love it," Angel responded, her voice squeaky from trying not to cry. She took a tissue from Beverly and blew her nose. "A year ago, I never would've thought I'd be surrounded by loved ones at such an important occasion. It means a lot to me. Karen, Beverly, Brielle, Ava." Then her eyes made it to me. "Mackenna. Thank you all for being here today."

I swallowed hard, her sentimental state contagious. From what Beverly had told me about Angel, it wasn't difficult to conclude that she didn't have a family. I'd almost declined the invitation to come because I thought I wasn't welcome. Now I was so glad I said yes.

When I moved to Tolson, the last thing I wanted was a social life. I didn't want wedding invites, friends, hugs from strangers, or a boyfriend.

Now I had all those things.

For a long time, I had shut off my emotions, saving them only for song lyrics. When I was writing, those were the times I let myself feel.

But something was happening to me. I couldn't seem to turn it off like I used to.

My phone buzzed in my lap, and I looked down to find a text from Jimmy.

**Jimmy: We're going on a date to-night. Be ready at 6**

Jimmy and I hung out all the time but we'd never gone out on an official date, and the thought made me nervous. I wasn't sure how to dress or act because I hadn't been on a real date in years. Would we go out to a nice restaurant?

I probably needed to put on something better than leggings.

Another text came through.

**Jimmy: Whatever you're thinking, lower those expectations. Really. Lower them a lot. I hate to disappoint you but we won't be going anywhere fancy because I'm broke as a joke**

I huffed out a laugh at his honesty and returned with an honest response.

**Me: That sounds perfect**

# CHAPTER 31

JIMMY

When I picked Mackenna up for our date, I didn't give her time to ask questions about where we were going. Just grabbed her hand and pulled her to the passenger side of the 'saggin' wagon'.

Taking advantage of the unseasonably cool weather, I rolled the windows down as I took a back road out of Tolson. One of the things I loved most about the Midwest was the fluctuating weather. Some people hated how it could be 95 degrees one day, then 72 the next. They didn't like the inconsistency.

But I liked a little change of pace every now and then.

Plus, it gave me a reason to see Mackenna sitting next to me while the wind blew through her hair.

She smiled over at me, the sinking sun behind her. Bright orange light filtered through her dark strands, making them look like they were on fire.

She was so gorgeous it took my breath away.

Right then, I wanted to confess my love for her. Right there, on a country road surrounded by cornfields, I wanted to tell her she was making me feel something I didn't even know was possible.

I wanted to let her know rule number three was completely fucked.

Instead, I removed my sunglasses and plopped them onto her face. She grinned as she pushed them up on her nose.

How could I possibly go on living my life without her after the summer was over?

The answer was I couldn't. Not an option.

Problem was, I didn't know how to convince her to stay with me. The best plan I could come up with was to show her how good we could be together. Show her that it didn't matter if we were in the same town or 300 miles apart.

I'd still love her regardless of where I lived.

We neared our destination and I slowed before turning left onto a narrow gravel road. I came to a stop about a quarter of a mile down, parking the car between tall trees on one side and big round haybales on the other.

Keeping the windows down, I turned off the ignition and let my eyes travel over to Mackenna. This was the first time I'd ever seen her in a dress. It was white with yellow sunflowers, and the hem just barely reached her knees.

I was in the middle of speculating what kind of panties she had on when she spoke.

"James Peabody Johnson, are you taking me parking?"

I laughed. "Sort of. To make up for the fact that this is probably going to go down as the crappiest date in history, I come bearing gifts." Reaching into the back seat, I picked up the paper sack. "Now, if you hadn't already smelled it, there's pizza in the back," I told her before raising the first item out of the bag. "And I have wine."

When I held up the bottle of Strawberry Boon's Farm, Mackenna snorted. "And how did you buy wine when you're not old enough?"

"I didn't. Travis did. Besides, it's for you. I'm the designated driver tonight." Smirking, I kissed her before removing her next present. "Don't get mad at me for the next one, okay?"

She gave me a look. "It better not be flowers. We already talked about that."

"It's not." Grinning, I put both fists in front of me. "Pick a hand."

Mackenna's lips tilted up as she tapped the right. For once, she guessed correctly. When I opened my hand, the starfish necklace dangled from my fingers.

Her jaw dropped open. "You got me jewelry?"

"Well, yeah," I said as it swung back and forth between us. "It reminded me of you."

"Why?" She tilted her head to the side.

Barking out a laugh, I rubbed at my jaw. "You might get pissed when I tell you... You know in the morning how you like to... 'cuddle'?" I asked, putting air quotes around the word.

"There's nothing wrong with snuggling," she shot back defensively, blushing bright pink.

"I agree with that. But you take it to champion-level cuddling. Like, if there was a contest, you'd blow everyone else out of the water. You're like a starfish. You know, how they have a bunch of limbs and all those little suction cups and they just—" I spread my fingers and made an obnoxious sucking sound.

Laughing, Mackenna grabbed my hand. "Oh, my God. I get it, okay?"

"So, you'll wear it?"

She responded by turning her back to me, gathering her hair up so I could get to her neck. Just as I finished hooking the clasp, she said, "No one's ever gotten me jewelry before."

"Never?"

Shaking her head, she glanced at me over her shoulder. "Well, one Christmas my aunt gave me a silver heart locket, but I'm pretty sure it was a re-gift from the year before."

"You deserve to have nice things."

"You didn't have to do all this." She turned to face me while fiddling with the starfish.

"I gotta bring my A-game." I tucked a strand of hair behind her ear. "I'm poor."

She giggled, and my favorite dimple appeared. "Stop saying that. Money isn't everything. Besides, your extremely large ego makes up for it."

"I'm really sorry I can't take you out on a fancy date."

"Jimmy." Bringing her hand up to my face, Mackenna did that thing again where she rubbed her thumb over my bottom lip, and my heart gave a hard thump. "I'll be honest with you. I don't like extravagant dates. If you haven't noticed, I don't really like being around people all that much." She looked around at the scenery, then her eyes found mine again. "This is the best."

"There's one last gift," I told her, lifting the box of

Magnums. I hoped getting them wasn't too presumptuous, and it occurred to me that Mackenna might be sore from the night before.

When her lips parted, eyes flaring with lust, I knew I'd made the right decision. Taking it from my hands, she ripped it open and took out one of the small square packages.

"Whoa." I stopped her and gestured to our dinner. "Don't you want to eat first?"

With a sexy smile, she shook her head. "Pizza can wait."

I set the pizza box on the dashboard before hopping out of the car, then I folded the back seat to make a large area for us to lie down.

As I spread out a fuzzy white blanket, I gave Mackenna a cocky look. "The saggin' wagon has its perks, huh?"

Grinning, she crawled over the middle console into the back with me and held up the condom with raised eyebrows.

Amused by her eagerness, I quickly shed my clothes, thinking she would do the same. I was surprised when she simply removed her white cotton panties, then turned around on all-fours. She wiggled her sunflower-covered ass at me, and all I had to do was lift the dress to get the irresistible view.

Rolling on the condom, I ran a hand down her smooth backside before giving her ass a squeeze.

"Are you sure you want to do it like this?" I asked, giving my dick a tug as I looked at her glistening pussy.

Doggie-style was a fairly dominant position. I knew I broke down some major walls with her last night, but still. I didn't want to do anything she wasn't ready for.

She sat up and looked at me over her shoulder. "You don't always have to be so careful with me. Not anymore." Then she whispered, "Feel how wet I am, Jimmy."

Well, okay then.

Reaching around the front of her body, my hand caressed the inside of her thigh before my fingers slid through her folds. She was drenched.

She fell back onto her hands and arched up, offering herself to me. I ran my tip along her slit, spreading her wetness around before I pushed into her heat.

It felt different with the condom on. Still really fucking good, though. This position made her pussy feel unbelievably tighter.

"Oh, my God," she panted. "You're going so deep."

I didn't bother telling her that I wasn't even all the way in yet. Using my thumbs, I spread her apart, loving the way I could watch my dick pump in and out of her.

Once I was fully seated, I ground myself into her while rubbing tight circles over her clit.

When her body trembled and her pussy clamped down on my cock, her fists clenched the blanket as she screamed.

Energy spent, her languid body sagged until she was lying flat on her stomach. Locking our hands together above her head, I gave it to her in slow deep thrusts.

Her moans echoed through the air, but no one could hear it. Not out here.

I milked one more orgasm out of her before I let myself go, gasping and groaning against the side of her neck.

Afterward, we stayed in the back, our bodies intertwined as dusk turned into night. We kissed, talked, and laughed until hunger won out.

Then we ate cold pizza in the dark while listening to the radio.

And when Garth Brooks' 'To Make You Feel my Love' came on, Mackenna let me lay my head in her lap while she sang.

I held onto her, rubbing my thumb over the smooth skin on her thigh while she ran her fingers through my hair.

In all my nineteen—almost twenty—years, it was the happiest moment of my life.

It was safe to say the date was a massive success.

# CHAPTER 32

MACKENNA

Sometimes weddings made me uncomfortable. I believed in true love, and I was fully supportive of the idea of having a ceremony to celebrate the union of two soulmates.

But holy shit. Why did there have to be so many people?

I peered through my living room blinds and surveyed all the cars on my street. Packed bumper to bumper, they lined both sides of the road, and I would've been willing to bet that it was the same everywhere in town. It was a good thing the weather was nice because there was no way I'd be able to drive anywhere today.

Jimmy wasn't kidding when he said the entire town of Tolson was invited. I was pretty sure a large portion of central Illinois showed up today. Part of that might've been because of the summer festival, but many people exiting their vehicles were dressed up and heading in the direction of the church.

Just the thought of having that many eyes on me as I walked down an aisle made my skin crawl. There was sure to be a big crowd today, but at least they wouldn't be looking at me.

Anxiously toying with my new necklace, I went to the kitchen to get a bottle of water while I waited for Jimmy.

This was our first public outing as a couple. I'd gotten a little too comfortable in our bubble, and I told myself it would be good for me—for us—to get out of the house for once.

A soft knock sounded through the quiet house, and I quickly pawed at the loose curls I'd taken so long to get just right. The simple strapless black dress I'd picked out was one of the nicest things I owned. I smoothed down the flowy knee-length skirt and hoped my red lipstick didn't end up on my teeth.

When I answered the door, I lost the ability to form words.

Jimmy looked good in everything. He rocked his auto shop uniform, giving hot mechanic a whole new meaning. He wore jeans like they were made for him. Hell, he even made an old apron look sexy.

But dressed-up Jimmy? I wasn't prepared for it.

He wore all black—even his tie. Most people wouldn't have been able to pull that off, but Jimmy did.

His slacks fit just right, hugging his narrow hips. The shirt was loosely tucked in around his waist and the sleeves were rolled up, showing off strong forearms and a peek of the peonies. His dark hair had been slicked back, but a few stubborn locks fell over his forehead.

"You gonna let me in?" he asked with a smirk, probably internally laughing at me for almost drooling.

"Yeah," I managed, stepping back to make room for

him. Once the door clicked shut, I tried—really tried—to talk myself out of jumping Jimmy's bones.

It didn't work.

I threw myself at him, and he made a surprised sound as his back hit the door. I kissed his mouth. Hard. Then I began to un-button his shirt while my lips latched onto the side of his neck.

"Mack," he whispered, his fingers digging into my ass as he ground his erection against my stomach. "Baby, we can't." He let out a moan when my hand slipped into his shirt and my finger flicked over his nipple.

"Why not?"

"Don't have time."

I pulled back a little. "Are you sure?"

Jimmy glanced at his watch, which worked now thanks to Hank. "We have to be at the church in fifteen minutes. Judging by all the people out there, we might have trouble finding a seat."

Disappointed, I let out a groan while resting my fore-head on his shoulder and desperately tried to get my libi-do under control.

Jimmy didn't realize it, but he'd awakened a monster.

A really horny monster.

Now that I knew how fun sex could be, I wanted it all the time.

He chuckled low, that sexy rumbling in his chest doing nothing to help my raging hormones.

"We can finish this later," he promised, and I lifted my head to gaze at his lips. Those lips curved up at the cor-ners. "Eyes up here, Mack."

"Sorry," I whispered. "I just can't help it."

In one quick move, he turned us so I was up against the door. He pressed his hardness into me again, and I let out a whimper of need and frustration.

"Don't ever apologize for wanting me. Do you have any idea how crazy you make me?" he asked. "Do you like doing that to me?"

Nibbling my lip, I nodded. He nipped at the lip I had between my teeth before licking over the spot.

Then he swayed back. "Well, it's only fair that I make you feel the same way." Giving my butt a light smack, he opened the door and made a sweeping motion with his hand. "After you, milady."

The ass knew exactly what he was doing to me.

Fine. If he wanted to make this a game of foreplay, I was down for that.

# CHAPTER 33

JIMMY

She was evil, I was sure of it.

At least she behaved herself in the church. But after that, all bets were off.

To everyone else, it just looked like Mackenna dropped her napkin on the floor and needed to retrieve it. An innocent mistake.

It wasn't a mistake. What they didn't see was her hand roaming up the inside of my thigh. Her hand finding my dick. Her finger flicking over the tip before giving my balls a light squeeze.

Just a few seconds of her 'finding her napkin' was all it took to make me hard as a rock.

These slacks weren't built to house a massive boner. I tugged at my collar, the room suddenly feeling like a sauna. I had a feeling this was her way of getting back at me for earlier.

Over the past several days, Mackenna had memorized my anatomy. And, usually, I loved her wandering hands.

But not in the middle of Travis and Angel's reception, surrounded by hundreds of people. Particularly, my grandma's knitting club friends at our table.

"So, James," a white-haired woman next to me said, "Beverly says you're staying with her over the summer."

Nodding, I made an affirmative sound while gulping the ice water the caterers placed in front of me. I was pretty sure she introduced herself as Alma, but having a hard-on messed with my comprehension skills.

"That's lovely," she continued, then her gaze shifted to my girl. "And who is this beautiful young lady?"

Seeing an opportunity to screw with Mackenna, I looped an arm around her shoulders and flashed the older women a toothy grin.

"My girlfriend, Mackenna Connelly. Honey bear," I started, and her head whipped toward me at the unfamiliar term of endearment. I tried not to laugh at her startled expression. "What do you think of this venue? Nice, huh?" Gesturing around the hall of the Tolson Community Building, I stroked the side of her neck with my thumb. "Better write that down in your planner."

Her eyebrows furrowed. "My planner?"

"Yeah, that wedding notebook you keep around. This venue—you like it, right?"

"Venue?" she croaked, catching on to what I was implying.

Alma squealed. "Beverly didn't tell me you were serious with anyone! When are you two getting married?"

A strangled sound came from the shocked girl next to me, and out of the corner of my eye, I could see her mouth open and close several times.

I smirked. "Nothing official yet. It's just so fun to talk about the possibilities."

A round of '*aww*' and a '*bless your heart*' came from the enamored women, and Mackenna's hand landed back on my crotch under the table. The squeeze she gave my balls wasn't so gentle this time.

"You'll have to excuse me," she said sweetly. "I need to use the ladies' room."

After she stood up, I kissed the back of her hand. "Hurry back, sweetheart. We don't want to miss the first dance."

Playing along, she sent me a dreamy smile. "While I'm gone, why don't you tell everyone how much you love Sweet Pea."

My grin dropped.

With a victorious smirk, she walked away. I couldn't help the way my eyes followed the mesmerizing swish of her hips.

Alma grabbed my forearm. "Oh, I'm so glad to hear that bird has a good home. It's what Bernice wanted."

I nodded stiffly. "He's really something."

"I would've taken him," another woman chimed in. "But I don't think he likes me. Every time I went over to Bernice's house, he called me horrible names."

"Oh, that's just how he says hello," I told her.

"Well, he pooped all over my handmade quilt," a woman across the table complained. "I was supposed to enter it in the county fair. Six months of hard work, gone!"

I laughed because it was kind of funny when it

happened to someone else. "Well, if it makes you feel any better, it wasn't personal. He does that to everyone. But I think he and I have come to an understanding. I feed him peanuts, and he doesn't crap on my stuff."

They all giggled.

Alma glanced at me. "Well, Beverly is a saint for taking him in. If it wasn't for her, who knows what would've happened to him."

Nodding, I looked up at the main table. Grandma was sitting there like a queen on her throne in her light-blue satin dress. It wasn't her wedding, but from the look on her face you'd never know it.

I'd never seen her this happy. She took a sip of her Champagne—pinky out—and seeing her have such a good time made me happy, too. If there was anyone in this world who deserved a moment to shine, it was Beverly Louise Johnson.

I endured some more flattery from the knitting club before they found a different topic to talk about.

I tuned them out as my mind went to how amazing Mackenna looked today. That dress. The red lipstick.

Absolutely stunning.

My phone vibrated with a text on the tabletop, and when I opened the message I almost choked on my water.

Mackenna sent me a cleavage shot. If her dress was pulled down any lower, I'd see nipples.

Another one came through.

Those full red lips were wrapped around her finger.

**Me: Well played, honey bear**

## Mack: Meet me outside the bathroom

Trying to hide my stiffy, I discreetly adjusted my-self before standing up. The hallway was empty as I approached the restrooms. Suddenly, a door swung open to my right and Mackenna grabbed me by the tie. Before I knew it, I was in complete darkness, my back against a door while my girlfriend's lips went to my neck.

I turned on my phone, using the light from the screen to see better.

"Is there a light in here?" I looked around. I saw old shelves with cleaning supplies and paper towels. A mop and bucket in the corner. Dust bunnies and cobwebs. But no light switch.

"Doesn't matter," Mackenna replied, pulling my face back to hers. After sucking on my bottom lip, she mumbled, "You're such a troublemaker. Within ten minutes, the entire town is going to think we're engaged."

"So?" I challenged.

"Have fun explaining that one to Beverly," she responded while undoing my belt.

She kissed me, slow and deep, before kneeling in front of me. It felt wrong to have Mackenna all dressed up and on her knees in a dirty broom closet. It also turned me the fuck on.

"What are you doing?" I asked, frozen in place.

With a flick of her fingers, the button on my slacks popped open and the zipper came down, giving sweet relief to my straining erection. "What does it look like I'm doing?"

"Uhh... Ah..." I sputtered. She took my cock in her hand, stroking up and down a few times before running her thumb over the tip.

I heard muffled cheering and clapping outside the heavy wooden door, reminding me that we were in a public place.

"Mack, are you sure—"

"Jimmy." Licking her lips, her eyes bounced up to mine. "Let me?"

"You're asking permission to suck my dick? Un-fuck-ing-believable." I laughed and raised my hands in surrender. "Have at it, baby."

The light from my phone went out, and I swiped the screen to turn it back on. I wanted to see everything. Eyes, lips, tongue. I didn't want to miss a second of it.

Music started up, and I could only assume we were missing the first dance. But as Mackenna's warm, wet mouth closed over my tip, I lost the ability to care. She gave a gentle suck.

"Oh, fuck," I breathed out.

Her fingers clumsily grazed over my length as she licked at my sensitive skin. The way she wrapped her hand around me was unsure. Curious and tentative.

It was obvious she wasn't experienced at this, but it didn't make it any less awesome. If anything, it made me impossibly harder. Watching her taste me as she ran her tongue over my slit. Watching her pull back with a gag when she took me in too far. Watching her discover how to make me moan.

Like always, I let her take control.

A grunt left me when she found a steady rhythm, her hand at the base of my shaft while her head bobbed back and forth. She glanced up at me, her eyes questioning.

"It's good, baby," I praised. "So fucking good."

The light on my phone went out again, and I growled. When I got the light back on, Mackenna reached for my other hand and put it in her hair, encouraging me to guide her. Gently gripping the back of her head, I made her go faster.

She moaned, and I felt the pressure build.

"I'm close," I told her as I tried to pull her off my cock. Sucking me harder, she wouldn't budge. "Baby," I warned. "Fuck. Fuck. I'm gonna come."

Her free hand came up to lightly squeeze my balls, and I couldn't hold back anymore.

With a hoarse shout, I emptied into her mouth. Mackenna's eyes got wide at the amount of cum I gave her, but she swallowed it down.

Releasing the hold I had on her hair, I sagged back against the door and the light on my phone went out again. I didn't have the energy to turn it back on. Mackenna started giggling before she even got off the floor, and I blindly reached out to help her up.

Falling onto my chest, she laughed, and I couldn't help but join her. I sighed as I held her, probably a little tighter than necessary. My fingers flexed around her back as I kissed the top of her head.

Mackenna found my mouth in the darkness and gave me a peck.

"Better get back out there," she said against my lips. "I don't want to miss the cake. I'll go first."

Before I could stop her, she was out the door.

A bit dazed, I staggered out of the broom closet and made my way back to our table, probably looking just as satisfied as I felt. Mussed-up hair. Loosened tie. My shirt partially untucked.

And a shit-eating grin I couldn't seem to wipe off my face.

Alma did a double-take when I sat down. She smirked, then dipped one of the cloth napkins in her water. She handed it to me and leaned in to whisper, "You've got some lipstick on your neck, dear."

I took it from her and wiped at my skin until she gave me a thumb's up.

Mackenna looked to the front and clapped as Travis and Angel kissed in front of the three-tier cake.

Alma winked at me, like we had a secret between us now. Pulling Mackenna close, I placed a kiss at her temple.

Hands down, it was the best wedding I'd ever been to.

# CHAPTER 34

JIMMY

Numbness settled in my fists as I pounded the bag over and over again. The distinct smell of sweat and rubber permeated the small gym, but it wasn't unpleasant.

Over the past couple of weeks, I'd become familiar with the Daywood workout center, building my endurance by running on the treadmill, then pummeling the punching bag until my arms couldn't take anymore.

Since Mackenna started spending Saturday nights at her parents' house, I had several hours to come here to train in secrecy.

And sometimes I worked out during my lunch break, like today.

"Damn, Jimmy." Colton's voice came from the bench press. "You got a beef with that bag?"

Part of the reason I was on edge was because the fight with Jaxon was in two weeks. No matter how much I trained, I felt like I had to be better, faster, stronger. There hadn't been anymore incidents since the car vandalism, but I knew Mackenna was worried.

I was worried, too.

The other reason I wanted to beat something to a pulp? Guilt.

Whenever Mackenna asked me what I did while she was gone on Saturdays, I told her I watched movies with Grandma—which was the truth. Part of it, anyway.

The lie didn't seem like that big of a deal at first, but as time went on, it got bigger. As my feelings for Mackenna grew, it expanded. Every time I went to the gym to train, it multiplied.

I told myself it was for her benefit, and that might've been true, but I still felt like shit about it.

Also, I hadn't been up front with Mackenna about my feelings. After a lot of internal debate, I decided not to tell her I loved her, mostly because I didn't think she'd say it back. My fragile ego couldn't handle that. So, I just kept it to myself and held onto the unlikely hope that she would say it first.

But time was slipping through my fingers. My summer in Tolson was more than halfway gone now.

Chest heaving from exertion, I stepped back and pulled off the gloves protecting my knuckles. "Nah," I told Colton with a forced smile. "Just feeling a little wound up is all."

"Alright." Getting to his feet, he made a 'come at me' gesture before balling his fists. "Let's duke it out."

I had to laugh at his bad form. Colton was in good shape, but bulk had nothing to do with fighting. Strength meant nothing if you didn't know how to use it.

"I think by 'duke it out', you mean get your ass kicked," I said with a laugh.

Fists still raised, he shrugged. "I've always been a lover, not a fighter. Now show me some moves."

"Well, first of all you need to bring up your left hand," I told him, moving it in front of his face. "You can't leave yourself wide open like that."

I kept my motions slow as I showed him a right hook and how to block. After a few minutes of circling each other and pulling punches, Colton was out of breath.

"Holy shit," he heaved. "I had no idea I was so out of shape."

I chuckled. "It's just a different kind of workout. We'll build up that endurance."

We headed to the locker rooms to change back into our coveralls, then went out to Colton's blue Ford pickup.

Just as I buckled my seatbelt, he spoke.

"Jimmy... I want to let you know we'll take care of Mackenna when you leave." He glanced over at me as he started the ignition. "After what happened with her car and everything... I know you're probably concerned."

"I'm terrified," I admitted, needing to confide in someone. "When I think about leaving her here—unprotected—I feel sick."

"I understand," he said with a nod. "But we'll look out for her. I promise. And if you ever need to talk about anything, I'm all ears."

"Thanks."

It made me feel a little better. It was nice to know Mackenna wouldn't be alone after I left.

I still had no idea what would happen to our relationship when the summer was over. I hadn't brought up the subject of long-distance since that night in the hotel, partly because Mackenna was so against it at the time.

I hoped she would change her mind, but the guilt I was feeling made me have doubts about that. I had successfully gained Mackenna's trust while also deceiving her, and I knew that was messed up.

How would she feel once she found out about the secret I'd been keeping? I wasn't foolish enough to think I could come out of the fight unscathed. I wouldn't be able to hide the bruises on my body, and I didn't want to. Once it was over, I had every intention of coming clean.

But would it be too late?

\*

After our lunch break, Colton left work early to take his daughter to the park, so it was just Hank and me at the shop.

I'd gotten the hang of things around here.

Filling out the invoices at the end of the day had become one of my jobs. I knew where all the tools were and how to clean them. And the guys had enough confidence in me that they let me do oil changes and tire rotations on my own.

Certain customers were starting to know me by name.

Norma Henderson came in at least once a week because she swore her Honda was making funny noises. Hank didn't have the heart to tell her that it was probably one of her hearing aids going bad. He also didn't have the heart to charge her when there was nothing wrong with her car.

However, I suspected she was coming in for the man

candy. One day I saw her bump into Hank and play it off like an accident. But I was pretty sure she just did it to cop a feel. I mean, she grabbed his ass to steady herself then left, looking flushed and a bit too satisfied.

Then there was Harold McCann. He walked by the shop every day at exactly 2pm with his cairn terrier, Roxy. We kept a jar of dog treats behind the counter just for her.

I'd just given Roxy her bone when Hank called me back inside. I watched the furball happily scamper off before heading to the office.

"What's up?" I leaned against the door way.

Swiveling toward me in his chair, he linked his hands over his stomach. "You caught that oil leak on Charlie's van yesterday."

"Yeah. Wasn't hard to spot it."

"That's fantastic." He smiled. "Charlie didn't even know about it, so that was a good find."

Hank had a way of making me feel like I did a great job, even when I wasn't quite sure what I was doing in the first place. I didn't think what I did was anything special, but his compliments made me feel warm and fuzzy.

"Thanks, Hank."

"Here's your next paycheck." He handed me an envelope. "Keep up the good work."

As I walked the three blocks home, I looked at the text Mackenna sent about an hour ago.

**Mack: Can't wait to see you. Just let yourself in ;)**

Truth was, I couldn't wait to see her either. I decided

to forego the shower I usually took at Grandma's just so I could see her ten minutes sooner.

Yesterday, she gave me my own key so I wouldn't have to knock all the time. We both tried to play it off like it wasn't a big deal, but it meant something to me. It felt like so much more than just a way into her house.

I palmed the cold piece of metal in my pocket as I walked up her porch steps.

I never would've thought Mackenna would be such a wild one in bed, but fuck.

She was insatiable.

She was like a kid discovering candy for the first time. Every night, as soon as I walked through the door, she was on me.

And it didn't matter where we were. The kitchen. On the couch. Halfway up the stairs. If she was in the mood, we fucked.

Sometimes I had to force myself to slow down so I could take my time, make it sweeter for her. But she liked pushing my buttons. She used any means necessary to make me lose control—her teeth, her nails, her tongue.

I'd gotten used to Mackenna launching herself at me, so I was surprised when I opened the door only to be met with eerie silence.

"Mack?"

Nothing.

"Mackenna?"

Fear spiked. A quick search of her downstairs, and I was taking two stairs at time.

"Mack!" I yelled out as I reached the second floor.

More silence.

I roughly raked a hand through my hair as a dozen awful scenarios ran through my mind. Just as I was about to lose my shit, her sing-song voice came from her bedroom.

"In here, Jimmy!"

My hand went to my chest, my heart racing like I'd just sprinted a mile. The door was cracked, and when I pushed it open I barely registered the drawn shades, the candles on the nightstand, or the hot naked girl on the bed.

When she saw my expression, she sat up and swung her legs over the side of the mattress. "What's wrong?"

Dropping to my knees in front of her, I wrapped my arms around her body, laying the side of my face on her stomach.

"Baby," I whispered shakily, then kissed her warm skin.

"What's going on?" she asked, concerned.

"When I couldn't find you, I thought..." I swallowed hard, not wanting to voice my fears out loud. Every time I was away from Mackenna, I was afraid her ex would go off the deep end again. That I wouldn't be there when she needed me. Sometimes I had nightmares about coming home to find her gone.

"Everything is fine." She ran her fingers through my hair in a soothing gesture. "I just wanted to surprise you."

I huffed out a laugh, not letting go of the hold I had on her. "I see that now." Resting my chin against her belly button, I glanced up at her face. "I was scared."

"Sorry, babe." The last of my fear melted away at the term of endearment. She'd never called me babe before. I liked it. Then her lips pulled into a naughty smile. "Wow, you're not even looking at my tits."

At the mention of her breasts, my eyes drifted to the dusky pink nipples just inches away from my face. "They're great tits. And I like it when you say tits."

She laughed and it made them bounce. I caught one between my teeth and her amusement turned into a moan.

"I need to shower," I told her. "I'm dirty."

To prove my point, I rubbed my thumb over her hip bone and left a dark streak of grease behind. Picking up my hand, she studied my blackened fingertips before dragging them over her stomach. I watched the lines appear on her pale, perfect skin, marking her as mine.

*Mine*.

Mesmerized by the physical evidence of my touch, I couldn't stop. Bringing my hand up to her face, I smeared my thumb over the place where her dimple would appear if she smiled. I drew lines down her neck, over her collarbone, to her left breast.

Mackenna's breathing picked up. "There. Now I'm dirty, too."

"I guess we both need a shower now," I said.

She stood up and held out her hand. Without hesitation I took it, willing to follow her anywhere.

When we stepped inside the shower, steam filled the air as she poured a large dollop of her body wash onto a loofa. The suds covered my skin as she scrubbed the dirt away.

"You're too good to me," I murmured.

"I like being good to you." She smiled. "As long as you give me what I want."

"And what do you want today?" I asked, amused.

"This."

I gasped as her hand made its way around my cock. "Baby, we ran out of condoms yesterday." My protest faltered when she rubbed her thumb over the barbell at my tip while sucking my nipple piercing into her mouth. "I—I haven't—shit, that feels good. I haven't had time to pick up more."

"I don't care," she said, breathless. "Just pull out."

We almost always used condoms, but nothing compared to the feeling of taking her bare.

It wasn't just about how her wet, silky walls felt around my dick. It was more than skin on skin. It was about the connection. Just her body and mine.

But first, there was something I needed to do. Dropping to my knees, I lifted her leg and set her foot on the ledge of the tub.

"What are you doing?"

I looked up to find Mackenna wide-eyed as she watched me move closer to her pussy.

"Something I've wanted to do for a long time," I replied. Using my thumbs, I spread her open, revealing her swollen sex. My mouth watered before I dove in.

Flattening my tongue, I ran it up her slit. I moaned at the taste of her while she gasped at the new sensation.

Her hand landed in my hair and the pull on my scalp

turned me on even more. I wanted her to guide me, to grind herself on my face, to use me for her pleasure. My tongue circled her clit before sucking it into my mouth.

Mackenna let out a loud whimper as her body went limp against the wall. My hand went to her stomach to hold her up.

"Jimmy," she panted. "This feels really good, but…" Her sentence turned into a moan.

I lifted my head long enough to ask, "But what?" Then I lapped at her some more, unable to get enough of her sweet taste.

"I want your cock," she managed through another gasp.

I laughed against her clit. My girl was so impatient.

"Alright, baby." Standing up, I gave her a light kiss before giving her what she wanted.

Pinning her up against the wall, I buried myself deep between her legs. I groaned at the feeling of her tight heat.

I would never get tired of this. The way her body fit me like a glove, her breath against my neck, her fingernails digging into my skin.

As I rocked into her, the emotions of the day came to the surface—anticipation for the fight, guilt over my dishonesty, and the fear I felt when I thought something happened to Mackenna.

Needing an outlet, I let it all out in the form of fast, rough thrusts. Her tits bounced from the force as I drove into her hard.

She didn't seem to mind, though. Panting loudly, she

clawed at my chest and shoulders, probably hard enough to leave marks.

I was glad. I wanted her to mark me, too.

And when I pulled out, my cum shot onto her stomach, branding her as mine again.

Rising up on her tiptoes, Mackenna kissed me slowly. Leisurely. Like we had all the time in the world. Hot steam filled the air while we basked in the post-orgasmic bliss.

When we parted, those big stormy eyes looked up at me, so innocent and trusting. Guilt gnawed at me again.

But then I tenderly peeled some of the wet, dark strands away from her forehead, revealing that scar.

That scar was my motivation.

As I placed a kiss over it, I vowed to do whatever it took to keep Mackenna safe—even if it meant keeping a secret.

# CHAPTER 35

MACKENNA

When I was a kid, summer always seemed to fly by at lightning speed. All year long, the school year dragged while I waited for it. Then, when it came, those couple of months disappeared in no time at all, leaving me with fond memories and the anticipation of next time.

This summer was kind of like that.

Only, there wouldn't be a next time.

It was hard to believe we only had a little over week before Jimmy was supposed to go back to Ohio. The past few weeks went by so fast. During the day, I stayed holed up in my house making music. Sometimes I spent time at Beverly's. Then at night, Jimmy was all mine.

I was so selfish when it came to him. Maybe part of that was because I knew we didn't have much time left.

So, when he told me he was going out with a friend tomorrow night, it took me a few seconds to recover from the disappointment of being without him.

*Geez, Mackenna. Dependent much?*

"Oh," I said, trying to keep my tone light as I gazed down at the rooster-covered table cloth. "I didn't realize you knew anyone around here."

"Yeah. You know Jay Langston?" he asked, taking a bite of chicken.

"Not really. He was a year or two behind me in school."

As Jimmy explained how they hung out while he was in Tolson when they were younger, I tried to put a lid on the 'crazy girlfriend' that wanted to burst out. Jimmy was a grown man. He didn't need me to warn him about rumors I'd heard about Jay.

But I did it anyway.

"Just be careful, okay? Jay gained a certain reputation in high school. People said he was trouble." If my memory was correct, the Jay I remembered didn't have a lot of respect for authority and spent a good portion of his time in detention. "I mean, I know more than anyone how inaccurate rumors can be, and maybe he's grown up since then," I said optimistically.

"Hey." Reaching across the table, he rubbed the back of my hand. "I don't want you to worry. Why don't you spend the night at your parents' house?"

I shook my head. "I'll just stay here. I'm not five, you know," I joked. "I can spend a Friday night by myself."

"Well, hopefully I'll be back before midnight."

"Okay." I forced a smile before pushing my mashed potatoes around my plate.

Jimmy looked like he wanted to say something else, his mouth opening for a second, but he didn't. Giving me that sexy smirk, he went back to eating his dinner.

And I went back to remembering that, soon, I would be spending every night alone.

Maybe tomorrow would be good practice for me.

# CHAPTER 36

JIMMY

Blood sprayed as my fist connected with Jaxon's face, the crunch under my knuckles satisfying. He staggered backward, holding his hand over his face.

Yeah, his nose was definitely broken.

I was winning by a landslide. He might've had more muscle mass than me, but I had revenge on my side.

What was his motivation? Money? Sport? The satisfaction of getting to inflict pain on another person?

My reason was better.

Obviously, he spent time lifting weights. His arms and shoulders were massive, making him appear as though he had no neck. But while he might've had me beat at bench pressing, I was taller and faster. His lack of agility would be his downfall.

The fight had been going on longer than people expected, and I could almost feel the anxiety and excitement coming from the crowd around us. Most assumed it would be over within ten minutes. Although I'd lost track of time, I had to guess we'd been going at it for at least twenty.

I could've ended it a long time ago but, like a predator playing with its food, I was toying with him. I enjoyed watching him struggle. I liked seeing his energy slowly dwindle. But most of all, I reveled in the flicker of help-lessness in his eyes.

I knew I was going to win and so did he.

Every injury I'd sustained was worth it. If I could make him feel a fraction of the pain he'd caused Mackenna, I would do this all night.

Miles from the nearest town and surrounded by tall cornfields, the abandoned farmhouse was the perfect spot for a fight. A couple trucks were pulled up around us with the headlights on, making sure everyone could see the action.

I wiped at the blood coming from a split in my eye-brow, and braced myself as Jaxon righted himself and came at me again. He crouched low and plowed me around the middle.

We both went down with a grunt. I took a hard blow to the ribs, but I got the upper hand when I flipped us so I was on top. I landed a quick punch to his cheekbone.

The faint wailing of sirens snapped me out of the zone I was in. When I glanced up, red and blue flashed far off in the distance. Jaxon took the opportunity to shove me off and we both staggered to our feet.

"Shit. Shit!" Jay shouted from somewhere off to my left. I could hear him yelling at Colin, the organizer of the fight. "Call it, man! We gotta get out of here."

Colin started to reply, but I tuned them out as I collid-ed with Jaxon, taking him back down to the ground. Hard.

Too concerned about the possibility of getting caught,

he'd just made the mistake of taking his eyes off me as he looked to Colin.

With panicked shouts, people fled the scene.

But I wasn't done yet. If I only had a minute to finish this, I was going to make it good. I didn't show any mercy as my fist slammed into his face again and again.

Someone grabbed my shoulders to pull me off, but I elbowed whoever it was in the face.

"That's it!" I heard someone say. "I'm out. Let the cops break it up."

"Fuck you, man! You can't just leave your own fight," Jay yelled in response.

I pinned Jaxon's arms down with my legs as I wrapped my hand around his throat, but I didn't squeeze hard enough to cut off his air.

I needed him to be conscious for what I was about to say.

"You will never contact Mackenna again," I growled low, not even recognizing my own voice. "Do you understand me?"

His eyes widened as he struggled to breath. "What the fuck," he wheezed. "I haven't seen that bitch in years."

"I know about the letter you put in her mailbox." My hand squeezed tighter. "And the damage you did to her car."

He tried to shake his head but couldn't. "I just wanted to scare her. I don't need that slut anyway," he rasped. "I've already got a new piece of ass."

Before I even knew what I was doing, I reared back

and brought one more blow to his face, effectively knocking him out.

A high-pitched sound repeatedly caused pain to radiate through my skull, and it took a second to realize it was more than just the sirens from the nearing police cars.

A screaming girl stood off to the side, wringing her hands. Tears flowed down her face, leaving dark tracks from her mascara. As I backed away from Jaxon's unconscious body, she rushed forward and fell to her knees beside him.

She glared up at me.

"What did you do?" she sobbed. "Why wouldn't you stop?"

With the long dark hair and light eyes, she had a striking resemblance to Mackenna. Only this girl was young—too young—probably not even seventeen. No amount of makeup could disguise her innocence, lack of developed curves, or the child-like roundness of her face.

"You're a pretty girl. You've got your whole life ahead of you," I told her, hoping she would listen. "Don't waste it on this loser. Do you even know why he was in jail?"

The sirens were getting closer and Jay was damn near frantic, but I couldn't walk away without warning her. If I could prevent this girl from ending up in the same situation as Mackenna, it was worth a shot.

"You don't know me," she snapped.

"No, I don't. But I know what guys like him do to girls like you. Get out before you end up stuck in a bad situation."

Her hard stare wavered as she looked down at the ground, and I got the feeling she'd already been a victim of his abuse in one way or another.

"I'm having his baby," she said quietly.

*Fuck.*

Jaxon had been out of prison for less than three months and the first thing he did was find some young, vulnerable girl to prey on. Then he knocked her up, tying her to him for the rest of their lives.

Pinching the bridge of my nose, I closed my eyes and gave her the only advice I had. "If you have supportive family members or a friend... Let them help you. You're going to need it."

Jay's red Corolla pulled up next to us and he rolled down the window. "Get in the fucking car!"

I hopped into the passenger seat and he hit the gas, tearing down the gravel driveway. In the rearview mirror, I watched one of the cop cars turn on to the deserted farm. My shoulders relaxed when I thought we might actually get away, but the second car kept going straight.

And he was gaining on us quickly.

"Pull over," I told Jay, already trying to figure out how I was going to explain this to my parents.

Shaking his head, he pushed the pedal down. "No."

"You can't outrun a cop," I reasoned. "Pull over and we'll just have to hope he's cool."

Jay started to hyperventilate. "I can't get pulled over."

"It was a fight, not a prostitution ring. Plus, you weren't involved." I pointed to my bloody face. "I'll take the blame for this."

"No. I'm high as a kite right now." He raked a hand through his reddish-brown hair. "I've got shit in my car. If they find it, I'm gonna be in so much trouble."

Shocked, I looked over at him. "What shit?" When he didn't answer, I asked again. "What shit, Jay?"

"No, no, no," he muttered before he hit the brakes and veered off into a ditch.

We came to a bumpy stop. Flinging the car door open, he took off, disappearing into a cornfield.

*Sonofabitch.*

The police car pulled up behind me, and I winced when the bright headlights reflected through the mirror.

Now that the adrenaline from the fight had worn off, I had one hell of a headache and I was becoming very aware of the bruises on my body.

As the officer approached, I stayed put in the vehicle, knowing that running wasn't going to do me any favors. Despite my previous encounters with the law, I had respect for cops. I just had to hope he would be understanding and cut me a break.

There was no way he wouldn't do a search after the way Jay took off.

Whatever he had stashed in the car was going to be a big deciding factor in the outcome. Alcohol? Not too bad, even though he was underage. Pot? Also not terrible, depending on how much he had. Coke, meth, or heroine? He was fucked. And I might be fucked, too.

I'd suspected Jay was into certain activities, and now I felt like an idiot for not being more cautious. Jay always seemed fidgety, nervous, and either hyped up or totally mellow.

I'd been so focused on getting the opportunity to beat Jaxon's ass that I overlooked all the signs.

And now I was going to pay the price.

# CHAPTER 37

MACKENNA

I woke up to the sound of ringing, and when I rolled over I almost fell off the edge of the bed.

No, not the bed.

I was on the couch. Why was I on the couch?

Then I remembered waiting up for Jimmy, and realized I must have fallen asleep at some point. The phone was still ringing, vibrating on the surface of the coffee table. Picking it up, I squinted at the flashing screen.

"Jimmy?" I answered groggily.

"Mack," he breathed out, sounding relieved to hear my voice.

"What's going on? It's—" I pulled the phone away and looked at the time. "—after 3 o'clock in the morning."

"I know. I'm so sorry, baby. I sort of need a ride."

I rubbed my eyes. "Where are you?"

"The police station."

Gasping, I sat up straight, feeling totally awake now. "What happened? Are you okay?"

"It's a long story." He sighed. "I got taken in, but I'm not being charged with anything. I just don't have a way home."

"Okay," I said, standing up. Stumbling around the room, I found my purse and flip flops. "I'll be there as soon as I can."

Most of the twenty-five-minute drive was spent with me playing out every horrific scenario I could think of. Given Jimmy's wild streak, combined with Jay's shady rep, it could be any number of different events that led to him ending up at the police station.

As I pulled up outside the large brick building, I caught sight of Jimmy on a stone bench outside, elbows on his knees and head bent down.

When he looked up, I gasped at the sight of his face. His body seemed stiff as he walked to my car and got into the passenger seat.

"Oh, my God," I breathed out. "Are you okay?"

"I'm fine." He tried to smile, but winced and brought his hand up to his split eyebrow. Two butterfly bandages covered the wound.

All my questions came out at once. "Are you going to fill me in? How did you end up here? Did you and Jay get into a fight?"

Hanging his head, he said, "I don't really know where to start."

"How about you start with what the hell happened tonight," I ground out, losing my patience.

When his eyes swung my way, it was hard to be mad. He looked so tired, not to mention he was injured. And honestly, I wasn't really angry. I was more worried than anything else.

"Jay's in big trouble." He leaned his head back and closed his eyes. "They found a pretty large amount of meth in his car."

"That shady bastard," I growled, and Jimmy chuckled.

"You're so hot when you're pissed."

"This is serious!" I hissed. "You go out with a friend and end up in jail. I feel like I don't even know you right now."

Immediately, all humor left his face.

"Don't say that. Baby, please don't be mad at me," he said quietly. "And, technically, I wasn't in jail. They just wanted to ask me some questions." He let out a tired sigh. "Could you just hold my hand right now? I promise I'll tell you everything when we get back to your house."

"Okay," I relented, linking our fingers over the middle console.

The rest of the ride was silent except for the low hum of the radio, but I was too wrapped up in my racing thoughts to listen to the music. I had no idea what kind of trouble Jimmy had gotten into or how badly he was hurt.

By the time we got back to my house, he was sound asleep, and from the pinkish glow on the horizon I knew the sun would be up soon.

"Hey." I gently shook his shoulder. "We're home."

Opening his eyes, he gave me a sleepy smile and started to yawn. The deep inhale must've been painful, because he let out a grunt as his hand went to his ribs.

"Do I need to take you to the hospital?" I asked, concerned.

"Nah." He attempted a laugh, but grimaced. "I'll be fine."

I bit my lip as I considered taking him there, regardless of what he wanted. "What if something's broken?"

"I'm just a little banged up. Been in enough fights to know the difference," he told me, reaching for the door handle. "I just need sleep and maybe an ice pack."

I followed Jimmy up to the house and, after getting him settled in bed, I went downstairs to get a bag of ice. When I came back, he was asleep again. I watched the steady rise and fall of his chest before reaching for his T-shirt. Lifting it up, I tried to figure out where he needed the ice the most.

I didn't have to look very hard.

A small gasp left me when I saw the redness and bruising on his left side. As gently as possible, I set the bag there. Jimmy's body jerked from the cold, but he didn't wake up.

I sat back against the headboard, and I studied him for several minutes while I let the ice do its job.

Although the cut over his eyebrow was the only open wound I saw, I could tell he'd been hit in other places. There was discoloration along his jaw, and one side of his lip was swollen. His knuckles were scraped up and red. His gray T-shirt had drops of blood on it, and I didn't know if the blood belonged to him or someone else.

I shifted on the mattress, trying to figure out where to lay. Jimmy's body was sprawled out in the middle, so there wasn't much room for me. It was probably best if

I didn't fall asleep in the bed. I didn't want to leave him, but I didn't want to hurt him with my 'champion-level cuddling'.

Deciding it was safest for us to sleep in separate places, I gently removed the ice pack, then grabbed my pillow and went downstairs to the couch.

# CHAPTER 38

JIMMY

For the first time in weeks, I woke up in bed alone. Worried, I jolted upright then immediately regretted it.

Pounding headache. Screaming ribs. Stiff muscles.

The next-day soreness was always the worst.

Events from the night before came back to me, and I wondered how much trouble I was in with Mackenna. The fact that she wasn't in bed with me was a bad sign.

Ignoring the ache in my body, I gingerly made my way downstairs. Mackenna was asleep on the couch. Taking a seat on the edge next to her, I absorbed a minute of peace before I faced the shit storm that was surely coming my way.

I woke her up with a forehead kiss. She smiled at me before a frown took over.

I tucked a rogue strand of hair behind her ear. "Guess you're pretty mad, huh?"

Scooting up, she shook her head. "I'm concerned."

"I got into a fight," I stated pointlessly.

"Well, that's obvious."

"With Jaxon."

With a blank expression, she blinked three times. "I'm sorry, what?"

I sighed and leaned down to give Mackenna one last kiss before she kicked me to the curb.

In one breath, I quickly explained how I'd contacted Jay several weeks ago, and that when I learned Jaxon wanted to fight, I knew I had my in. I told her about how the cops showed up, but not before I finished what I'd started.

"I'm not sorry I did it, but I am sorry that I lied to you," I said. "I just knew if I told you what I was doing, you wouldn't have wanted me to do it." I sent her a charming grin to help my case. "And I really, really wanted to kick that motherfucker's ass."

Her eyes glistened and her chin wobbled.

My face fell.

I would've preferred anger over sadness any day. I wanted her to yell at me. Anything but tears.

"How much groveling do I have to do to fix this?" I asked, rubbing my thumb over her legging-clad knee. "Because I'll do whatever it takes." Unable to handle the sight of her crying, I glanced away.

"You fought for me?" The question came out in a shaky whisper.

My head whipped back in her direction. "What?"

"You fought for me," she said again. She didn't look pissed.

"You're not mad?" I asked, and she shook her head.

"I can't believe you did that."

I tilted my head to the side. "Why are you so surprised?"

Biting her lip, she shrugged. "No one's ever done something like that for me before."

I remembered what she told me that night in the hot tub. How all her so-called friends abandoned her. The harassment she'd endured. How alone she felt.

"Mackenna, I would do anything for you."

"Fighting him was dangerous." Her lips flattened into a straight line. "And you're right—I would've tried to convince you not to if I'd known about it."

I nodded. "I might've done it anyway."

"How much trouble are you in?"

"Surprisingly, none. The cops weren't even called because of the fight. They were there on a drug bust, and they got what they were looking for."

"What are you going to tell Beverly? Your face..." Her fingers ghosted over my injuries.

"The truth," I responded before placing a kiss on her palm. "I might not tell my parents, though. I've given my mom enough gray hairs as it is."

"I'm staying with you tonight," Mackenna stated.

"What about going to see your family? Don't feel like you have to cancel your plans for me."

"I had already planned on spending the night with you. It's our last Saturday..." she trailed off with a frown.

Mackenna never spoke of our limited time together. I felt like this was a good opening to talk about our future together—and we *would* have a future together.

But I didn't get the chance.

Scrambling up onto her knees, she took my face in her hands. Her fingertips softly roamed over my cheeks, my nose, the cut on my eyebrow, as if she was seeing the damage again for the first time. The last touch was her thumb gently sweeping over my bottom lip.

Bringing her face to mine, she kissed me slowly. "How hurt are you?"

"Just bruises. Nothing a couple days' rest can't fix."

"I need you," she whispered against my lips. "Right now. Are you up for that?"

Smirking, I glanced down. "See for yourself."

She put her hand over my cock, which was already standing at attention. My eyes closed when she lightly scratched the material of my jeans, the rough denim texture causing a vibrating sensation with every scrape of her fingernails.

"Wait." I stopped her because there was still more to last night's story. "I really hope the fight was enough to make Jaxon stay away from you. And it seems that he's already moved on…" I took a deep breath before I continued. "He had a girl with him last night. And when I say girl, I mean practically a kid. God, she couldn't have been more than sixteen. Maybe younger."

Mackenna's expression turned horrified. "Of course he would go after someone like that. That's what predators do."

"That's not all," I said before voicing the worst part. "She said she was pregnant."

She gasped, and her mouth opened and closed a few times before she started rambling. "What's her name? Maybe if I could find her, I could warn her. She can't stay with someone like him, especially with a baby. I have to do something—"

"Slow down a second," I interrupted, rubbing up and down Mackenna's arms. "I understand why you'd want to do that, but we need to think it out first. The last thing you want to do is put yourself on his radar any more than you already are."

"You're afraid that if I get involved, he might come after me again," she said warily.

Just then, my phone pinged with a text.

**Jay: Call me if you're not locked up**

I turned the screen toward Mackenna before dialing Jay's number, then put it on speakerphone. As it rang, she got up and anxiously paced the room.

When he answered, I skipped the pleasantries. "Man, what the fuck?"

"I know," he said, sounding remorseful. "I screwed up. I'm sorry for leaving you like that, but I just panicked."

"They took me in, but they didn't charge me with anything," I told him. "You're in trouble, though. What were you doing with drugs in your car?"

He hesitated, like he didn't want to tell me, then let out muffled curse. "I've been dealing. It was good money, you know? Then I started using and it just got out of hand."

"They took your car, and I'm sure there's a warrant out for your arrest."

He sighed. "You're not telling me anything I don't already know. I'm turning myself in later today."

"I'm sorry," I apologized, even though I knew this was his own fault. "You did me a favor setting up the fight, and I'm grateful for that."

"Hey, it's no big deal. I should've known this lifestyle would catch up with me eventually. But that's not why I called. I've got news."

Mackenna finally stopped pacing and sat down in the armchair.

"What news?" I asked.

"Apparently, I wasn't the only one dealing meth. When the cops showed up last night, they found a couple hits in Jaxon's pocket. It gave his parole officer reason to search his house. Guess they found a shitload of it, packaged and ready for sale."

My jaw dropped. "Holy shit."

"Yep. He's going back to the slammer, probably for a long time."

I glanced over at Mackenna. Expression hopeful, she was sitting up straight while gripping the cushion so tightly her knuckles were white.

"Are you sure?" I asked Jay, needing confirmation.

"Positive," he said, and Mackenna deflated with relief. "I do have some bad news, though," he continued. "You're not gonna get paid for the fight. Colin is pissed. Says you didn't fight fair."

"I don't even care about the money. It was never about that."

"No, I guess it wasn't," he mused, and I could hear the smile in his voice. "Anyway... I've gotta get going. Time to face the music and all."

I nodded, remembering a time not too long ago when I had to do the same. "Good luck, man. And thanks for letting me know."

"Wait!" Mackenna rushed out, nearly falling off her seat.

"Who's that?" Jay asked, sounding a little paranoid.

"Mackenna," she replied, then added, "Connelly."

There was a three-second pause before he chuckled. "Well, I'll be damned. Guess I don't have to wonder why you wanted to fight Jaxon anymore. 'Sup Mackenna?"

Moving to the seat next to me, she spoke softly into the phone. "I need a favor, Jay."

"Lay it on me, Beautiful."

Shaking my head at his shameless flirting, I put an arm around my girl.

"There was a girl with Jaxon last night," Mackenna said. "A young girl. Is there any chance you know who she is?"

"No, but I can find out. Tell ya what. This'll be my last hurrah. I'll do some digging before I turn myself in," he said. I had no idea how he could sound so cheerful when facing significant jail time, but that was Jay.

Seeming relieved, her face relaxed. "Thank you. I really appreciate it. And I'll even forgive you for almost getting my boyfriend arrested," she added with a laugh.

After Mackenna rattled off her number and Jay said he would text her with the information, we said our goodbyes.

I set my phone on the coffee table and our eyes locked.

# CHAPTER 39

MACKENNA

"Now, where were we?" I asked, going back to the button on his jeans.

Lightly pushing Jimmy's shoulders, I had him sit back on the couch while I kneeled in front of him. After unzipping his pants, I tugged them down.

Jimmy's voice stopped me again.

"So you're really not mad at me?"

When I looked up at his face, battered and bruised, I ached for him. He'd done something incredibly selfless.

I knew how easy it was for people to look the other way when it came to domestic violence—I lived it. Even after people found out about the secret hell I'd been living in, they didn't stand up for me. They didn't lend a helping hand or a kind word.

Because of Jimmy, Jaxon was back behind bars and the heavy fear I'd been carrying around was lifted. I wouldn't have to carefully survey my surroundings every time I left my house. I wouldn't have to lay awake at night, wondering if tonight was the night I would have to face my demons.

Jimmy literally fought my war for me.

His vulnerable eyes searched my face before he continued. "I've spent so much time earning your trust, Mack. But I don't even deserve it."

"You didn't lose my trust," I told him with a shake of my head. "I understand why you didn't tell me. Honestly, I'm grateful for what you did. But I have to say, I hate seeing you hurt."

"It was worth it," he said confidently. "Please forgive me?"

I nodded. "Absolutely. Now are you going to get naked or what?"

He snickered, but it turned into a groan when I wrapped my hand around his thick shaft. I pumped up and down a few times before sucking on his tip. He loved it when I did that.

I was rewarded with a sexy grunt and a jerk of his hips.

Then I stood up to shed my clothes. When Jimmy tried to lift his shirt over his head, he let out a hiss of pain.

"Let me help," I whispered. I got his arms out one at a time, then carefully avoided the injuries on his face as I lifted it over his head.

My eyes fell to his ribs, the daylight shining through the window lighting up everything. I placed a light kiss over the area before moving up to a bruise on his chest. Next was his jaw, his cheekbone, his lips.

"You don't have to do anything." My mouth brushed against his. "I'll take care of you, okay?"

His pouty lips parted as he watched me straddle his lap. A quick breath left him when I positioned his dick at my entrance. Some of my hair fell over my breasts and he smoothed the long strands away before resting his hand on the side of my neck.

"So beautiful," he said huskily, rubbing his thumb over my pulse point.

"Tell me when you're close, okay?" I leaned in to rub my nose over his.

Seeming lost for words, he just nodded.

I started sinking down onto his cock, loving the familiar, slightly painful stretch. Even with how wet I was, getting his size inside me took work.

Once he was fully seated, I rotated my hips in circles. With a gasp, Jimmy's head fell back against the wall behind the couch.

"Am I hurting you?" I asked, concerned.

"Baby, the last thing I'm thinking about right now is the pain."

This was a position we hadn't done yet. Usually, I loved letting Jimmy take control. On top. Behind me. Against a wall. It was so freeing to surrender to him.

But this.

I felt a sense of power as I moved over him. I watched his face while he watched my body. His hands came up to cup my breasts and he pinched both nipples at the same time.

I let out a shuddering moan as I rocked faster.

His palms traveled down to my ass, and he grabbed handfuls of my flesh.

Panting, I ground my clit against his pelvic bone and

my eyes rolled back at the sensation of his cock hitting my G-spot.

"Baby, you gotta slow down," he rasped. A naughty smile spread over my lips when I did the exact opposite. His fingers flexed on my ass cheeks. "I'm serious, Mack. You're gonna make me come already."

"I'm almost there," I breathed out as I felt my inner walls flutter.

With a rough grunt, Jimmy closed his eyes. Like maybe if he couldn't see me, he would last longer. It didn't matter, though, because I wasn't kidding about being close.

A keening sound ripped from my throat and my fingers curled into the back of the couch behind Jimmy's shoulders. The feeling of coming on his cock was indescribable. For several seconds, my body reached levels of pleasure I didn't know existed.

Jimmy's hands moved from my backside to my waist, and he lifted me up and down several times, pumping my body over his cock. His strength never ceased to amaze me, the way he was able to pick me up like I weighed nothing.

Suddenly, I was flipped onto my back and he was thrusting hard.

I gasped at how deep he went.

He drove into me four more times before pulling out, and ropes of cum shot onto my heaving chest and stomach.

Like always, the sight of Jimmy stroking his dick caused me to want him all over again.

Resting his forehead against mine, he gave me a grin before kissing my lips. "So good, baby. Always so good."

When he reached to the floor to get my T-shirt, he winced and his hand went to his ribs. I took the shirt from him and cleaned myself off.

"I'll go get us some clean clothes," I told him as he carefully reclined on the cushions. "And you need ibuprofen."

"And kisses." He grinned.

"And kisses," I agreed before leaving the room.

The rest of the day was spent with me spoiling Jimmy. I changed out his ice packs, brought him food on the couch, and kissed every hurt place on his body.

And I fell even harder for him. He wasn't just my boyfriend.

He was my *best* friend.

And now he was my hero, too.

# CHAPTER 40

MACKENNA

Taco Tuesday at Buck's was insane. Apparently fifty-cent tacos drew a big crowd. I'd been warned about how popular it was, but I wasn't prepared for half the town to be packed into the narrow tavern.

The roar of laughter and voices made me flinch.

I was definitely out of my comfort zone, but I reminded myself that this was for Jimmy.

Just for this occasion, I'd traded out my leggings for skinny jeans, and my usual T-shirt for a white summery top with a lace trim around the low-cut neckline. And of course, my starfish necklace was right where it belonged—over my heart.

Lacing my fingers with Jimmy's, I led him to the back for his surprise. Three tables were pushed together, and the whole gang was there. The social anxiety I was suffering was totally worth it when I saw Jimmy's face.

Grinning from ear to ear, he looked to me. "What's going on?"

I made a sweeping motion to everyone. "Well, with the help of Angel, I sort of put together a send-off party."

Angel and I had been texting back and forth over the

past few weeks since she got back from her honeymoon. We hadn't hung out yet, but I had a feeling I would need her friendship in the coming months as I coped with Jimmy's absence. I couldn't even imagine what life was going to be like without him.

Hank spread his arms. "Surprise!"

Jimmy's smile fell, and his eyes moved from Beverly and Ernie at one end of the table to his coworkers and friends at the other. He glanced back at me. "You didn't have to do this."

I gave his hand a squeeze. "I wanted to. We're all so happy for you."

Forcing out those words was difficult. Keeping the smile on my face was even harder as I told the bold-faced lie. The last thing I wanted to do was celebrate Jimmy leaving, but he deserved to have this last gathering with people who were important to him.

We took our seats and Colton told us he already put in an order for one hundred tacos. Leaning forward, he flipped the lid on a rectangular box in front of us.

It was a cake. A hilarious cake. The white icing had black lettering that said 'We wish you the best... Just kidding. You're dead to us now.' Then there was a drawing of a guy in auto shop coveralls getting hit by a car.

Jimmy laughed. "Wow. That's pretty morbid."

"It was a custom order," Angel supplied with a giggle. "We got it from the same place we got our wedding cake." She nudged Travis, and he handed Jimmy a blue envelope.

Jimmy ripped it open and took out the card. The front

said 'Good luck!' and he guffawed at the inside. Scrawled with a blue pen, someone had written 'Seriously, though. You're dead to us now.'

"Ah, shit guys." Snickering, he held up the satirical card. "Very funny."

Our dinner arrived on three different trays full of tacos, various toppings, and dips. Plates were passed around and we dug in.

In between scarfing down tacos, I silently observed the conversations happening around me.

Jimmy was exchanging playful jabs with Colton about his terrible boxing skills. Everyone laughed when Travis relayed the latest auto shop story about when they found a cat hiding in Loretta Davey's car—and the best part was, the animal wasn't even hers. Angel chattered on about Brielle's upcoming wedding in the fall, while Beverly and Ernie seemed lost in their own world, canoodling in the corner.

Everything was fine until questions about Jimmy's school year came up.

"Where are you going to live?" Brielle asked. "The dorms?"

Jimmy nodded slowly. "That's the plan."

"What class are you looking forward to the most?"

"Well." He paused to take a sip of his Pepsi. "I thought speech 101 sounded pretty cool when I signed up for it."

As Brielle started talking about her nursing classes, I felt an unwelcome pressure behind my eyes, a tightness in my throat, and a burning in my chest.

This was supposed to be a happy occasion, so it was a bad time for me to get emotional.

Needing a break from thoughts of Jimmy's departure, I excused myself to the bathroom. The heavy door swung shut, blocking out some of the noise.

Blowing out a breath, I gripped the edge of the sink and stared at my reflection. I didn't recognize the desperate, lonely look in my eyes. I wasn't this girl, dependent and needy. I was Mackenna Connelly, reclusive songwriter extraordinaire.

Jimmy didn't need to see me like this. We had a deal. I'd offered him a summer of no-strings-attached fun in exchange for intimacy, and we both got what we wanted.

A second later, the door opened and Angel slipped inside.

"Hey, are you okay?" Her blue eyes held so much empathy, it made me want to spill everything. Instead, I went with the short answer.

"Honestly, no."

"I know what you're going through right now. Travis and I almost had to do the long-distance thing. I'm glad it didn't come to that, but it wouldn't have been the end of the world. When you're in love with someone, you stick it out," she said optimistically.

I didn't know what to say, so I just nodded. When her arms wrapped around me, I had no choice but to hug her back. Even if I didn't know Angel that well yet, it was nice to get comfort from someone who understood my pain.

But what she didn't realize was that Jimmy and I weren't supposed to last forever.

Angel pulled back to give me a kind smile.

"Take as long as you need in here. If anyone asks where you are, I'll just tell them you're having taco-induced diarrhea," she said brightly.

I laughed, unsure of whether she was joking or serious, and she walked out, leaving me alone with my turmoil once again.

After allowing myself a minute to wallow, I went back out to the table with a smile plastered on my face. I ate tacos, contributed to some conversations, and I laughed at the appropriate times.

But all the while, I thought about what Angel said. She wasn't wrong about sticking it out for someone you love.

The problem was, I didn't know how Jimmy felt about me.

And I hadn't exactly been open about my feelings either.

Later that night, I tried to show him. As soon as we got home, I led Jimmy up to bed and made love to him like it was the last time.

No words were spoken, but I used my body to communicate all the things I was too afraid to say.

*Thank you.*

*I wish you didn't have to go.*

*I love you.*

*Goodbye.*

# CHAPTER 41

JIMMY

Over these past couple months, my priorities and goals had changed. I'd come to Tolson on a mission to prove I could stay out of trouble and earn a second chance at college.

But I'd gained so much more than that.

This morning when I woke up with Mackenna star-fished to me from head to toe, I couldn't imagine being anywhere else.

I couldn't leave her.

I couldn't leave the job I'd come to love.

I was supposed to move back to Ohio on Saturday, so it was a little last-minute to be making life-altering decisions. But at my going-away party last night, everything felt wrong. Talking about my classes and my future away from Tolson—it was all so wrong.

I wanted to stay.

But before I went shouting it from the rooftops, I needed to get my ducks in a row.

I paced the floor outside Hank's office. I'd gotten done with my work over an hour ago, but I was stalling so I could get a chance to talk to my boss alone. Colton had just left for the day and Travis was gone on a haul, so it was just us now.

During my time here at the shop, I had worked hard. I'd tried my best to learn the skills they'd taught me and keep up with the workload.

And in the process, I found my passion. A career I was excited about. Mechanics. Motor oil. Trucking.

I wanted all of it.

Hank's jovial voice carried out into the garage. "You're gonna wear a hole in the concrete if you keep walking back and forth like that."

I smiled at Hank's no-bullshit attitude.

It was now or never.

Walking into the office, I gestured to a small chair against the wall. "Can I sit? I have something I want to talk to you about."

His computer chair creaked as he leaned back. "Of course."

I squared my shoulders as I took a seat. "I've really liked working here. Loved it, actually. I know when I started it was meant to be temporary but, the thing is, I'd like to stay in Tolson. Become a certified mechanic. Get my CDL. I know my last day is supposed to be Friday, but would you consider keeping me at the shop permanently?"

Hank's face remained passive during my rambling. My future depended on what his next words would be, and I held my breath as I waited for his answer.

Suddenly, he threw his head back and laughed. In an

instant he was out of his chair, hugging me and slapping my back a few times.

Letting out an uncomfortable chuckle, I returned the action.

He was still smiling when he sat back down. "Well, I'll be damned. I owe Colton fifty bucks."

"What?"

"We had a bet going on whether you were gonna go back to Ohio or not. He won."

Placing a hand over my chest, I pretended to be wounded. "Nice to know I'm just a bet to you guys."

Hank smiled. "We got ourselves another Tolson resident. I guess we're almost up to a population of 325 now."

I grinned, but he still hadn't given me the answer I needed. "So... That's a yes?"

"Hell yes, that's a yes! Welcome aboard, son." He grappled with some papers from his desk. Pointing at various numbers on the spreadsheet, he started talking about the trucking company. "Now, I think we're going to change some things. Travis and Colton don't need to be away from their families on long hauls, and you can't take deliveries across state lines until you're twenty-one. We've got enough local business to keep it going. Hank and Sons *Midwest* Transport." His hand glided through the air as he told me the new company name. "What do you think?"

"I think that sounds great," I told him, happy that he valued my opinion enough to ask.

He went back to excitedly shuffling papers and

punching numbers into his calculator. While we discussed the details of my future as a mechanic/truck driver, a sense of rightness came over me.

I had finally found my path.

# CHAPTER 42

JIMMY

I couldn't wait to tell Grandma the news. My usual stroll home from the shop turned into a jog. I passed Mackenna's house, figuring I would head over there after I made the announcement to Grandma.

Excited, I bounded up the cracked porch steps.

But as soon as I stepped into the house, something felt different. It wasn't unusual for Grandma's house to be quiet, especially if she wasn't home, but some indescribable weight in the air made my hair stand on end.

"Grandma? You home?"

As I passed the dining room, I noticed the door to Sweet Pea's cage was open. He was huddled in the corner, which wasn't like him when he had free time.

A bad feeling settled over me.

I went from room to room, terrified of what I might find. The Pepto-Bismol bathroom was empty. Grandma's bed was made, neat and tidy, and so was mine.

My last stop was the kitchen.

When I looked down to the floor, I saw a glimpse of Grandma's fluffy pink housecoat and her curly dark hair.

"Grandma!" Grief consumed me as I rushed toward

her limp body. "No. No, no, no. Grandma, wake up. Please, wake up."

I wasn't ready for her to be gone.

As I picked up her lifeless hand, I thought about Twinkies, whiskey, and the countless twenty-dollar bills she'd slipped to me. Over the years, she'd given me endless laughter and priceless words of wisdom. She was the one who taught me how to tie my shoes. The first time I ever heard the f-word, it was from her mouth.

There was no one else in the world like Beverly Louise Johnson.

Her papery skin was pale and her forehead felt cool to the touch. I did a quick assessment for injuries, but found no cuts or bruises. Pressing my fingers to the side of her neck, I felt a pulse and noticed the rise and fall of her chest.

That was a great sign.

The next minute felt like a lifetime.

Whipping out my cell phone, I punched in the number for 9-1-1.

When the operator answered, I barked out Grandma's address along with the fact that she was unconscious but breathing. She asked about Grandma's age, her medical history, and general health—most of which I didn't have a great answer for.

"Uhh, she's pretty fucking old. I think she'll be eighty this year. She drinks like a fish and eats mostly snack cakes. I know that sounds bad, but this woman is hell on wheels. Nothing gets her down. She's sharp as a tack and swears like a sailor." I cringed at the next piece of information.

"Oh, and I know for a fact that she and her boyfriend have an active sex-life. That's healthy, right?" My eyes stung as I added, "I love her and I can't lose her."

I barely heard the voice telling me an ambulance was on the way because Grandma moved. With a painful moan, she lifted a hand to her forehead. I dropped the phone and it clattered to the floor.

"Hey, hey. Easy now." Grabbing a dishtowel off the side of the sink, I folded it up and gently put it under her head.

"Jimmy?"

"Yeah, I'm here."

Making an incoherent sound, her eyes drifted closed again and I started to panic. "Grandma, stay with me. Help is on the way, okay?"

"I feel kinda shitty," she mumbled.

Squeezing her hand, I tried to see through the tears filling my eyes.

"I'll bet you do. But you know what? You can't leave me. I'm staying in Tolson," I told her, hoping the exciting news would keep her awake. "I'm moving here for good, so I'm gonna need you around. Just hang on, okay?"

"Oh, for crying out loud, I'm not dying," she grumped. "Good golly, have you always been this dramatic?"

Laughing, I wiped at the wetness running down my face. "Yeah, I guess so. I think I got it from you."

She let out a '*hmff*' but gave me a small smile. "Did you mean all those things you said about me?"

"What things?"

"What you said—" She waved her finger in the air before her arm fell limply to her side. "—on the phone just now."

"Yeah. Well, they wanted to know your medical history and I didn't know what else to say."

"I've never been so flattered in all my life," she said with a loving smile, and I chuckled. Only my grandma could make such a serious situation so fucking funny. "And are you really staying in Tolson for good?" Her eyes gleamed with happiness and I nodded. "Oh, this is just the best day ever. I knew it. I knew I could get you to stay."

My mouth dropped open as realization hit me. "Did you set me up with Mackenna on purpose?"

"Well, of course I did. You two need each other."

"And did you break my car so I'd have to go to Hank's, too?" I asked, wondering how far her devious plan went.

"No," she scoffed. "Your car's just a piece of shit."

Flailing her arms, she tried to sit up but failed.

"Whoa," I said, going back to concerned. "I'm not sure you should do that. Let's wait for the paramedics. Can you tell me what happened?"

Her lips pressed together. "I fell and hit my head."

I glanced around the kitchen, wondering what could have caused her to lose her balance. "Were you dizzy?"

"No."

"Did you trip?"

She huffed. "No."

"Well, what then?" I asked, confused.

Frowning, she looked away. "I slipped in bird shit."

That time my laughter came out loud and long. The hilarity of the situation combined with relief made it easier to see the humor of the circumstances.

"I think it's time to set some ground rules for Sweet Pea," I told her. "Less playtime outside of the cage?"

With a sigh she nodded, and I heard the far-off squeal of the ambulance in the distance. I never thought I would be so thankful for approaching sirens, but it was music to my ears. Red lights flashed through the kitchen window as it got louder, and I sternly told Grandma not to move before meeting the paramedics at the door.

I stood back as they checked her over and asked her questions. Not more than a minute later, I heard two different panicked voices coming from the living room.

"Where's Beverly? Let me through, damn it!" Ernie sounded frantic.

"Jimmy! What's going on?" That was Mackenna.

Reluctantly, I left the kitchen. When I rounded the corner, my eyes landed on my girl first. There was a large smear of mustard down the front of her white T-shirt, letting me know she'd probably dropped dinner in her hurry to get here.

Ernie looked disheveled. The suspenders he always wore hung loosely at his sides, and his Army ballcap was absent. His thinning hair stuck up at odd angles, like he'd been running his hand through it.

"She's okay," I reassured them, and Mackenna engulfed me in a hug. Kissing the top of her head, I glanced up to find Ernie wringing his hands. I gave him a nod.

"She fell in the kitchen and hit her head, but she's just as spunky as ever. I'm guessing they'll probably want her to go to the hospital, though."

His face twisted up, causing the wrinkles around his eyes and mouth to deepen. "Good luck to them. Boy, she's gonna give 'em hell."

His prediction was spot-on because we were interrupted by Grandma's angry voice carrying through the house. "Absolutely not! You're not putting me in that paddy wagon of death."

Ernie sighed. "I'll handle this."

The tiny kitchen was cramped with so many people in it, but Ernie hurried to Grandma's side, dropping to his knees on the checkered floor. "Bev, if they want you to go, you should go."

"I don't want to," she whined.

"Now, listen," Ernie started. "You could have a concussion or a broken bone. If it was me on this floor, wouldn't you want me to go? If it was Jimmy—" He pointed up at me. "—wouldn't you want him to get checked out?"

Grandma looked from me to Ernie, then back to the EMTs waiting for her response. Heaving out a sigh, she nodded. "Okay. But only because you asked me to."

"I'll meet you there." He gently patted the side of her face. "I love you, Bev. For the rest of my life, and then some."

Grandma beamed as she placed a hand over his heart. "I love you, too."

Feeling like an intruder on a sacred moment, I backed out of the kitchen to give them some privacy.

Mackenna didn't ask any questions as they loaded Grandma into the ambulance. She just held onto me. Or maybe I was the one holding onto her. I was still shaken up from thinking I'd lost one of the people I loved the most.

With a wave of his hand out the window, Ernie sped off in his car, intent on getting to the hospital to be by Grandma's side. Several concerned neighbors still loitered in their yards.

"It's okay." I projected my voice down the block so everyone could hear. "She just had a bad fall."

Satisfied with the update, most murmured "thank you" and went back into their houses.

"Are you okay?" Mackenna asked softly as we trudged up her porch steps.

"Yeah," I answered, a bit dazed from the events of the afternoon.

We both slumped down onto her couch. I was glad Mackenna already knew what happened because I didn't want to rehash everything. Still, I couldn't seem to shake off the lingering fear.

"When I first saw her... I thought—I thought—"

"Shh," she soothed. Lying back, she pulled my head down to her chest. Her fingers idly stroked my scalp. "Everything's okay."

I wrapped my arms around her middle, sinking into her comfort.

I loved that she let me do this. Let me be vulnerable. I didn't have to try to be tough around her. I could just be myself.

Exhaustion replaced the adrenaline rush, and suddenly I couldn't keep my eyes open. With Mackenna running her hands through my hair and the sound of her heart beneath my ear, I drifted off.

When I woke up, it was almost dark outside. Mackenna and I were still in the same position but her eyes were closed, her breathing even.

"Mack." My fingers danced along her collarbone and she blinked a few times. "I gotta go next door to feed Sweet Pea."

"Do you want me to do it?" She yawned, then pursed her lips. "You're not planning to kill him, are you?"

I chuckled. "No. Pretty sure Grandma might kill me if I did. I left my phone over there anyway. I should call my parents and let them know what's going on."

"Okay." Mackenna nodded before running her thumb over my lower lip. "Dinner's still in the Crockpot. I'll fix you a plate for when you get back."

My stomach growled at the mention of food. With all the excitement, I'd forgotten to eat.

When I got to Grandma's, I passed by Sweat Pea's cage. He was still in there, looking ashamed of himself.

Good.

My phone was on the kitchen floor where I'd dropped it. I frowned when I saw the three missed calls and the texts from my parents.

**Dad: Ernie called us. What happened? Call asap**

**Mom: Jimmy? Where are you? We're**

**worried**

**Dad: Do we need to come to IL?**

**Dad: That's it. We're packing**

Shit. Now I wished I hadn't taken that nap. I pressed the call button on Dad's number. He answered on the first ring.

"Jimmy? Is Mom okay?"

He rarely called my grandma 'Mom'. Our whole family was in the habit of calling her 'Grandma', regardless of their relation to her. It reminded me that she was his mother—the woman who gave him life, raised him, and loved him unconditionally. Of course he was going out of his mind.

"Sorry I didn't call earlier, Dad," I said, feeling guilty for letting him worry for so long. "I was totally wiped out after everything."

"We just want to hear the story from you. Ernie told us what he could, but he wasn't there for all of it."

"What happened?" My mom's voice came through the phone, and I figured they probably had me on speaker.

Taking a deep breath, I explained how I came home from work, found Grandma on the floor, and called 911. I left out the part about how I cried like a baby because I thought she was gone.

Dad sighed. "I'll bet that was pretty scary for you."

"It was," I confirmed as I tinkered with the latest note tacked to the fridge with a butterfly magnet. This one simply said '*Get more Twinkies*'.

"We're so glad you were there with her." Mom sounded like she was crying.

"Me too," I said, sitting down at the kitchen table.

"Yeah," Dad agreed, a little choked up. "If you hadn't been there..."

"That spitfire would've woken up and gone about her day as usual," I filled in with a light-hearted chuckle.

"You sure are right about that." He laughed. "But if it had been something serious... You being there could've saved her life."

I had wondered how to broach the subject my sudden change of plans. While today sucked, it led to the perfect opportunity to bring it up.

"Speaking of that... I have something I want to talk to you guys about. How would you guys feel about me staying in Tolson?" When I was met with stunned silence, I clarified, "Permanently."

Dad spoke up first. "Jimmy... Is that really what you want? Your classes..." he sputtered, sounding shocked. "Don't change your whole future just because of what happened today. If we need to hire someone to care for Grandma, we'll do it—"

"Dad," I stopped him. "Actually, I had already decided to stay. I even talked to Hank about it this afternoon. I've got a job for as long as I want it. If I cancel my classes now, you should get a full refund for this semester."

"And do you want that? To be a mechanic?" Mom asked.

"Mom, for the first time in my life I feel like I really know what I want. I'm going to cancel my classes at Ohio State. There's a community college in Champaign that offers a mechanic certification program, and I want to apply."

Dad cleared his throat. "Now, does this have anything to do with a certain young lady?"

"Yes." There was no reason to deny it. "It's a combination of things, but Mackenna is a big part of that."

"And how does she feel?" Mom piped up, ever the concerned parent. "Does she want you to stay in Tolson?"

"I haven't talked to her about it yet, but I think so. I didn't want to say anything to her unless I had talked to you guys first."

"Jimmy," Dad started, "I think I speak for both of us when I say... We're so proud of you."

There it was. The approval and praise I'd been wanting for so long. Hearing it was just as good as I'd imagined. "You have no idea how much it means to me to hear you say that."

"I think we do," he said. "You've turned into a fine young man. You apply for that program and we'll pay for it."

"Thank you for supporting me in this," I told them. "It might not be the life you envisioned for me, but I really want it."

"We love you and we just want you to be happy," Mom said softly, then added, "And preferably not in jail."

I laughed. "Love you guys, too."

We discussed the plans for a few more minutes, and after we hung up I couldn't keep the smile off my face.

It was time to tell Mackenna the news.

# CHAPTER 43

MACKENNA

The thing about lying to yourself is that it only works for so long. Sooner or later, the truth comes to the surface whether you like it or not.

I tried not to fall for Jimmy. I tried even harder to deny that it had happened.

And after I had to face the fact that I was in love with him, I tried to convince myself I would be able to let him go when the time came.

But it was a lie.

When he came back from Beverly's, he scarfed down his dinner, then grabbed my hand and dragged me to the car. He seemed excited and happy—more so than usual. I asked him what we were doing, but he told me it was a surprise.

My heart beat a little faster when he took the back road out of Tolson, because I knew where we were headed.

This gravel lane had become our spot. The fireflies were our candlelight. The crickets and cicadas, our music. Who would've thought being in the back of a car could be so romantic?

But the haybales were gone now, reminding me that

summer was fading and fall was looming. Soon, the fireflies would disappear and the leaves would change.

And I would go back to the isolated existence I had before Jimmy came into my life.

Our time was almost up.

I wondered if I would still come back here after Jimmy was gone. If I would park my Buick next to this field and remember our time together. If I would always feel the pain I was experiencing now.

Reaching over the middle console, Jimmy switched on the radio and pulled a plastic bag into the back seat with us.

I forced a smile. "What surprises do you have for me tonight?"

Shrugging, he smirked. "Another cheap date."

As he poured a bottle of Boon's Farm into a Solo cup for me, the song 'Strawberry Wine' came on the radio. I inwardly cursed the bad timing. This song had a history of making me teary-eyed, and that was without any relatable circumstances.

I really, really didn't want to cry.

Shit. I was totally going to cry.

As Deanna Carter sang about the loss of innocence, I took an unsatisfying sip of my wine. Then I set the drink into the cup holder and turned toward Jimmy.

"Two months ago, I never would've believed you if you'd told me I was going to get busy with you in the back of the saggin' wagon," I joked, trying to lighten the heaviness in my chest.

Jimmy didn't laugh like I thought he would. Didn't even crack a smile. A few seconds of silence passed.

"Mackenna." His face was serious. "This has been the best summer of my life. And—"

I stopped him by putting my fingers over his lips. I couldn't bear to hear him tell me it was over. Not without telling him I'd changed my mind about staying together.

I was about to become a weepy mess, but I pushed on anyway.

"I think—" I hiccupped. "I think I want to try long-distance. That is, if you still want to. I tried not to get emotionally attached to you. I really did. But I don't—" Holding back a sob, I struggled to keep myself together. The next words came out in a shaky whisper. "I don't want to say goodbye."

A huge grin broke out on Jimmy's face.

The tears I tried to blink away spilled down my cheeks. "Why are you smiling at me like that? I'm being serious here."

"Baby." He cupped my face. "You have no idea how happy it makes me to hear you say that. But I don't want to do long-distance."

My heart plummeted. "You don't?"

He shook his head, still grinning. "Because I want to stay."

"What?" I asked dumbly, unable to comprehend what he was saying.

"I want to move here. For good."

I took three deep breaths as I processed his words. "But what about college?"

"I can still go to school here, but it won't be a university. I love my job," he said, sounding excited. "I could apply to the mechanic program at the community college in Champaign. And I can get my CDL so I can start truck driving."

"You've thought about this," I surmised.

He nodded. "I've thought about it a lot."

Hope and happiness made my stomach flip, and I couldn't stop the huge smile stretching my face. "You're really moving here?"

"My parents want me to sleep on it," he told me. "But they're supportive of whatever I want to do."

With a laugh, I connected my lips with his.

Wine forgotten, clothes were shed and our limbs tangled together as giggles turned into gasps, and gasps turned into moans.

Sex with Jimmy was always mind-blowing, but this time it didn't feel like a goodbye.

It felt like a promise for the future.

# CHAPTER 44

MACKENNA

The squirrels got into my garbage again this morning. As cleaned up the wreckage of water bottles and leftovers on my lawn, I remembered the day they spread tampons all over my yard and how embarrassing that was.

And how *long* ago that was.

I hadn't had a period since then, which meant I was late. Really late. It wasn't unusual for my cycles to be irregular, but I'd never completely skipped a period before.

After Jimmy left for work, I hightailed it to Walmart to get some pregnancy tests. And now here I was, staring at my future.

Two pink lines.

At some point, every sexually active girl thought about what it would be like to see those lines. Depending on the situation, some would imagine themselves being elated. Some devastated. Some shocked.

Once I got over the shock part, I was pleasantly surprised to find myself in the first category as I stared down at the stick on the bathroom counter.

I didn't feel anything other than happy. So unbelievably happy.

I tore open another box of digital tests I'd gotten because I didn't trust one result. After dipping two more sticks into the cup I'd peed into, I set them down and waited. Less than two minutes later, both showed the same word.

*Pregnant.*

And that was when the full impact the situation hit me. Seeing it spelled out like that had me sinking to the floor while I stared blankly at some spot on the wall.

In the blink of an eye, the vision of a dark-haired, chubby-cheeked baby popped into my mind. It'd been a long time since I'd held an infant. Not since Krista was born. I was young then, but I still remembered the smell of her skin and the way it felt to have her smile at me for the first time.

Having kids of my own had been the furthest thing from my mind, but now I wanted it.

I wanted it more than I'd ever wanted anything.

This definitely hadn't been part of the plan. I knew Jimmy and I took our chances when he didn't use a condom, but we'd only done that a handful of times. We just got so caught up in the moment that I didn't consider the consequences.

No. Not consequences. I refused to think of it that way.

What would Jimmy's reaction be? Would he share my joy?

Jimmy's future was still uncertain. Not only was he younger than me, but he was just starting out in his career at Hank's. He was still trying to find solid ground after the year he'd had at school, and this news was enough to rock that foundation off its axis.

Then I thought about the night before. How he told me he was staying in Tolson and the way he made love to me like I was the most important person in the world.

I thought about what it would be like to see Jimmy cradling a newborn, and my stomach swooped. That image was enough to make any woman's ovaries spontaneously combust.

We could do this. We could be good parents. Sure, we hadn't been together long, but I was head over heels in love with him.

The fact that this tiny human was half Jimmy gave me the warm fuzzies.

My heart pounded as I thought about how to tell him the news.

Texting was out of the question. I could announce it at dinner tonight. I had all the ingredients for the beef stew he liked.

Trying to make myself presentable, I slipped on my sunflower dress. My hands shook as I brushed out my hair.

The first thing I needed to do was calm down. Having a panic attack wasn't going to help the situation.

I grabbed my guitar and went out to my front porch. As I sat down on the swing, I let my fingers do the worrying for me as I strummed out a random melody.

I had just started to feel a sense of peace when an unfamiliar car pulled into Beverly's driveway. The gray car was sleek and new-looking. A girl about my age with shoulder-length strawberry-blonde hair stepped out as she looked at the sage green house. She smoothed down her flowy blue tank top before climbing up the porch steps.

Scooting down in my seat, I tried to keep myself hidden. If there was one useful thing I learned growing up in a small town, it was the ability to spy without being noticed.

She knocked and a minute later, Ernie answered the door. Beverly had gotten discharged from the hospital early this morning with a clean bill of health, but Ernie was refusing to leave her side.

"Hi," the girl said sweetly, "Is James here?"

"No," I heard Ernie reply. "He's down at the shop, I believe."

"The shop?" she asked.

"Hank's Auto Shop. He's probably there if you need to find him."

"Oh, okay." The girl smiled before turning to walk away. "I'll try that. Thank you!"

I had no idea who she was or how she knew Jimmy. But I wanted to find out.

Curiosity got the best of me. As the car zipped away, I decided to follow.

Like a crazy stalker girlfriend, I quickly walked the three blocks. I arrived just in time to see Jimmy and the mystery girl sitting down at a table outside of Buck's. Tiptoeing to the side of the building, I stood out of sight while I eavesdropped.

"It's like you fell off the face of the earth these past couple months," the girl said. "I've been worried about you."

"No need to worry," Jimmy responded. "Just needed some time to get back on my feet."

"Ezra's probably gone crazy without you this summer." She followed up with a feminine chuckle.

Jimmy laughed. "Yeah. I miss that bonehead."

The familiarity between them was unmistakable, but nothing about their conversation told me who she was.

"So when are you coming back?" she asked. "You are coming back, right?"

The answer that followed wasn't what I was expecting.

"Yeah," Jimmy said. "I can't wait."

"When?"

"Sunday," he replied.

My face screwed up in confusion and my stomach dropped.

He'd just told he was staying here. In Tolson. But thinking to the night before, Jimmy never said he was 100% certain. He seemed so excited, but then I remembered how he'd said his parents wanted him to sleep on it.

Had he changed his mind already?

The rough concrete exterior of the building dug into the skin on my back while I held my breath and waited to hear more.

"So, what's going on, Erica?" Jimmy asked, his tone neutral.

Erica... Did I know an Erica? I tried to wrack my brain for any time Jimmy might've mentioned that name, but I came up with nothing.

"Ezra's not the only one who misses you, James," she said quietly.

"Erica—"

"Just hear me out, okay?" she cut him off. "When your parents said you were starting back at State this semester, I knew it was our second chance. And that's why I'm here. I wanted to talk to you—about us—before we go back to school. We were good together once, and I think we could be again. We'll be in the same place, so it would make sense for us to get back together..."

The sound of my own pounding heart drowned out the rest of her words as I put two and two together. Erica was Jimmy's ex. The one he'd been so upset about last year.

She came all the way here to offer him the life he always wanted. A life with her at the college they'd both planned on attending.

A life I couldn't give him.

If he'd already changed his mind about staying in Tolson... That meant he might've changed his mind about me, too. I had no idea what would've swayed his decision so suddenly, but the reasons didn't matter if he was leaving.

Her voice faded away as my feet carried me in the direction of my house. I couldn't listen to it. I couldn't listen to Jimmy and his ex-girlfriend's reunion.

And she was pretty, too, in a refined, elegant sort of way. I could almost imagine them walking hand in hand together on campus. Standing side by side on their graduation day. Getting married and having adorable babies.

Babies.

Placing my hand over my lower belly, I considered the biggest concern of all. What about our baby?

The baby Jimmy didn't even know about.

As much as I loved Jimmy and wanted him in my life—in our lives—I refused to be a consolation prize. I didn't want him to stay here out of obligation. If I told him about the pregnancy now and he decided to stay, I would never know if he did it out of a sense of duty.

After I made it through my front door, I sat down at the pathetically tiny kitchen table where we'd shared so many meals together.

I imagined what it would feel like to have him look at me with pity while he explained his change of heart.

Then I imagined the look of horror and disappointment on his face when I told him about the pregnancy, and my gut churned.

Suddenly, that churning turned into nausea and I was bolting for the bathroom. I wasn't sure if it was morning sickness or because I was so upset, but everything I ate for breakfast came up into the toilet.

After I had nothing left to throw up, I went to my room and curled up on my bed. The sheets smelled like Jimmy. I closed my eyes, and if I tried hard enough I could almost feel him next to me.

I sat up.

I couldn't be here.

Every room in this house reminded me of Jimmy and the times we'd shared. Every inch of this town had his mark on it.

Overwhelmed, confused, and devastated, I made an impulsive decision.

I decided to do something I was really good at.

I ran.

# CHAPTER 45

JIMMY

The last person I expected to see in Tolson was my ex, so imagine my surprise when she showed up at Hank's Auto Shop, looking extremely out of place in her white capris and high heels.

When she asked me if I had a few minutes to talk, I'd almost been too confused to form a sentence.

And now she sat across from me, rambling on about getting back together, and I felt like I was trapped in some bad episode of *The Twilight Zone.*

"Wait," I interrupted her seemingly rehearsed speech. "That's why you came all the way here? Because you think we're getting back together?"

"Well..." She paused, looking unsure. "I was hoping for it, I guess. I've had a lot of time to think about us and—"

I cut her off with a shake of my head. "We're not getting back together."

"Oh." Frowning, disappointment was written all over her face. "I just assumed with you coming back to school and all..." She trailed off with a shrug, like it was obvious.

"That I would come running back into your open arms?" I finished for her.

There was no heat or anger behind my question. I had no ill-will toward her, and that was one of the best things about being over someone. No bitterness. No resentment. Just indifference and a mixed bag of memories that would always stay in the past.

She huffed out a laugh. "It sounds kind of silly when you put it like that."

"It's not silly," I told her. "It's just not gonna happen."

"So that's it, then?" she asked, toying with the strap of her purse. "You're going to stay mad at me forever?"

"I'm not mad at you." I ran a hand through my hair as I thought about how to explain my feelings. "I'm just... over you."

"Ouch." She flinched. After a pause, her next words were laced with regret. "I never should've broken up with you."

"No, you did the right thing. We weren't right for each other, and I respect the hell out of you for being able to recognize that."

As I thought about the times we'd had together, a feeling of nostalgia came over me. Football games. Homework. School dances. Movie dates. Curfews.

So many memories.

But the fondness I felt had nothing to do with her.

It was the fact that those memories revolved around a time when life was simpler. When decisions were easier. When the weight of the world didn't rest on my shoulders.

But even with how good those times were, I wouldn't trade it for what I had now.

"It'll be hard seeing you around campus," she said sadly, reaching across the table to put her hand on my arm.

I moved back because I didn't want her touching me. As far as I was concerned, every part of my body belonged to Mackenna.

"No, it won't," I told her, "because I won't be there."

"What do you mean?" she asked, confused. "You just said you were coming back this weekend."

"I'm not coming back to school. I'm going to my parents' house to get the rest of my stuff because I'm moving here."

Eyebrows raised, she looked out at the empty streets of Tolson and I knew what she saw. Through her eyes, it probably just looked like a podunk, nothing-ever-happens-here town.

And that was partly true. But what she couldn't see were the people I had come to think of as good friends and the pride I felt when I worked at Hank's.

She couldn't see the love I felt for the gorgeous-as-fuck girl next door.

Her gaze landed back on me. "So, who is she?"

"Who is who?" I played dumb.

"The girl you've obviously fallen in love with."

Okay, so maybe she could see the love-struck look on my face. Just the thought of saying my girl's name made me grin. "Mackenna."

"Wow. You've got it bad." A small smile appeared on Erica's face, and I was glad that, despite the rejection she was facing, she was happy for me. "Well, I hope she realizes how lucky she is to be with you."

Still grinning, I shook my head. "No, I'm the lucky one."

*

After the short conversation, Erica and I said goodbye. The encounter with her had been unexpected, but I felt a pleasant sense of closure on that chapter of my life.

When I got off work, I practically sprinted the three blocks to Mackenna's house.

Tonight was the night I would finally tell her how I felt. I planned to take Mackenna out to our lane and tell her I loved her.

For weeks I'd been afraid she didn't feel the same, but after last night I didn't have doubts about that anymore. The fact that she'd been willing to try long-distance spoke volumes.

My strides slowed when Mackenna's house came into view because her car was gone. On my way up the porch steps, I shot her text.

**Me: Hey, where are you?**

Figuring I'd just wait for her to get back, I let myself into her house. I went to the kitchen to grab a bottle of water from the fridge. That's when I saw a note on the kitchen table.

> *Jimmy,*
> *If you're reading this letter, then you know that I'm gone.*
> *I've never been great at goodbyes, and I want our last memories of each other to be*

*good ones. I'll never forget the way your hand felt in mine, the way your laugh gave me butterflies, and the way the setting sun lit up your face as you smiled at me. Those are the things I'll think of whenever I miss you.*

*This summer, you gave me happiness I didn't think was possible. You healed something inside of me that I didn't even realize was broken. And although I always knew our time together was temporary, you showed me what it felt like to be loved, even if it was just for a small moment in time.*

*It's important to follow your dreams, regardless of what anyone else wants.*

*Have confidence in yourself when you go back to Ohio State. You're smart, passionate, and when you set your mind to something there's no stopping you.*

*Best wishes,*

*Mack*

What. The. Fuck.

Confused as shit, I read over the letter at least five times as I paced around her house. Her guitar and laptop were missing from their usual spots. There were no water bottles scattered throughout the living room.

Mackenna was gone.

She wanted me to leave? And she didn't even stick

around to say goodbye face to face. All I got was a lousy fucking letter.

*Best wishes?* What kind of shit was that?

Why would she do this?

Pulling out my cell phone, I dialed her number. Usually, we texted. But I needed to hear her voice. I needed her to explain to me what the hell she was thinking.

It didn't even ring. Just went straight to voicemail. I tried again a few more times, knowing the result wasn't going to be any different. When it was clear that she'd shut her phone off, effectively shutting me out, it felt like my entire ribcage was caving in.

I struggled to breathe as I leaned my elbows on the kitchen counter. I thought I'd experienced heartbreak before, but I was wrong.

What I felt after my last breakup barely registered on the Richter scale.

This was a fucking tsunami.

Slamming the front door so hard the house shook, I stomped down her porch steps and my pain morphed into rage.

I felt the old me rise to the surface, and I needed an outlet for my anger.

The flimsy garbage can was the closest thing to me, and it became my unfortunate target.

My fists landed on the metal over and over again. Every dent was a representation of my mangled heart. It crunched and groaned until it was an unrecognizable heap of steel. At some point, the garbage bag inside burst open and trash went flying everywhere.

I gave it one last kick, realizing the neighbors probably witnessed my meltdown.

I didn't give a fuck.

Out of breath and drained of energy, I slumped down onto the lawn and hung my head between my legs.

What was I supposed to do now? Wait for Mackenna to come back? Hunt her down, just like her ex?

Then what? Experience what it was like to have her rip my heart out face to face?

I was so fucking confused.

Then my eyes zeroed in on an object in the grass by my foot. A small, thin white piece of plastic with a pink cap on the end.

I might've been a guy, but I knew what it was.

The stick was facedown and my heart raced at what could be on the other side. My hand shook as I reached for it. Pausing, I took a deep breath before quickly flipping it over.

Two pink lines side by side. What did that mean? Was it good? Bad?

Not even caring about what a lunatic I looked like, I crawled around on all fours, searching the garbage for an instruction pamphlet.

I didn't find it. What I did find was even better—another stick. This one had a blue tip and there were no codes to crack.

*Pregnant.*

One word, and my whole world flipped upside down.

Mackenna was pregnant. I was going to be a father. Happiness unlike anything I'd ever known filled my body until it was a physical, tangible thing. I could feel it in my heart all the way to my toes.

I wanted this life. With Mackenna. With our baby. We were going to be a family.

But then my stomach lurched.

Is that why she left me that letter? Did she want me to leave because she didn't think I'd be a good dad? Was I really so much of a fuck-up that she didn't even think I should stick around to be there for my kid?

I thought Mackenna was different. I thought she saw past the tattoos and the mistakes, and saw me for who I was on the inside.

I took out the letter and read through it again, even though every word was burned into my mind.

She didn't say anything about a baby. Which meant she didn't want me to know.

The failure and disappointment I'd experienced at the beginning of the summer was nothing compared to this. This wasn't about skipping class or not studying enough for a tcst.

This was real life shit.

This was the kind of permanent thing Grandma talked about two months ago. This was what all the other little mistakes were supposed to prepare me for.

Did Mackenna really think they were better off without me?

That was the only possible conclusion I could come to,

and tears of anger and sadness filled my eyes. Only this time, the feelings were so overpowering that there was no possible outlet.

No punching bag was big enough. No amount of alcohol could dull my senses.

As I wiped the wetness from my eyes, I stuck the pregnancy test in my pocket, and went to Grandma's garage to grab a new trash bag. I diligently cleaned up the yard and set the new bag by the curb.

I barely registered Grandma's voice as I flopped down onto the edge of my bed and buried my face in my hands.

"Jimmy? Jimmy. You're freaking me out." She nudged my shoulder. "What the hell is the matter with you?"

"I think Mackenna broke up with me," I rasped out.

"What do you mean you 'think'? Either she did or she didn't."

I shook my head. "She left me a note. Said she was gone and she wanted me to go back to Ohio."

"I'm confused." Her voice turned sympathetic. "That doesn't make any sense. That girl loves you, Jimmy. I've seen the way she looks at you."

I didn't want to tell Grandma about the pregnancy. Because then I'd have to tell her the real reason Mackenna didn't want me to stay, and it was too painful to say out loud.

"She doesn't even want to talk to me," I said quietly. "She turned off her phone and everything. I'm guessing she's probably at her parents' house, but I don't know where they live."

Grandma left the room and when she came back a minute later, she threw something heavy onto the bed next to me.

"It's called a phonebook, Jimmy. Ryan and Grace Connelly. Go get your girl." She let out an exasperated sigh before leaving again, muttering something about '*fucking kids these days*,' 'Google,' and 'Skypetime.'

I stared at the phonebook, knowing this was a pivotal moment in my life.

I could push my ego aside. I could find her parents' address, go demand an explanation, and beg her to stay with me.

Instead, hurt and anger clouded my judgement and I made a different decision.

Reaching under the bed, I pulled out my old duffle bag and started to pack my shit.

# CHAPTER 46

MACKENNA

I absentmindedly tossed woodchips into the bonfire, mesmerized by the orange flames.

There were so many questions running through my mind, but I didn't want to know the answer to any of them.

I'd been hiding out at my parents' house, refusing to turn on my phone. The thought of listening to Jimmy tell me why he wanted to leave—and ultimately, why I wasn't a good enough reason to stay—was too much to bear.

I was such a coward, and I knew it.

It'd been three days since I saw Jimmy, which meant he was gone by now. A small part of me held onto the hope that he'd changed his mind and decided to stay.

Tomorrow, I would find out for sure.

"Don't hog all the woodchips," Krista said, holding out her hand.

I dropped several pieces into her palm and she joined me in the pointless game.

As if she could sense something was wrong, she'd been my constant companion over the last few days. She forced me to watch action movies, insisted on painting my toenails at least five times, and even convinced me to teach her how to knit—and she'd always hated knitting.

She was the best distraction, and I was grateful for her company.

"Mackenna?"

I glanced her way. "Yeah?"

"I've loved having you here this week." She looked over at me. "But whatever it is you're running from, eventually you're going to have to face it."

A surprised laugh burst from me. "Who are you right now? Dr. Phil?"

"I'm serious." Her quiet voice carried over the crickets and crackling logs. "I heard you cry yourself to sleep last night. And the night before."

"Things are just a little complicated right now." I sighed, not wanting to get into the details. Sometime in the near future, I would be telling Krista that she was going to be an aunt. And it would be really difficult for me to explain why Jimmy wasn't in the picture anymore.

Of course, I planned on telling him, too. Just not right now. And probably not tomorrow, either. I just needed some time to come to terms with my new reality.

"Is this about Hot Shirtless Guy?" she asked.

I scoffed. "When did you get so smart?"

"I'm fifteen. I'm not a kid anymore." She cut me a look, then her eyes softened. "I'll always be here for you. Mom and Dad, too."

"Thanks," I said quietly.

What she didn't realize is that I would need them now more than ever.

# CHAPTER 47

MACKENNA

Before I went home, there was something I had to do first.

After checking into Jay's thorough report about the young girl at the fight, I found her. Very easily, in fact. I had no idea how he got so much detailed information so quickly. And, honestly, I didn't want to know.

Casey Maxwell. She had just turned sixteen—mere months older than my sister—and was supposed to be starting her junior year at Brenton High School.

At least, she would've been if she wasn't preparing for motherhood.

Brenton was a small town about fifteen minutes east of Daywood, consisting mostly of trailer parks and low-income housing—a perfect spot for someone like Jaxon to fly under the radar. He'd been renting a trailer there, and I had to assume that was how he met Casey.

She didn't have a driver's license, but there wasn't much need for it when she didn't have a car. I learned she worked at a diner half a mile away from the doublewide she lived in with her mom.

I also knew she had a shift in less than an hour.

And that was how I ended up parked about fifty yards away from her little yellow home.

I sat up a little straighter when she walked out her door. Her dark hair was pulled into a ponytail, and she wore jeans and a white T-shirt with a logo over the left breast pocket. From the puffiness under her eyes, I could tell she'd been crying recently. And, given her circumstances, that was completely understandable.

She came from poverty, and her baby would be born into poverty.

She was too young to be a mother.

And as grateful as I was that Jaxon wouldn't be involved in their lives, I knew how terrified she must be to do it alone.

Because I was terrified, too, but at least I was an adult who had financial security.

Slinging her purse over her shoulder, Casey hopped down the steps of the rotting wooden porch before getting onto a rusty blue bike.

I felt like a creeper following behind her at a safe distance as she pedaled to work. When she got there, she leaned her bike against the side of Gloria's Diner. The older building was modeled after those old train cars. It was a little rundown, with some rusty spots in the metal exterior, and the light behind the 'G' was burnt out.

But at least it was a job.

Casey didn't go right in. Hanging her head, she took a moment to place her hand over her lower belly—the same way I'd done so many times since finding out I was pregnant.

Just like me, her flat stomach concealed a precious secret. There were two heartbeats inside her body. Two souls. She carried an extra set of arms and legs and tiny toes.

Then a small smile appeared on her lips.

She loved that baby already.

And that's how I knew I was doing the right thing.

After Casey went inside the diner, she slipped on a black apron and got to work. As she bustled from table to table, I gripped a medium-sized Manila envelope in my hand. I ran my fingertip along the edge as I tried to figure out how to get it to her, anonymously.

When an elderly couple exited their black Lincoln Town Car, I had my answer.

"Excuse me." I flagged them down, walking toward them while clutching the envelope to my stomach. "Are you going to Gloria's?"

The petite woman smiled behind her giant glasses, and she reminded me a bit of Beverly. "Yes, we come here every Monday for lunch."

"Would you be able to give this to a waitress inside?" I held up the envelope. "Her name is Casey Maxwell and it's really important that she gets it."

"Of course, dear," she replied, taking the important package from my hand. "We know her. Such a sweet girl."

I thanked them and they shuffled up the diner steps.

They approached Casey right away. I wasn't a lip-reader, but I could see the confusion on her face as she questioned them about where the package came from. The couple gestured toward the parking lot, then shrugged.

With a smile that didn't quite reach her eyes, Casey slipped the unopened envelope into her apron before leading the couple to a booth in the back. She got called over to several tables for food orders and coffee refills, but I waited because I wanted to watch her open the gift.

When she finally got a moment to herself, she slipped behind the counter. I couldn't see her hands but I knew she opened it. The expression on her face said it all.

Casey's hand flew to her mouth as she looked down at what I gave her: five-thousand dollars in cash, and a short letter with words of encouragement and a list of local resources for teen moms and battered women's shelters.

I told her things she probably needed to hear. That she wasn't alone. That she'd be okay. And to use the money wisely for her and the baby.

Stuffing the envelope back into her apron she hurried toward the door, probably to search for the anonymous do-gooder.

I hunched down in my seat for a minute, and when I poked my head above the dashboard, she was gone.

# CHAPTER 48

On the drive back to Tolson, the familiar chords of 'If Only' came through the radio, followed by the vocals from The Princess and the Pariah.

Normally, I would change the station because I'd heard this song a thousand times, but something made me keep it on.

Most people assumed this was a breakup song when, in fact, it was about the duet's father. But as I listened to the lyrics, they took on a new meaning while I thought about going back to my empty house.

*I can almost hear your voice,*
*Through the halls of the house that we built,*
*Days go by and your memory won't fade,*
*A piece of me died when you walked away,*
*I hope you find what you're looking for,*
*Because I'd give anything to hold you in my arms again,*
*You could take the pain away,*
*If only... If only for a day...*

When I turned onto my street, I held my breath as I searched for Jimmy's station wagon.

I didn't see it.

I pulled in to my driveway and craned my neck, desperately searching for that damn car. The saggin' wagon was nowhere to be found.

But I still needed closure.

I stepped out of my car and bypassed my house, walking across the yard to my neighbor's front porch. Giving myself five solid seconds to mentally prepare for any outcome, I took a few deep breaths while anxiously shuffling my feet.

Then I knocked.

When the screen door creaked open, Beverly's head popped out. "Well, hi!"

"Hi, Beverly." I forced a smile. "How are you feeling?"

"I'm feeling great," she said, her voice hushed. Quickly glancing behind her, she turned back to me. "But don't tell Ernie. He's doting on me something fierce, and I'm milking it for all it's worth."

That time I smiled for real. She was so crazy.

Mustering up the courage, I asked her what I came over to find out. "Is Jimmy here?"

"Oh, I'm sorry, Mackenna," she replied with a sympathetic look. "Jimmy moved out two days ago."

"Oh," I breathed out, my heart breaking into a million pieces.

"I'll tell you what." She smiled broadly. "You come visit me tomorrow, and I'll have a fresh batch of lemonade for you, okay?"

Swallowing hard, I nodded. "Okay."

After the door shut, tears filled my eyes. It was so silly of me to think he'd be here waiting.

At least now I had my answer.

Forcing myself to put one foot in front of the other, I traveled the short distance back to my house while trying to work out the details of the future in my head.

I could be a single mom. I made enough money to support myself, and working from home would be ideal for raising a child. Once I told Jimmy the news, I could let him decide how involved he wanted to be.

I had yet to turn on my cell phone, and I dug it out of my purse to do just that. Stopping in the grass, I stared down at it.

Changing my mind, I dropped it back into my bag.

No phone calls today. No texts. I just wanted to give myself one more day to grieve while eating mass quantities of ice cream sandwiches.

Then I would face reality.

Before I could reach my door, I stopped. There was a purple guitar pick taped to the knob. When I grabbed it, I realized there was a tiny piece of paper taped to the back.

My heart pounded as I unfolded it.

*Rule #1- I hope you think of me every time you use this pick.*

This was it. This was his goodbye.

The night we made those silly rules seemed like a lifetime ago, and I hadn't thought about them much since then. But Jimmy remembered the part about the guitar picks.

The first thing I did when I got inside was head to the kitchen, ready for my ice cream sandwich binge. Hot tears streamed down my face and a sniffle turned into a hiccup as I dropped my purse onto the counter.

The silence I used to love so much was unsettling.

Hollow.

So lonely.

I could hear the faint ticking of the clock on the mantel in the living room, and every quiet *click* taunted me.

Then I looked down at my belly. This house wouldn't be quiet for much longer. Part of Jimmy was still here—would always be here—no matter what.

I walked to the fridge, but I stopped short again because another pick was taped to the freezer door.

*Rule #2- I hope you sing to me every day.*

Face scrunching up in confusion, I walked into the living room, trying to figure out what the hell that meant.

I screamed when I saw someone sitting in my favorite chair. Instantly, I recognized the green eyes looking back at me.

"Jesus, Jimmy!" I put my hand to my chest where my heart threatened to beat right out of my body. "You scared the crap out of me. What the hell are you doing?"

He rubbed a thumb over his lower lip. "Waiting for you."

I gaped at him for several seconds. "Where's your car?"

"In Grandma's garage. I wanted this to be a surprise." With an unreadable expression, he spread his hands. "Surprise."

"But Beverly just said you moved out." Baffled, I pointed in the direction of my neighbor's house.

"I did," Jimmy confirmed, then hiked a thumb over his shoulder. "Welcome home, honey."

My eyes landed on a stack of five cardboard boxes labeled 'James Peabody'.

It was then that I noticed other new objects around my house. A black blanket was folded over the back of my couch. Three different types of men's shoes were lined up inside the front door.

A hiccup left me when I saw the framed picture on the mantel.

A new wave of tears filled my eyes when I picked it up. It was Jimmy and me at the wedding. We wore bright smiles as we sat together at our table. He'd had Alma take a picture of us sometime between the cake and the Hokey Pokey dance.

My eyes bounced back to Jimmy. "You can't be serious."

"Oh, but I am."

"You moved into my house?" I asked incredulously.

He nodded. "It's gonna take more than some crappy letter to get rid of me, Mack."

"But—but," I sputtered. "I thought you were leaving. Aren't you supposed to be back in Ohio right now?"

Instead of answering me he glanced down, his face full of pain. "Why did you want me to leave?"

"I—I didn't. I don't," I said, exasperated. "But that's what you said. You said you were leaving."

Now he looked confused. "When did I say that?"

There was no way for me to admit how I'd learned that information without revealing the fact that I'd basically stalked his ex. Blowing out a breath, I decided to be honest.

I told him how I saw a girl show up at his grandma's house asking for him, how I followed her, and how I eavesdropped on their conversation.

His lips twitched. "I take it you didn't stick around to hear everything?"

"No." I crossed my arms over my chest. "I didn't want to be a bystander to your reunion."

Throwing his head back, Jimmy laughed.

"Glad to see my heartbreak is entertaining to you," I grumbled.

His smile slowly fell away. "The truth is, I did plan on going back to my parents' house, but it was just to get some more of my stuff before I moved here for good. And I was going to ask you to come with me."

"Oh," I breathed out awkwardly. "So you're not getting back together with your ex?"

"No."

"Oh," I repeated, suddenly feeling ridiculous. Happy and relieved, but ridiculous nonetheless.

I'd just made a pretty big mess over nothing. If I hadn't made assumptions, my misery over the last few days could've been avoided.

And now that I took a closer look at Jimmy, I noticed the stubble on his jaw and the dark circles under his eyes.

I wondered if he'd been just as miserable.

He'd spent the last two months showing me that he was worthy of my trust, and at the first sign of doubt, I bailed.

And I felt terrible.

"I'm so sorry, Jimmy," I said sincerely. "I made a mistake. A really big mistake."

"No, *I'm* sorry." Holding up the letter I left him, he waved it in the air a couple times. "If you have any doubts about the way I feel about you, that's on me. See, I wasn't completely upfront with you about my feelings."

"What do you mean?"

"Come here," he requested and my feet obeyed, closing the distance between us. He held out his fists with a smirk. "You know what to do."

I tapped his right hand and his smile grew. "Good choice."

When he opened it, another guitar pick sat in his palm. I unfolded the strip of paper on the back.

*Rule #3- Fuck rule number three. I love you.*

I stared at it for several long seconds, trying to catch up with the emotional whiplash overloading my system.

Jimmy loved me.

He wasn't leaving.

He freaking *moved in* with me.

"Mack, I've loved you for a while now," he said. "I don't even care if you don't say it back. All I can do is hope that someday you'll love me as much as I love you."

Climbing onto his lap, I placed both hands on his face.

I rubbed my thumb over his bottom lip before confessing my feelings.

"Knock-knock."

A slow grin appeared on Jimmy's lips. "Who's there?"

"I love you, too, Jimmy."

"That's not even a joke," he responded quietly.

My face serious, I slowly shook my head. "No. It's not."

His eyes got watery, and he blinked a few times before looking down. Seeing this big strong guy brought to tears was nearly my undoing.

"So you didn't leave because you thought I'd be a bad dad?" he whispered, his voice shaking a little.

The blood drained from my face. "What?"

Reaching into his pocket, he pulled out one of the pregnancy tests I'd thrown away. "When were you going to tell me about this?"

I gasped. "How did you find that?"

Looking sheepish, Jimmy shrugged. "I might've gotten into it with your trash can after I got your letter. I was pretty pissed." He glanced down at the stick. "Then I found this."

I connected the dots in my mind. Jimmy thought I left because I didn't think he'd be a good father to our child.

"No, babe. No." I kissed him and wiped away the tear that spilled down his right cheek. "I think you're going to be a great dad." I kissed him again. "The best." Touching my forehead to his, I breathed in his comforting scent. "I was planning to tell you. I just didn't want that to be the only reason you stayed."

"I'm staying for *you*, Mack. The baby? He's just a bonus."

The smile I gave him was wide and goofy. "He?"

"I've just got a feeling," Jimmy said before placing his hand over my stomach. "I'm so fucking happy."

"Me too," I returned. Then I frowned. "I wish you hadn't found out about it this way. I wish I could've made it better. Like one of those awesome Pinterest pregnancy announcements."

He smirked. "What is that exactly?"

"You know, where they do something creative with baking or balloons. Or they spell it out in pepperoni on a pizza."

He ran his fingers through my hair. "There's always next time."

Grinning, I raised my eyebrows. "We haven't even had this one yet, and you're already planning for more?"

"Hell yeah. Remember rule #4?" Bringing his left fist out, he opened his hand. A simple white gold band sat in the middle of his palm. "You're mine for as long as I'm here. And I plan to be here for as long as you'll allow it. Marry me?"

"Jimmy," I gasped. He slid it onto my ring finger, and I started crying all over again. "Yes."

"I'll get you a better one when I can afford it," he added. "With a big diamond."

"You most certainly will not." Holding my hand in front of me, I admired the simplicity of it. I'd never been a fan of gaudy jewelry, and the symbolism of the band was enough for me. "I can't imagine anything more perfect than this."

Pressing my lips to his, we kissed slow and deep until we couldn't hold back our smiles anymore.

"I love you," I told him again, because it felt so good to finally say it.

"I love you, too, baby." His face got serious again and he paused before adding, "And I'm not like your ex. If you didn't want to be with me, I wouldn't force it."

"You moved yourself into my house," I pointed out with a laugh. "But I'm not unhappy about it. I know you're nothing like him. Why would you even think that?"

"The day I found out you were pregnant..." he went on, gently trailing a fingertip over my ring, "all I kept thinking was that it meant we were tied together for the rest of our lives. That we would always be connected. And I was glad. I want that."

"That's not a bad thing, Jimmy. Do you have any idea how happy I am that I get to keep this piece of you forever?"

"Baby." He put my hand over his heart. "You get to keep all of me forever."

# EPILOGUE

JIMMY

Over the past year, I'd had a lot of proud moments.

I was proud of myself when I became a certified mechanic and got my CDL, securing my career at Hank's Auto Shop.

I was even more proud when Mackenna became my wife on a sunny September day, in front of a small gathering of family and close friends. She'd insisted on a no-fuss courthouse union. She wore a purple dress and requested an ice cream cake. Instead of a reception, we had a cookout in Grandma's backyard. Nothing about it was traditional, but I didn't care about the details as long as she let me be her husband.

But I'd never been more proud than I was right now, holding my newborn son while his worn-out mother slept in the hospital bed. The nurses couldn't stop talking about his hair—thick and dark—just like mine. With big stormy eyes, he was extremely alert for an infant. Mackenna said he had my lips.

He was perfect.

William—named after my grandpa—let out a small cry as he looked for a place to latch on to my bare chest.

JAMIE SCHLOSSER

"Sorry, dude. I don't think I have what you're looking for," I told him with a chuckle.

"You're making ovaries explode all around this place." Mackenna's tired voice caused me to look up. "I'm starting to think that whole skin to skin thing is just a ploy to get hot, shirtless men to hold babies."

I snickered as I stood up and wrapped William in the blanket Mackenna had knitted, swaddling him just like the nurses taught me. Then I placed the blue bundle in her arms.

Mackenna's hair was a mess, the unwashed strands piled up in a loose bun on top of her head. There were dark circles under her eyes. The hospital gown she wore was horribly unattractive.

As always, she was so gorgeous she took my breath away.

Pulling the top of her shirt down, she offered William her breast. He rooted around for a few seconds before getting a good latch. His hand found the starfish necklace and he gripped it in his tiny fingers while he fed.

I sat on the edge of the bed with them, and Mackenna scooted over to make room for me.

"I've lost all sense of time." She yawned. "I don't even know what day it is."

Out of habit, I looked down at my watch, then remembered it gave out on me again last week. I decided not to have Hank fix it. Two days ago, right after William screamed his way into this world, I set it to the time he was born.

11:11am.

And that's where it would stay until I gave it to him someday.

I couldn't wait to get to know him. To hear his laugh. To watch him grow. I couldn't wait to teach him new things, like how to box and how to change a tire. I'd tell him that it's okay to have Twinkies for breakfast every now and then. And when Grandma slipped him twenty-dollar bills, I'd pretend to look the other way.

And when he grew up, I'd tell him not to be afraid of failure. I'd tell him that sometimes our biggest mistakes are really just blessings in disguise.

Then I'd tell him the story about how I fell in love with the moody girl next door.

"What are you thinking about?" Mackenna asked quietly, and I glanced down to find our son passed out with milk dribbling down his chin.

I brushed a piece of hair away from her face. "Just thinking about the time you walked in on me when I was wearing nothing but an apron."

She laughed lightly. "And those hot as fuck undies."

I hummed in agreement before placing a kiss over her scar. "Knock-knock."

Her lips tilted up. "Who's there?"

"Dropping out of college was the best thing that ever happened to me," I said softly. "Because it brought me to you. And to him." I gently held my son's hand, observing the massive size difference before locking eyes with my wife. "You're the love of my life, Mack. And he's my greatest accomplishment."

Her eyes glistened with happy tears. "That's not even a joke."

"No." I smiled as kissed her lips. "It's not."

# THE END

DROPOUT PLAYLIST
"Cheeseburger in Paradise" by Jimmy Buffet
"Burning House" by Cam
"If Only" by Dallas Schlosser
"Dream On" by Aerosmith
"Barbie Girl" by Aqua
"It's Five O'clock Somewhere" by Alan Jackson featuring
Jimmy Buffet
"John Deere Green" by Joe Diffie
"Crash" by Dave Matthews Band
"Weak" by Dallas Schlosser
"To Make You Feel my Love" by Garth Brooks
"Strawberry Wine" by Deanna Carter

## MACKENNA'S HONEY MUSTARD CHICKEN

2 lbs. chicken breasts
¾ cup yellow mustard
¾ cup honey
1-2 cloves of garlic, minced

Place all ingredients in a slow cooker. Cook on low for 4-5 hours. Enjoy!

# ACKNOWLEDGEMENTS

Behind every writer, there's a huge support system. I wouldn't be able to do this without my family, friends, acquaintances, complete strangers, beta readers, editors, cover artists, formatters, my personal assistant, promotion companies, bloggers, and readers!

To my husband and kids- Thank you for your support and your patience. You see everything that comes along with this journey: the triumph, the excitement, the success, the self-doubt, the frustration, the tears, and the occasional mental breakdown. When I started writing, I didn't realize I could experience every single one of those within an hour. Ha! Thanks for all the hugs and words of encouragement.

Kate Squires- You were my first mentor and now you're "my person." Thanks for laughing at me when I talk about quitting. And thank you for giving me a judgement-free zone where I can be the hot mess that I am. #YetiLove

Alexa Riley- You're like a wizard. An awesome, perverted wizard. You know how to get stuff done. Your guidance and friendship has been amazing, and no amount of panda flasks can repay you for your generosity. P.S. there's a little something extra in that shower scene just for you.

Jen Frederick- Thanks for being the best table assistant ever, and for teaching me the art of pushing a free book on someone. You've got skills.

To my betas- Kim Harbaugh, Brittaney Campbell, Liz Castillo, Melissa King, Miranda Arnold, and Amie Knight.

Thank you for being the first to read *Dropout*! Your input helped to make this story better.

Kim Huther, my editor- My first manuscript could have been a total train wreck, but you were eager to work with me from the very beginning. I'm very thankful for that.

Hang Le, my cover artist- You are a genius. Really. I have no idea how you took an idea from my mind and made my cover exactly how I pictured it. You nailed it!

Susan Garwood, my logo designer- When I messaged you in a panic because I procrastinated (big surprise there), you whipped up the whole package for me in less than 24 hours. Because of you, I didn't look unprepared and un-professional at my first signing. You're awesome!

Rebecca Poole, my formatter- You're so easy to work with and you save me the giant headache that can come along with all things formatting.

Amber Goodwin, my personal assistant- What would I do without you? You're the best book pimper ever!

I have to give a big thank-you to the promotion companies that make my book releases so awesome. Colleen Noyes at Itsy Bitsy Book Bits, Neda Amini at Ardent Prose, and Lydia Harbaugh at HEA Book Tours- thank you so much for your hard work!

To ALL the bloggers out there- your passion for books is what fuels this industry. You spend countless hours reading books, talking about those books, and promoting books. All for the love of books! I'm so thankful for all of you.

And, of course, my readers. Thanks for loving the good guys just as much as I do!

# ABOUT THE AUTHOR

Jamie Schlosser grew up on a farm in Illinois, surrounded by cornfields. Although she no longer lives in the country, her dream is to return to rural living someday. As a stay-at-home mom, she spends most of her days running back and forth between her two wonderful kids and her laptop. She loves her family, iced coffee, and happily-ever-afters. You can find out more about Jamie and upcoming books by visiting these links:

Facebook
https://www.facebook.com/authorjamieschlosser/
Twitter:
https://twitter.com/SchlosserJamie

## ALSO BY JAMIE SCHLOSSER

TRUCKER (The Good Guys Book 1)
A Trucker Christmas
DANCER (The Good Guys Book 2)

68323322R00233

Made in the USA
Columbia, SC
09 August 2019